The Night Chasers
Cosmic Ark Book Two

Scott Boss

Dedication
To my Peach.

Part I

Prelude

Translated Alien ship log.
Expedition from planet Pelosia.
Scribe: Amun.
Day 1: We touched down on a beautiful, temperate planet. There are waterfalls, lakes, and green mountains. The only thing reminiscent of Pelosia are the sand dunes leading to the huge lake near our landing place. Though, the lakes have all dried up back home. Why do I even call it that anymore? It's not home and hasn't been since I boarded the ship six months ago. I'm happy my name was chosen for planet five's exploration team, as four and six are less hospitable in appearance and readings. Favor to the team we dropped on four, but I surmise we'll make our final settlement on planet five. Maybe they'll name it after me, Planet Amun. I like it.

We landed on the far side of a field, at the foot of a range of mountains that seems to split the dark and light sides of this planet. The crops seem to be thriving in the constant sun. They're tall and stalky, with bright-green leaves going in every which direction. Most importantly, we can grow food. Father is happy about that.

There doesn't appear to be much wildlife. We've spotted what we'd classify as some type of livestock, but our sensors are picking up a semi-complex language, and they're clothed. Tonight, we're going to sleep on the ship. The techs want to run tests on the oxygen and such. We all need rest. We've been up the last cycle and a half, dropping the other team as well as preparing for touchdown. I'm excited to be on land again. So excited, I don't know if I can sleep.

Pelosin ship log, Day 2: The oxygen checked out for our exploration. The radiation levels are much lower than Pelosia. We may really thrive here. Our team hit the soil and my father was on his knees. I could hear his hysterical laugh starting, the one that said he'd made it as far as he could go and a few more days on the ship and he would've snapped. He pulled himself together as we met a few of the locals, the Clothed Livestock, as we're calling them. Hopefully, they can't translate that. They were calm, gentle beings, out harvesting some of those stalks from the field. They treated us with suspicion at first—who wouldn't?— but weren't hostile. They didn't seem prepared to fight and the only thing that resembled weapons were these short-handled tools they used to shuck the stalks clean. We offered them some of our last livestock jerky as a gift. They declined and my father was slapping his head, realizing they are likely herbivores. We'll try again tomorrow.

Pelosin ship log, Day 3: Success. They accepted our gift of dried thistle-weed and exchanged some of the crop they'd been harvesting. Good thing because none of us could stand another bite of the thistle-weed. They ate it on the spot. Good fortune to them because that stuff is nothing but fiber.

I spent the better part of the day speaking with them. They call themselves Wyans. The planet as well. There are many more in the next village over. It's only a few miles down the path. I'll be going tomorrow, escorted by my new friend Balowg. He was very excited to talk to me and it sped our process along much quicker since the others have been less willing to communicate. There is so much we can learn from each other. I have no more time to write. I need to continue piecing together their words in my dictionary. It's small now, but by tomorrow it will be expanding and so on.

Pelosin ship log, Day 4: The other village is much bigger. I was a little overwhelmed but Balowg kept things peaceful. I've found they are indeed herbivores, right down to eating the trees themselves. They are peaceful, as far as I could tell. Balowg told me they were just fearful of new encounters. We'll learn to live together. I tried to explain that there are more of us on their neighboring planet, but each time I did, they'd just say "Melinger" and wave it off. I'm furiously putting all this in my dictionary. I have an idea what it means but I don't want to embarrass myself just yet.

2

My father has been communicating with our party on Planet Four. We'll be out to get them soon as it sounds like they are having less luck than us. It was expected, but the Wyans have made our plans to visit Planet Six less of a priority. My father has called for colonizing already, only a few days in. The others in leadership have opposing ideas, but the data is there. Wyan is habitable.

Pelosin ship log, Day 4: Today was weirder. The hospitality from the townspeople changed. The progress I felt I was making yesterday reverted. Only Balowg would give me a minute. He seemed like he was in a hurry. He kept saying, "Mal-dirum, Mal-dirum." Which I deciphered to mean, "the night comes." When I lay it all out, it makes sense. Melinger, the planet, is just a dark spot in the sky to them. They don't have telescopes or anything similar. Wyan mostly faces the sun. Melinger does the same, so it would just be a black shadow in the sky to them when it's close enough to see. They may not even realize it's a planet. I'm hoping when I share this information with them, they'll understand and give me their trust. Back to Mal-dirum, or, the night comes. From our observations, Wyan rotates just enough to occasionally have nighttime. It's very uncommon, as it was on Pelosia toward the end. Some of the kids here may have never seen night. Unless they went to the other side of those mountains, that is. For them, the night is likely a frightening thing, maybe even a superstition or religious experience as witnessed in lower intelligent lifeforms. If we could just explain to them it's a simple rotational pattern, I think they'd understand. For now, they're all afraid of the dark and have locked themselves in. Tomorrow, I'll try again, but it is getting darker. I'm not sure how long it will last. The shadows have reached the ship as I write. Father told everyone to be in by the time they covered the fields. Looking out at the fields from my viewpoint, it's like a giant darkness has overtaken their crops. This is probably why the Wyans hate it, their precious crops, their...

I must have been staring at this screen for too long. The shadows in the field look like they're moving. Even the crops...no, the crops are tumbling down in places. Are the Wyans making one last effort to harvest these crops before night? No. I've never seen any of them move that fast.

~ * ~

I locked the door to my quarters. I saw...I don't know what it was but Marlay was coming back from the field when a shadow swooped over him. His scream made my whole body shake. It was so short though. Within seconds he stopped, then I heard Jualan. It was the same process, a quick scream, then silence, only. Jualan is down the hall, or *was*. No one is answering the coms. Something is on the ship. I can hear footsteps outside the door. I... (end of log)

Chapter One

--Ship manifest for the Mack--

Returning crew:

Captain Williams: Pilot

Lana: Mission Chief

Walters: Panel Tech

Percy: Mechanic

Julie: Medic

Wyan Ambassadors:

Bruuth

Doth

Gow'on

Belt Refugees:

Captain Davis: Pilot

Arjen: Mission Chief

Isolde: Crew Chief

Admani: Scientist/Medic

Marlin: Panel Tech

Peter: Security Guard

Zane: Earthling

Marlow: Earthling

Avani: Child of Marlow and Zane

It was almost eight weeks since they'd left the Belt when Marlow stood anxiously by the door to the cryo-room. Avani bounced in her arms. Her slick of dark hair was fuller and fluffier, and Marlow didn't think she could ever bring herself to cut it. She ran a hand through it, tufting it into a mohawk-pompadour combo, then mashing it back down. Avani reached up, swinging a chubby hand that opened and closed, trying to grasp onto something.

"You ready to see your daddy?" Marlow cringed at her own comment.

Zane was Avani's dad, that was true. How he became her dad? Well, that would be a weird conversation, but the more she thought about it, *nothing* about Avani's childhood would be "normal." Not even Belt-normal. They were hurtling through space toward a planet they'd never seen before, full of aliens who would view *them* as the extraterrestrials. Their mission—as Lana explained it over the past month and a half—was to join in with the Wyan people and gain their trust, so together, they could fight the wicked, monstrous Night Chasers and stop them from killing every living thing on the planet.

Marlow was pretty sure explaining that Avani's dad was just a good friend, albeit a gay friend, wouldn't be anywhere near the weirdest, or hardest part of her upbringing. Hell, having Zane *and* his boyfriend Peter around wouldn't bother her in the least. Her arms needed a break. Babies were not built for space travel.

The big door cranked open and Lana stepped out.

"How are they?" said Marlow, peering over her shoulder.

"Coming along nicely," said Lana. "Hand me Avani and you can go in."

She handed Avani over and entered the cryo-room. It was warm and oddly humid, smelling musty. The crew was spread around, most of them propped against the walls as their muscles were getting used to movement once again.

"Zane." Marlow spotted him in the low lighting and went over to find him gazing at Peter, their hands on top of each other's. Their movements were much like Avani's and it made Marlow laugh. She pulled Zane in for a hug then made sure he didn't slump over when she let him go. "I have so much to tell you."

He nodded and forced his cheeks into a smile. She could see Avani's eyes in his face. She hadn't had the chance to notice it before in the whirlwind of leaving the Belt.

"I'll let you recover a bit, but we have a lot to talk about."

He mumbled something and pointed to her head.

"Yeah," said Marlow. "I cut my hair. Avani was pulling it."

He smiled bigger.

"Wass-thah?" said Arjen, a few feet away next to Isolde.

Marlow pointed a finger at him. "Your girlfriend..." then shook her head. "Never mind. We'll talk. We'll all talk. I'm happy you're all awake again."

Ice slumped a hand onto Marlow's leg and winked at her. Marlow wasn't sure if the wink was purposeful as it never seemed to end.

"Okay, I'll be back."

There was a slurred yell from across the room. "Gets your hand out of my lap, Purse."

"It's Percy," someone yelled back, "and I'm trying."

Marlow shook her head as she walked out.

~ * ~

The group gathered around the conference table much like they had before the cryo-sleep, only now, many things had changed. As word of the Night Chasers filtered through the room, the unrest began seeping into their pores.

The room was split in two. The Belt crew was on one side: Marlow and Zane from Earth, their daughter Avani, the gatherers Arjen and Ice, Captain Davis, Marlin the NutrientPanel tech, Peter from belt security, and Admani the scientist and older sister of Ice. Lana's crew was on the other side: Captain Williams, Julie the medic, Percy the mechanic, and Walters the former 'Panel tech who found real food rendered his job obsolete. It was a reality that Marlin would soon have to endure. The Wyans were missing from the meeting as Lana explained the travel made them sick. They needed to be back on their own soil as soon as possible. Thankfully, that was only a few days away.

Lana stood in front of them. "We have a lot to discuss."

"Damn right we do," said Zane. "You lied to us."

"Now," started Arjen. He stood at the head of the table, one of his feet near Lana's team with another by Ice and the rest. There was a strong, metaphoric tug-of-war going on inside his chest.

"No," Zane cut him off. "We had it good in the Belt. We could've tried to work through our differences and—"

"They assaulted me and cut Avani out of me against my will." Marlow's eyes were on fire. "I couldn't ever work through that. Not in my life."

Zane turned, raising a hand to make a point, the same point he'd tried to make when Arjen and Ice first found them on Earth. "How can we trust *her*?"

"We've worked it out," said Marlow. "She did lie. Apparently, that's what everyone does to get you to trust them." She glared at Arjen as she spoke. "But now we're heading for Wyan and there's not much we can do about it."

"Mar..."

"I'm not going back to the Belt, Zane."

"I know."

"So, hear Lana out."

Marlin spoke up. "You may remember, Little Earthling, that we're not all fighters like you. What are we supposed to do against these *Night Chasers*?"

"If you'd just let me speak." Lana crossed her arms.

"Yes," said Arjen. "Everyone give her a chance."

"Easy for you to say," said Peter, crossing his arms. "You're fucking her."

"All right." Lana put a hand through her hair.

Her determined eyes searched the ceiling for an answer. "I understand some of you feel like this was all a bait and switch, but you have to see the bigger picture. When you left the Belt, you thought you were just going to live on someone else's planet as a foreigner, an immigrant, but hear me out: the Wyans are a peaceful, docile race. If we help them solve their problem, we become citizens of their planet. We don't just live on their land. We get our own land. This is better than the Belt. We can start a real colony of humans again without the problems they're having back in the Belt."

The room grew silent before Captain Williams cleared his throat.

"If I may. Our crew found this planet on the verge of our own deaths. There were ten of us then and five of us when we came back. We need you, but you need us. We know the land, the people, some of the language, and we know what it takes to save them, to protect them, but we'll need all of us working together to pull it off. It won't be easy and it's highly unlikely we all make it to the other side, but Lana's not telling you the full reward. If we can put an end to the Night Chasers, we won't just be citizens of Wyan, we'll be kings."

Chapter Two

"Well, that was inspiring," Peter said to Zane, as they walked arm in-arm toward their bunks. "I especially loved the part about how most of us will die."

Zane nudged him playfully. "He didn't say that."

Peter sniffed. "It was implied."

"Baby..."

"No." Peter stopped and freed his arm from Zane's. "This was supposed to be like a vacation, a way for me to get away from that shitty security detail, working for Lana's tyrant dad Maynard and drinking their god-awful swill just to pass the time."

"I never said it would be a vacation."

"No, but you said it would be a new start for us. Some pretty place like Earth with no ex-boyfriends to worry about, but now we're flying to our death, all for your nostalgia."

"It's not just for me. It's for Marlow and Avani. I couldn't just let them go."

"I know," Peter looked away, "but I'm beginning to wonder who you love more."

He walked off on his own.

Zane watched him go and his face went hot. He wanted to yell something after him, he was about to do so when he felt a hand on his shoulder.

"I'm sorry." Julie, the *Mack's* medic stood next to him. "I know we don't know each other that well yet but fights are no fun."

Zane turned to see a shy, short and curvy woman who looked older than him but not by much. She had a wave of braided red hair trailing behind her with no end in sight. It was a little darker than Peter's hair and Zane wondered with the small population of humans left if she were somehow related to Peter.

"Hey," said Zane. "You heard that?"

She nodded with sympathetic eyes. "Yeah, small ship. I mean, relatively."

"I guess." He was looking toward the hall Peter went down. His bunk was that way as well, but he was too hot to have another run-in with his boyfriend.

Julie seemed to read his thoughts. "Wanna come back to my bunk? I have something that might cheer you up."

Zane narrowed his eyes at her. "*Something...?*"

"Not...Just come on, I'll show you."

She led him by the arm to her bunk.

Meanwhile, Marlow sat around the conference table with Marlin, Percy, and Walters.

"Man, we should've grabbed a couple decks when we went back," said Percy.

He still looked young and bright-eyed, despite all the space travel he'd been through. He laid down a jack and picked up a king. "I have no idea what I'm doing, by the way."

"Me either." Marlow dropped her hand. "Can we go back to blackjack?"

"Fine." Walters tossed his hand in. "Give 'em to me. Damn kids."

Marlow looked to Percy and he shook his head.

"He doesn't mean it. He loves kids, don't you, Walt?"

"Maybe that baby you have floating around. Once they get much older than that, they're just trouble. Speaking of...?"

Marlow looked over her shoulder. "She's with Admani and Ice."

"The sisters from another mister?" Walters smirked.

"God," said Percy. "I knew you were going to say that."

"Then why didn't you beat me to it?"

"Because it's not funny."

"You're not funny."

"Well, neither are you."

Walters shuffled the deck poorly, a few errant cards flying out of his grasp. "Why don't we ask the table? Between the two of us, who's funnier?"

Marlin held up his hands. "I just wanna play cards. Seriously."

They turned toward Marlow, Walters tipping his head for an answer.

"I don't know. I'm just wondering why we thawed you from cryo-sleep so soon." Marlow smirked at the pair.

"Ah, we'll ask Williams later." Walters started his deal. "Blackjack, you said?"

Arjen was passing by the conference room with Lana. They were carrying dirt-covered tree roots as he heard Marlow talking. They continued down the hall toward the Wyans' bunks.

"I can't believe she's okay with all this," Arjen whispered.

"Well, she wasn't at first," said Lana. "We had a lot of time to talk it out."

"Good, because we need her."

Lana stopped, letting go of her end of the tree. It thumped on the floor with a bang, shaking dirt off as it did.

"I know you think she's special, but on Wyan, she's just another body, just another person to help with the colony."

"I get it," Arjen crossed his arms, "but you have to understand, she's a leader, even if a quiet one. Where she goes, Zane goes, where Zane goes, Peter goes. Hell, even Marlin has a thing for her."

"What does that mean?"

"Not like that. Just that he cares for her. I mean, as far as I know."

Lana rolled her eyes, bent down and grabbed her end of the root. They continued down the hall.

~ * ~

"This is crazy," said Zane, putting on a cowboy hat. "You got this stuff from a gathering trip?"

Julie was propped on her bunk, nodding with pride. "Yeah. We've been back twice now since we've moved out to Wyan."

"Twice?"

"Once before, then this last time before we went back to the Belt."

"Why didn't you come back to the Belt? Why didn't you tell them you weren't lost?"

"That's a question for Captain Williams and Lana. I've stayed out of that." Julie clipped a holster around Zane's waist and admired him. "Let me find the guns."

"Guns?" asked Zane.

"They're toys." She rummaged under her bunk.

"Okay." Zane watched her for a minute. "Don't you have anyone back in the Belt though?"

"Huh, not really." Julie grunted as she stood up, holding two plastic guns with red caps on the end. She tucked them in his holsters and smiled.

Zane looked down. "Guess I'm a cowboy now."

"Not without the boots. What size do you wear?"

"Nine?"

As she dug around more, Zane grabbed her shoulder. "Julie, will you sit for a minute?"

She rose, reluctant and they sat side-by-side on her bunk, Zane in the cowboy getup and Julie with a dark wig with a white stripe down the middle of it, streaks of her red hair escaped the sides.

Zane looked at her, her eyes darting away from his. "You're telling me there's nobody you care about back in the Belt?"

She tossed her arms up. "I don't know. I just...my mom wasn't exactly supportive of my decision to become a gathering ship medic. My dad situation is even more complicated. I had a few friends, but you know...gatherers don't really stick around much. Then we found Wyan and everything changed. It felt like it was the place I was meant to be. As soon as I touched the ground, it was just different. It's alive. That's probably the best way to describe it. The Belt is just so dead. So *scientific*.

Earth is beautiful in a way, but toxic. Wyan is a real, living planet. It's home, or it will be officially when we...you know."

Zane nodded. Just kill the Night Chasers and they'd have their perfect utopia again. Somehow, he didn't think it would be that easy.

"Have you seen them?"

Julie's face went somber, she pulled off her wig and held it to her chest like a hat during a funeral.

"We have a few rough images of them, of their movement over the mountains in the dark." She stared at her lap. "I can't look at them anymore. They give me nightmares."

Zane put a hand on her shoulder. "I'm sorry. I didn't mean to—"

"It's okay." She patted his hand and stood up. "Now let me find those boots. I want to see you in the full outfit."

Chapter Three

Bruuth stood at the head of the conference room table. He was paler than he'd been when they first met him. His eyes sunk into his head and his long neck slumped. He looked to Lana for cues and she had him wait. All the humans sat around the table with translators in their ears and data-pads ready.

Lana began, "With the help of my trusty assistant, Marlow, we've tested all of your translators over the past few weeks, but this is the best chance to work out any bugs before we get to Wyan. Bruuth will say a sentence and you log it verbatim into your data-pad, then we'll compare. Is everyone clear?"

There were nods around the room as Lana turned to Bruuth.

"Are you sure you're up for this?"

He gave a short reply and eyes lit up among the listeners as they heard the word, "Yes," come through their translator. Lana opened the floor to Bruuth. He grunted out a sentence and furious typing began. When they stopped, Lana raised a hand.

"Walters, you care to start?"

Walters nodded. "When the haddish crops reach your head, it's time to harvest. That about right?"

"That's it," Lana confirmed. "Anyone get something different?"

"I didn't get the name of the crop," said Percy. "I mean, I know what it is called in Wyan, but it didn't come through. The rest was the same."

"Noted. Anyone else?" She looked around, smiling at the lack of response, then turned to Marlow. "Way to go us. Let's try a few more."

Bruuth called out more of the Wyan language as the humans made notes. The translators were a major success. Outside of Percy's, none of them needed tweaking.

"Remember," Lana said, as Bruuth spoke his last line, "these are tools to help you learn the language. Rely on them but learn the words as you go. One day we won't need them at all."

She patted Bruuth on the neck as he headed out. Before he crossed the doorway, he looked back to the group and mumbled something. Those with their earpieces still in heard, "Don't let her get a stone face."

"Bruuth." Lana smiled as he went out.

"What's a stone face?" asked Zane.

Lana shook her head. "It's like a big head. Conceited. You know. He was making a joke. I'm glad to see he's feeling well enough to do that."

They watched him go as Lana addressed the group again,

"All right, eating practice for those that need it will be back here in an hour."

There were groans from the recent Belters.

"Hey, listen, I know it's no fun, but we've seen the long-term effects of the NutrientPanel. It should be used sparingly, only to get us back up to proper nourishment."

"Choke me with a cornstalk." Marlin reached in his pocket. "Anyone who wants to, I'll be sticking around to play cards."

"I'm in," said Walters.

Peter headed out the door as Marlow gave Zane a look.

He shrugged. "He needs to grow up."

"I'm sorry," said Marlow. "Want to hold your baby?"

She held Avani out toward him as drool rolled down her chin.

"Oh, she's *my* baby now?"

"Technically she's always been your baby, but I just need someone else to try to entertain her. I need a break."

Zane took Avani and she started fussing, reaching back for Marlow right away.

"Jeez, she's gotten so much heavier. I still can't get over that."

Marlow raised her eyebrows to say, "Yeah, I know..." She pleaded with Avani to just give her shoulders a few minutes.

"I might have something." Julie stepped over to make a face at the baby. "Want to bring her to my bunk?"

"Yes," said Zane. "Mar, you've got to see what she's got in there."

The three of them went off as Marlin dealt out the first hand of cards to Walters.

"So," said Marlin, "what do you do on Wyan if you don't use the 'Panel?"

"Oh, this and that." Walters ran a hand through his short, shaved hair. "I do some fishing. I'm having Purse teach me some mechanics. We're working on a couple machines back on Wyan for processing medicine and stuff like that. It will be good to know. I just feel like I'm so far behind with all this stuff."

"Tell me about it," said Marlin. "I have yet to accept my baths are gone. I'll probably be in denial until we get there."

Walters gave a knowing nod. "Well, I'll tell you a little secret. Purse and I found a hot spring that even Lana doesn't know about. When we get settled again, I'll take you there. It's the closest thing to a bath you'll get."

Marlin brightened up. "That sounds good to me."

Walters leaned in and talked in a husky whisper. "Think you can get any of the ladies to come down there with us?"

Marlin looked around. "Hmm, probably a better chance if you don't have me with you."

Walters slapped the table in a laugh. "Ah, surely we can get someone to turn up. I'm sick of it being just me and Purse."

Marlin looked around and kept his voice low. "Well, Marlow is a little young, even for Armageddon, and you know, the baby and all. Ice, well, the name says it all, her sister, Admani, she's always got her nose in the lab...you tried Lana?" Walters made a face. "Right," said Marlin. "She's back with Arjen anyway. Julie?"

Walters shook his head. "Nope. I wouldn't touch that. Just...no."

Marlin raised his hands. "Fair enough. Options are a bit slim then unless there are any female Wyans I should know about."

Walters choked back his laughter. "The only way I'd ride one of them is if this were the wild west and they were my horse."

"What in the hell are you two talking about?"

It was Captain Williams. He stood tall next to the table, stroking his thin mustache as he regarded them.

"Nothing worthwhile," said Walters. "Care to play a hand?"

"Don't mind if I do."

~ * ~

A few days later, they were down to the last hours before arrival and not a moment too soon. The Wyans aboard were all bedbound. Bruuth, the strongest, lasted only a few hours after his help with the translators. Their bodies needed the nutrients from their planet. The plants aboard were almost gone and not cutting it anymore.

Lana paced the bridge. Arjen stood back, watching. Her chestnut hair flipped with each turn of her head, but her expression kept him back. She was disquieted with the whole situation. He could see how much the Wyans meant to her, to get them back safely, and he knew how much she regretted bringing them at that moment. Arjen wanted to walk over, turn on his charm and put her at ease. It worked on almost anyone else, but he knew it wouldn't work with her. Lana was a challenge, one that he'd accepted willingly, but at the moment it made him feel helpless.

Captain Williams sat back in his chair, chatting with Captain Davis about the gravity and atmosphere on Wyan.

"It is what it is," said Ice, a few feet behind him, leaning on a wall. Arjen jumped when he heard her.

"What?"

"I'm saying, they make it a few more hours or they don't. We've done all we can."

He looked away from Lana for a second. "That's pretty cold, even for you."

"Just saying, you pacing around up here isn't going to change it."

"And you propose...?"

"You come eat something. You've skipped your last two meals."

She lowered her dark eyes at him.

"You keeping tabs on me now?"

Ice shrugged, making her way toward the door. "Just saying, even though you got *her* back, doesn't mean I don't care about you anymore. You'd think she would too."

Arjen put his hands on his hips. "Now come on, she has the whole ship to take care of."

Isolde waved a hand and was out the door.

Chapter Four

The whole crew stood, fighting for room to see the wormhole come to an end. It had been two months since they left the Belt. Some of them had been awake for less than a week, but it didn't completely wipe out the passing of time. They were all desperate for a new view. Any view.

The light from the star showed first, glowing as an orange orb through a dark window. There were shadows across it, like spots when you stare into the light too long.

"Are those asteroids?" asked Zane.

Julie shook her head next to him. "Planets. Probably like Mercury, if you know what I mean. We've hit it at just the right point in the orbit, thanks to Williams. The real prize is coming up."

A few more minutes passed as they shed the wormhole, opening completely into a new solar system. There were the Mercury-esque planets, but directly in their path was—

"Sweet mother," mumbled Captain Davis.

"There it is," said Lana, a smile finally crossing her face.

The deep blues of Wyan's oceans jumped out first, then the green of the hillsides. Rocky ledges rose then toppled into darkness at the terminator line. Marlow's mouth dropped open, watching puffy, white clouds flow across the surface like a cotton comforter. It was Earth. Only, it wasn't Earth. It was like Earth's prettier little sister and she was breathtaking.

Those in the room were in silent awe. Zane whispered to Marlow, "Remember the picture my dad would show us?"

"Of the Earth from that textbook?" she replied.

"Yes. He always said, this is not what it looks like anymore, but one day we'd see it return. If we just stuck around, we'd..." His voice caught in his throat and Marlow put an arm around him.

"We're seeing it," she whispered. "Just like he wanted."

~ * ~

Captain Williams made them all strap in for landing. The planet grew larger in their view. More definition of rolling hills, crops, and even civilization showed. The *Mack* teetered with the dark side of the planet, flying straight down the terminator line before turning toward a plain lying between two mountain ranges. The reverse thrusters kicked in to slow them and pushed their insides into their throats. Stalks swayed in the fields as the *Mack* touched down.

Lana and Walters rushed a stretcher to the exit ramp. Percy trailed behind, making sure Bruuth stayed in place as they hit the grass. The rest of the crew followed, watching as they ripped one of the stalks out of the field and presented it to him. With weak hands, he guided the root into his mouth, soil and all. Marlow and Zane cringed, listening to him crunch it between his teeth, but the smile on his face told them all they needed to know. He'd made it in time. He would be okay. The roots and soil were like oxygen for them. It would turn out his friends were not as lucky.

"We're here," said Zane. "Look at it."

Marlow couldn't stop. She was looking around frantically, holding Avani close.

"No, no-no-no. Is it happening already? The Night Chasers?"

She'd had more than one nightmare about that moment. The darkness taking over the land, and the beasts being unleashed.

The sky was all bright sun and a few clouds, but Zane followed her gaze. They'd landed in a Wyan village, only every house was destroyed. There were no Wyans in sight.

"Tell Lana," said Marlow. "We have to get back to the ship."

Zane was about to run to Lana in the field when a hand caught his shoulder.

"Hold on guys." Julie was next to him. "It's not what you think The Night Chasers did this, but it was years ago. Look closer."

Marlow squinted at one of the nearest houses about fifty fee away. The walls were torn, and it barely stood on parts of the frame, bu the signs of decay were there.

"But what...?" asked Marlow. "Where are the people, th Wyans?"

"Next village over. We park here. They aren't fond of the ship The main village is about two miles through there."

She pointed to a path past the field. There were mountains risin on either side, but a small walkway clearly went up and through it.

"Gotta grab our stuff," said Julie. "You coming?"

She headed back toward the ship.

Marlow and Zane stood, catching their breath. Marlow remembered the horrors of being on the ship, caring for a helpless chil while being told she was the Night Chasers' next meal. Lana brushed i off too quickly, and she had no one else to turn to during the next month Avani had been her only comfort and companionship. They'd slept clos all that time and Marlow was paying for it. The baby never wanted t leave her side.

She scanned the wrecked huts when she felt Zane's hand.

"I'm gonna go get my stuff. Want me to grab yours?"

Marlow didn't look at him. "No. I'm coming."

After one more look around, she followed.

Chapter Five

The path through the mountain was rugged, but worn. They couldn't go more than two-by-two at many points. Marlow clutched Avani close as she slept through the bouncing trek. Zane carried her bag and his own. Peter lagged at the end of the group.

Lana led the group with Arjen at her side as Captains Williams and Davis were next in line. Their data-pads stopped working as soon as they left the ruined village. Lana mentioned that was the way it was until they came up with a better relay.

The rocks were dark, almost black in places and marbled in others. They closed in, hugging the group in a claustrophobic fashion as they squeezed through.

"Guys." Zane was looking up. "What is that watching us?"

A face peered over the ledge twenty feet up. Black eyes and a stony crest twisted with each shift of its head.

Lana looked up. "It's a mercow. You'll hear their call now and then. Sounds like *mer-coh, mer-coh.* Hence the name. They're kind of like cassowaries on Earth. Did you ever...? No probably not. They're not generally mean unless you give them reason. They can fly a little, but they're better runners. Just stay out of their way and you'll be fine."

Zane admired the bird with fear and awe. He looked away when it tried to meet his eye. He didn't want to set it off, regardless of what Lana said.

The dark rocks gave birth to swaying grass and open air. The breeze was cool, despite the constant sun. Marlow took a deep breath, testing the air as it spun around her in an invisible caress. It wasn't the poison from Earth, and it wasn't the stillness from the Belt. It was fresh and just right. There were wide-based trees plotted around the open area. They grew up to thirty feet in diameter and some were fifty feet tall.

A few huts began to appear beneath the shade of the trees. They were round with conical roofs built from the trees. Other destroyed huts lay further back, taken down to their foundations. Two bigger buildings were just past the standing huts. One of them was partly in the sunlight. Its roof shone with some type of weather sealant.

Lana looked back to Admani, then pointed to the building in the sun. "That's the lab. Doesn't look like much, but we've got all our tech in there."

"Can't wait." Admani's freckled face glowed with true excitement.

"Are these your houses?" asked Zane.

"Some." Lana pointed across the way at another group of huts emerging from behind one of the giant trees. "There are the rest." They were similar to the others, cylinders separated by ten feet of wild grass. "We're going to have to bunk up for a bit until we can build more. The well is behind the lab if anyone needs a drink."

Peter looked back the way they'd come.

"Why not just use the ship?"

Lana shook her head and looked to the others for confirmation. "Part of our integration with the Wyans is living among them. They are very distrusting of our tech, but they view us as friends, equals, when we are down here 'in contact with the land.' When we sit in the ship, it gives them bad feelings."

Captain Davis scoffed.

Captain Williams patted him on the shoulder. "I said the same thing." Then to the whole group. "We keep bending to these animals and we're going to be under their rule instead of the other way around."

Lana had her hands on her hips. "Williams...you know the plan. Stick to it and everything is going to work out."

He waved a dismissive hand at her, put his arm around Davis's shoulders and said, "Let me show you, my quarters."

They started off toward the second set of huts.

Lana watched them go, staring as if she meant to say something, then shook herself out of it. "We should probably discuss our living situation. We have six huts and our lab. It will take time to build more, time that we will reserve for after the Night Chaser attack. Anyone who helps us through that will have a mansion on the other side."

"Are you talking Heaven or Wyan?" asked Marlow.

There were laughs from some of the crew, but not from Lana.

"They will be one and the same in a few months. You have my word."

She shared a stare with Marlow until Marlow looked away.

"All right, it looks like the captains will be bunking together." Lana looked around. "Walters, can you make room for Marlin?"

Walters nodded and led Marlin to his hut.

Admani raised a hand. "We'd talked about me staying in the lab a couple days ago. Is that still an option?"

Lana put her hands together and gave a quick bow of thanks. "Yes. That would be great."

She looked to Marlow, holding Avani, trying to keep her from fussing. "What would be the best...?"

"They can stay with me," said Julie.

Zane shot her a surprised but relieved look. He'd accepted his role as donor, but he still hadn't come to terms with being a father. If they'd stayed in the Belt, he was pretty sure it wouldn't have been an option. Somehow Robin Visser would be on the birth certificate if there was still such a thing. On Wyan, he had other objectives. There was a mountainside to explore, trees to climb, and an invasion to withstand. Eventually, he'd need to have a real talk with Peter and if that failed, have a talk with Percy, because his gay-dar had been screaming at him since they boarded the ship.

"Marlow, is that okay?" asked Lana.

Marlow furrowed her brow at Zane for a few seconds, trying to read him, to give him time to say anything. When he didn't, she said, "Sure. That's fine."

Then to Julie, she said, "If you don't mind waking up at all hours."
Julie shrugged. "I'm up all the time anyway. No worries."

Marlow lifted Avani and sniffed her. "Yeah, I'm gonna need a place to change her soon. Zane?"

He reached out her bag. "The cloth diapers are on top."

Julie waved for her to follow.

Lana continued. "There is the matter of Ken's house. It's been empty since we lost him. We could put two of you in there." She looked over to Zane and raised her eyebrows.

"Uh..." said Zane.

"Yeah." Ice stepped up. "Zane and I could take it. We're not afraid of ghosts, right?"

"Right." Zane smirked back at her.

He was having trouble sharing the open space with Peter at the moment, much less a tiny hut.

Lana looked around at the remaining homeless. Percy gave her a knowing nod.

"Guess it's you and me, Peter," said Percy. "I'll show you the way."

Peter crossed his arms and followed, giving a death glare toward Zane. Zane considered that he'd just let his boyfriend bunk with the only other gay guy on the planet.

"All right," said Lana. "Everyone get settled. Arjen and I will take Bruuth home."

The immigrants made their way to their new homes for their first day on Wyan.

Chapter Six

"You've lost two of my people and almost killed one of my best men."

The voice ripped through the air as an angry grunt, then came out in Arjen's translator in emotionless English. It would be comical in many other settings, but not this one. Arjen was still taking in the scene. He and Lana stood before the village leader, Karath. She was shorter than Bruuth and aged to a leathery gray shade. Bruuth sat up on the stretcher, his four legs beneath him, arms helping hold himself upright, listening, while Arjen looked to Lana for clues.

There were several huts in a semicircle around a gray stone well in the middle of the village. It had a big bucket attached to a pulley system that swung gently in the breeze. Bigger buildings lay behind, all falling into the same rustic architectural style of the Wyans. The huts were like the ones the humans used in the wrecked village another mile back. Worn, dirt paths led from the well to the rest of the village. There were two other Wyans flanking Karath. Arjen couldn't tell if they were also females or not. They didn't have the same violet coloring on the side of their faces. They never looked at him, only Lana to discuss the issues.

Lana grunted a reply that translated in Arjen's earpiece. It was very odd to hear it come back into English. "We didn't know the effect the travel would have on them. We thought we'd prepared enough resources. I am eternally sorry."

Karath stomped a foot, raised up on only her back two legs, reaching over seven feet when she did. Arjen thought of the god Vishnu from folklore he had read growing up.

"What good has come of it?" Karath asked.

"I've brought more help," said Lana. "There are thirteen of u₃ now, not counting the child."

"And two less of us."

Lana bowed her head. "I cannot expand my apologies more. Wᵣ will do much good in the coming time of darkness."

Karath seemed to chew on Lana's words for a minute, looking t₀ her companions for assurance.

She settled onto her four legs again and raised her chin to Lana "We will trust you again, but no more travels. You stay here, you help us and our deal will be complete."

"Thank you."

Bruuth had taken the time to get his feet under him. He rested ₐ hand on Lana's shoulder, blinked twice deliberately and walked slowly into the small village beyond the huts. He never spoke.

Lana took the stretcher and Arjen helped her wheel it back towarₑ the humans' dwellings as a crowd watched their departure.

"So, she's the queen I assume?" asked Arjen.

"Yes, reluctantly." Lana let out a breath. "It's all a show."

"A show? Pretty good show I'd say."

"Yes, but her bark has no bite. In the end, the Wyans are helpless They used to number in the thousands, as far as I can tell from theiᵣ stories. Now, that's it. What we just saw was it."

"And that was what? A hundred?"

"Maybe two, all counted. That's why they need us."

Arjen helped lift the stretcher over a rough patch, relieved thaₜ Bruuth was not on it any more.

"I'd say so. If they're so docile, how come there are any left?"

Lana stopped to catch her breath, perched on a rock, overlooking the village they'd left. She was so beautiful and so conflicted.

"They started a ritual when their numbers were at their peak. Thiₛ would've been twenty years ago or so. As with any society with largeᵣ numbers, there was crime, groups ganging up, testing their boundaries₊ The leadership at the time had to stop it, but again, they're not int₀

28

weapons, prisons, or fighting of any kind. They just want to live in peace with each other, so the obvious punishment came into play, banishment."

"Oh, God." Arjen leaned on the rock next to her.

"Yep, they sent the criminals, if you will, over the mountains to the dark side. They didn't know what lived over there. The criminals must have come across the Night Chasers, giving them a taste for Wyan blood. When darkness fell, the Night Chasers were thirsty for more. It wasn't many the first time, but soon word must have gotten out. The following darkness there were more. Karath said it became a ritual for them. She tried reason, but the Night Chasers are mindless beasts. The last time they wiped out those two villages you saw. The one where we landed the *Mack* and the one we're staying in. Their stories don't make it clear how many Night Chasers there are, only that when they come, they destroy and kill everything in their path. We don't know what goes on, on the dark side of this planet. We probably don't want to know. We only know the Night Chasers wait until darkness, meaning they don't like the light. I've been picking every brain here for information about them. The more we know, the better chance we have of defending Wyan."

Arjen took her hand in his, stroking it gently. "And it became your mission to save them? Why not the Belt?"

She pulled her hand back. "Because people like your father only see their way. Just like my father. Nothing we could do would ever truly appease them. We'd spend our lives searching, scavenging for them, for what? So, we could bring back whatever we found, get a pat on the head, then be sent back out for months to find them more. I'm done with that, Arjen. I've found the best treasure yet and I'm not sharing this one with them."

Arjen felt his face heating up at her speech. She'd articulated thoughts he'd never been able to.

"You knew I'd agree with that. Is that why you came back?"

She reached for his hand and they connected again. "We needed help. I knew you could pull together at least a few people that would defect."

"So that's it, huh?" He raised his eyebrows.

She smirked. "And, I kind of like having you around." She leaned in for a quick kiss then jumped down from the rock. "Now come on, we need to get back to the troops."

Chapter Seven

Marlow laid Avani down and stretched her back, hearing no less than three pops from her joints. Julie put her hands together on her cheek and mimicked sleeping. Marlow nodded but kept her eyes wide to signify it could end at any minute if they made too much noise. She whispered to Julie, "Have you seen Honey?"

Julie looked puzzled.

"It's the toy duck I made her out of old jumpsuits and bedding. She loves it but I haven't been able to find it since I unpacked."

Julie motioned to the door. "Think it's on the ship still?"

"Probably if it's not here."

"You want me to go check?"

"Would you mind if I do? I know the usual hiding places. I won't be gone long."

Julie waved a hand. "Go ahead. She's probably pretty tired. She should sleep, right?"

"Should. If not, call her dad." Marlow made a face.

"Ah, I'll be okay."

"Thanks."

Marlow headed out of the hut. The air felt good. The few minutes of freedom would feel good as well. As much as she'd wanted to see people again after they woke everyone up, she was ready for a moment alone. She went down the path they'd come. Lana mentioned the ship would be open if they needed to get any supplies they hadn't carried in on the first round. They only had to follow the one rule, that they would live in the huts.

The rocks called to her and she took off, leaping over ones in her way and darting between the rising walls on her sides. The jog invigorated her. It reminded her of how fit she'd been when they were in the Belt. At least, before she was pregnant, then all she was good for were walks. She thought back to those dull days with sadness. They were bland and seemed endless, but Honey was there with her, eventually Marlin showed up, and then the whole Rami situation. There were some good memories, but they always ended in pain. Rami was killed right in front of her. No one knew every detail from the wild exodus of the Belt, but she'd lost her two companions, just like Jason, just like her mom. She feared getting close to anyone again. Even Zane seemed to be distancing himself. Maybe it was for the better. If they could really build a life on Wyan, it would be Marlow and Avani against the world, or *universe,* the same as it had always been.

The ship came into view. A large, ugly lump of titanium sticking out like a sore thumb amongst the beauty of the planet. She imagined it was what people on Earth felt like when trains and cars started showing up. Sure, they were cool, intriguing and most of all useful, but at what cost in the long run? At what cost were skyscrapers, cell phones, and nuclear weapons? She was one of the few left to witness their price. Wyan was mostly untouched by all that, and Lana seemed intent on keeping it that way. That was one thing they agreed on.

Marlow continued her jog until she hit the ramp. It wasn't that she was in that much of a hurry. Avani might wake up crying, but she'd been fed. She'd be okay. If not, Julie would ask somebody. She would, wouldn't she? Marlow dashed up the ramp and down the halls until she found her bunk. It was dark on the ship, making it eerie as she looked around. Thankfully, the solar panels were sucking in the sun that never stopped. She was able to turn on a few lights and found Honey tucked behind the bunk. Marlow held it up, examining her handiwork. It was blue, like the old jumpsuits they'd worn when they were first picked up. Its eyes were carefully aligned buttons from one of the suits and its bill was a pocket flap that she folded and sewed onto the end of the head. Honey was full of mattress stuffing she'd picked out a little at a time and contained one feather directly in the middle. Marlow found it in her bag when they were aboard the *Mack*. It was the first day she felt well enough from her incision to get up and do an inventory of what she'd packed and what made it out of the Belt with her. The feather was stuck in a pant leg and it fell out when she gave them a shake. She'd picked it up with no lack of tears as she ran her fingers along it. One day, she'd tell Avani the story of Honey the duck. Until then, Honey would be with her whether she knew it or not.

Marlow tucked Honey under her arm and exited her bunk. She was passing the seats they used for takeoffs and landings when she heard a banging, then scrambling across the floor. There was someone, or something in the ship with her. It was dark in the hall, only the faint glow from the ramp thirty feet ahead. The sound came from the seating area. She could hear breathing—throaty, loud breaths and she wondered what kind of animal had made its way onto the ship. Had she really landed on a new planet and taken off on her own with no fear of what might be out there?

"Hello?" she called. She locked her gaze on one of the far seats, almost sure there was a lump of shadow out of place. "Is someone back there?" The shadow moved in one quick lunge behind a set of two other seats across from it. There was another bang as it settled against the seats.

"Shit-bitch," came a voice. It was odd, almost guttural, like a teenage boy whose friends' voices have all changed and he's trying to keep up with them.

"Who's there?" asked Marlow.

She clutched Honey close.

"Barchek," came the voice.

It sounded more childish this time.

"Barchek?" repeated Marlow. "Who are you? What are you doing on the ship?"

"Barchek, shit-bitch."

"Right." Marlow's fear was easing away, and her intrigue was picking up. "I hear you know some good swear words. Wanna come out so I can see you?"

33

There was a mumbling of the Wyan language and Marlow hurried through her pocket to put in her earpiece. She caught the tail end o something about its mom being mad.

"Please come out. I won't tell."

The shadow grew behind the seats, moving closer until the light from the ramp hit. It was a Wyan child, probably four feet when it was or all fours. It had its hands raised at her to signify no harm. Apparently, tha signal was universal.

"Hey. You're okay. What were you doing in there?" Marlow realized she was still asking the poor thing questions it couldn't answer "Sorry, you can't understand me."

"Cunt," said the child.

Marlow furrowed her brow. "I hope you didn't mean that. Who taught you those words?"

She spoke slowly, hoping if the Wyan had learned some curse words she may have learned others as well.

"Walt...Purse."

Marlow's eyebrows shot up. "Walters and Percy?"

The Wyan nodded.

Marlow shook her head. "Those bastards are teaching you curse words but nothing useful. Figures."

"Bastard." The Wyan nodded in agreement.

"Right. You probably know that one." Marlow leaned down by the Wyan. "We've got to teach you some useful words." She pointed at herself. "I'm Marlow."

The Wyan squinted. "Mar-low?"

"Yes, and you..." She pointed. "Barchek? Is that your name?"

"Barchek," the Wyan confirmed.

"Awesome, progress." Marlow waved for the Wyan to follow. "Will you come off the ship and maybe we can talk more."

Barchek looked confused.

"Just follow me." Marlow took Barchek by the arm, noticing the violet coloring on her cheeks. Barchek was a little girl.

Barchek lowered her head and started walking, mumbling in

Wyan again. This time Marlow picked up the whole sentence about Barchek's mom being mad that she'd snuck onto the ship.

"Bal," Marlow repeated. "Is that Mom?"

"Bal." Barchek nodded.

Marlow wasn't sure if Barchek was confirming she had the right word or just repeating things. She hoped for the former.

"Okay, I won't say anything to Bal." Marlow made as many hand motions she could think of to reassure the child.

When they hit the ground again, Barchek looked around, waved at Marlow and took off running towards a group of wrecked huts. Marlow watched for a minute as the Wyan tucked behind one and disappeared. Marlow considered going to find her and making sure she was okay, then she looked down at the stuffed duck in her hand and realized who the alien was on the planet. She decided it was time to jog back and make sure Avani wasn't screaming Julie's ear off yet. She waved goodbye at the wrecked huts, hoping Barchek saw and understood.

Chapter Eight

After a rest period, the humans met in the center of their village. They were lacking in a real town hall but settled on some wood blocks for chairs.

"I'm starving," said Peter.

"Food's coming soon." Lana watched the path to the Wyan village. "Though today we do need to discuss sustaining this many people long term. We've been here off and on for the past two and a half years, but we've never settled in properly. Now that our numbers are up again, we'll have to assign jobs and work on our colony."

"There are so few of us though," said Captain Davis. "I thought you had more of your team here." He stood up, looking around as if he'd see the rest of their numbers hiding behind the trees. "Are we really it?"

Lana nodded. "We lost half our team on an expedition shortly before our trip to the Belt." Lana looked down in shame, shaking her head. "We were trying to learn more about the Night Chasers. We never heard from them again. You were recruited because we believe we can truly make this planet the next Earth. But we need all the help we can get."

"Then why didn't you stay longer?" said Peter. "When you came back to the Belt. Why didn't you pitch it to all of them? If we had everybody—"

"Robin Visser and the founding families would not have let that happen. You know it as well as I."

"It's true," said Arjen. "My dad lives and dies with the Belt. It's his life's mission, and we could only tell so many back there; in fear, they would turn us in and none of us could come here."

"Wish they would've," Peter muttered.

A swishing of feet in the grass was heard. The group looked up to see two smaller Wyans carrying baskets overflowing with produce. They stopped to talk to Lana for a second as she thanked them, then they were off.

"Dig in," said Lana.

Everyone seemed to forget their discussion for a moment while they rifled through the baskets. The humans who'd been there before knew where to start. They led the others in the proper ways to peel and shell the produce.

Marlow bit into a piece of fruit. It looked like an eggplant, but tasted more like a melon.

"So, the females have the violet markings," said Marlow, catching some of the juice dripping down her chin with the back of her hand. "The males, like Bruuth, are a little bigger with wider faces..." She looked after the two Wyan deliverers as they disappeared into the rocks.

"There is a third gender," said Lana, "or *non*-gender, if you will. Those two that brought the food are called Wits, which roughly translates to it or them."

Marlow raised her eyebrows. "They call them it?"

"Not exactly. The Wits are actually genderless. They cannot reproduce. They have no sexual organs. Their only purpose is to serve."

"So, they're like slaves then," said Zane. "Sounds pretty bad to me."

"They're not slaves. They just know their role in society here."

"So, if they can't reproduce," asked Marlin. "Why haven't they died off?"

"The women give birth to them," said Lana. "It's completely random as far as we can tell. Sometimes they have males, sometimes females and sometimes Wits. They live with the results. Like I said, everyone knows their role."

"Still sounds fucked up to me," said Zane.

Marlow nodded at him in agreement.

"While we're on the subject," said Captain Williams. "Nobody get pregnant."

The group turned to stare at him. He was stone faced as if he'd just said the grass was green.

"I'm saying once we get through the time of darkness, we can focus on that. Until then, we can't have anyone out of commission."

"Pregnancy isn't a disability," said Marlow.

Williams turned to her with his lips pursed. "Oh yes, would you like to be carrying around a fetus while you're being chased by those *things*?"

He pointed a thick finger toward the mountains in the distance. The tallest peak, called Ruh'la, stared down at them as its caps were darkened by the blackness behind.

Arjen stood. "I think the point is, we don't need anything else on our minds when the time comes. Afterward..."

"We'll have an orgy," yelled out Walters, leading to erupted laughs from the group. "Just tell me the time and place."

Lana put her head in her hands.

Walters clapped his hands. "All right, let's get this show on the road. Who's coming fishing with me today? I am not eating another vegetarian meal. In case nobody's noticed, they don't have great toilets out here."

"I'll come," said Marlin.

"Me too," said Zane.

"Follow me to the storehouse." Walters stood. "We'll need a couple poles and the machetes."

"Jesus," said Marlin. "What kind of fish do they have out here?"

"You'll see."

Lana watched them go. "All right then. Admani, I want to show you some samples I've collected for the lab. I could use your expertise on a few of them."

"Let's do it," said Admani.

They walked together with Arjen trailing behind.

"Arjen said you have some medical training as well?" asked Lana.

"Some. I can help out where needed. I learned a lot through

Marlow's pregnancy for sure."

"Great."

One by one, the group found places to be until it was only Marlow, Avani, and Isolde.

"What do you make of all this?" asked Marlow.

Ice leaned forward on the log seat. "I'm still taking it all in."

"Did you ever imagine...?"

"That I'd completely turn my back on the Belt? On my mother?"

Marlow propped Avani against one of the seats, sitting next to her on the ground for support. "I was gonna say that you'd be helping colonize a new planet?"

Ice huffed out a breath. "Not really. The trips *we* went on were for collecting, not looking for a new home."

"Do you regret it?"

Ice shrugged. "Too early to know."

"I guess so."

"What they did to you there..." Ice began. "I see why you left. I don't blame you. It was the right choice. The rest of us? We'll have to see, but I feel better knowing I don't live in a place with someone who would make that kind of decision."

Marlow looked around. "As far as we know."

Ice nodded. "As far as we know." She stood up and stretched, her long braid swinging over her shoulder. She caught it and held it up. "I'm thinking of cutting my hair."

"Oh yeah? Did I inspire you?"

"Maybe, but first things first, I'm going back to my hut for a nap. Zane snored something awful last night, or should I say, *rest period*. Still getting used to that. At least with the TechBubble we could turn down the lights."

"Right," said Marlow. "Zane mainly snores when he's on his back. You just gotta roll him over."

"Noted." Ice gave a half-salute to Marlow and turned back toward the huts.

"What do you say Vani?" Marlow grabbed the baby's hands.

"Want to meet my new friend?"

Avani cooed a reply and they were on their way.

~ * ~

Walters led Marlin and Zane through a lightly worn path in the forest behind the huts. There was a chorus of chirps, howls, and hoots from unseen animals. Bugs flew by but seemed uninterested in the humans, as if they didn't recognize them. When the trees thinned out sand began showing up underfoot. Soon there was just a spattering of bushes and a panoramic view of the ocean. The sun reflected off the water on a cloudless day. They were standing on a giant sand dune. Zane and Marlin each held a fishing pole, scavenged from Earth, and Walters had a machete in each hand like some kind of jungle warrior.

"Quite the view, ain't it?" Walters rolled his sleeves back to the elbows, revealing dark, thick arm hair. "You ever run down a dune?"

"Can't say that I have," said Marlin. "Can't say I've ever been on a dune."

"No," said Zane. "We weren't allowed near the beaches growing up."

Walters put his fists on his hips, a machete sticking out of each still. "That's a sad story. I'd say it's time for a little fun."

He pointed a blade toward a flock of mercows near the water line. "Watch this."

He shuffled his feet out of his shoes and took off in a full sprint down the dune. It was a fifty-degree slope going a hundred feet down to the water. Walters was picking up speed as sand flew in the air behind him. His two companions watched with fear that he'd trip and impale himself on one of the machetes.

The flock didn't notice him until he was twenty feet back, then there was pandemonium. The birds, who were taller than Walters with the crests on their heads, scattered, but none of them planned which way they'd go. A few ran into each other, letting out loud "*Coh, cohs!*" When Walters reached them, the last mercow jumped out of the way just in time to avoid the swing of his blade. Walters hit the water at great speed, splashing hard, trying to keep his balance when a small wave took him out at the waist, and he went headfirst into the blue.

Zane looked at Marlin with concern, then back out to the water where Walters was standing up, waving a machete and laughing.

"Fucking cold," he yelled. Despite the constant sun, the atmosphere only let in so much heat from the small star. It was just enough to keep it warm, but the water was another story.

"Come on," yelled Walters.

The birds regained their composure but had no intentions of hanging around the crazy man with the weapons any longer. They made their way down the beach.

"All right," said Zane, looking at Marlin. "You up for it?"

"No way. I'll take it slow, thank you very much. You go ahead, but why don't you hand me your pole first?"

"Thanks." Zane gave him the fishing pole, dumped his shoes and took off.

He went down the warm sand, falling a couple times and rolling to a stop before he got back up, shook off the sand and continued on. By the time he reached the water he was breathing hard, splashing into it and feeling the shock on his skin.

"Jesus."

Walters was a few feet away.

"Told you."

They convened on the beach, laughing about the run, the water, and the mercows.

"See this?" Walters spread out his arms, still dripping with water, and turned in a circle. "This is why we couldn't stay on the Belt."

"What about Ceres?" asked Zane. "Ceres had oceans."

"Not like this, and nothing had been living on Ceres until we showed up. There aren't millions of years of species around, natural grass or trees. It's all artificially put together there. It's not right. This, on the other hand, is where we belong."

Marlin ran a handful of sand through his fingers. "You've got a point. This is nothing like Ceres. Now how about these fish? If you didn't scare them all off."

"We'll move up the beach," said Walters.

They followed, set up their poles, then waited for bites. Walters was whistling a tune when Marlin finally asked, "Something up with you we should know about?"

Walters checked the pole then raised his eyebrows in question.

"You just seem a lot happier today than usual."

"Fine, I'll tell ya, but you can't say anything to anyone else."

"Okay."

He put his hands out to tell his story. "I went by the lab before breakfast and talked to Admani. I told her a few jokes, got her laughing and she agreed to take a walk with me later."

Zane and Marlin shared confused looks.

Walters ran a hand through his hair, sending sand and water springing out of it.

"That's Wyan-speak for going on a date."

"Oh..." said Marlin. "Does *she* know that?"

"Well, I'm sure she does. I mean, why else would I ask her to take a walk later?"

"She's a scientist, dude," said Zane. "Maybe she thinks you're going to show her something interesting to study and sample."

"Oh, shit. You think?"

"I don't know, but you should probably ask her before you make any moves."

"Damn women. Still confusing even when there's only five of 'em." He shook his head, looking out at the water. "Still, there's only so many of us guys and who knows how many of you are gay. Process of elimination. I've got a chance. I've got a chance..."

Marlin and Zane shared another look when they saw a tug on one of the lines.

"Oh yeah," said Walters.

He started reeling it in as the others watched. Walters got up and walked to the water's edge, continuing the slow turn of the reel. He was squinting at the bright waves coming in, looking for a sign when a dark blue fish popped out of the water. It tucked back in and fought the pull as Walters talked to it. "No, you don't. Come on."

He stopped reeling and started pulling the line hand over hand until there were only a few feet left. The fish gave up pulling and made a lunge out of the water directly at Walters' head. He cried out as it grazed off his face and landed on the shore, flopping around, tangling itself in the line.

"Motherfucker." Walters held a hand to his cheek while the other kept the line. There was a trail of watery blood running through his fingers. "It attacked me."

Zane and Marlin were examining it from a distance.

"Those fins look sharp," said Marlin.

"No shit," said Walters. "Somebody hold the line a minute."

Zane took it, keeping a fair distance from the flopping fish. Walters had Marlin check out his cheek.

"Not too deep," said Marlin. "Good thing it didn't get your eye."

Walters dabbed the blood on his shirt then reached for a machete. He held it up over the fish, who was barely fighting anymore, but he didn't bring it down.

"Walters?" said Marlin.

Walters was looking to an uneven spot on the edge of the sand dune. "I've got a better idea." He brought the machete down on the fishing line, cutting it a few feet from the fish's head, then he lifted it up and smiled. "How would you guys like to catch a dragon?"

~ * ~

Marlow circled the *Mack* with Avani strapped to her chest. She felt like she was back in Isolde's strength-training class. She caught just a glimpse of Barchek's rear through one of the broken-down huts. Marlow shushed Avani and reached down for a rock. She snuck near the back of the hut knowing Barchek and her perky ears would pick up on her any second if Avani didn't give them away first.

Marlow tossed the rock on the other side of the hut. It skidded through the grass five feet ahead of Barchek and she was frozen, watching the movement, trying to figure out what caused it.

Marlow snuck up until she was a couple feet back then yelled, "Hey."

Barchek jumped and turned at the same time, losing her balance as she did and fell to her side. She craned her neck to look up at Marlow and Marlow feared she would cry.

Barchek burst into a honking laugh. She rolled onto her back and continued. Avani watched her with wide eyes, turning her head the best she could from her position.

"It's okay," said Marlow, patting Avani's back. "I guess I didn't scare her too bad."

Barchek flipped herself up in an impressive motion and was in Marlow's face.

"'Gain, 'gain."

"Ah-gain," said Marlow.

"Ah-gain," said Barchek.

Marlow sighed. "Okay, just one more time, then I need to go." She held up a finger to confirm."

"Wun mo."

"Okay, okay. I'll count." Marlow covered her eyes, feeling almost as much excitement as the little alien child did for repeated games of hide-and-seek. The look on Barchek's face made it worth it, her rows of flat teeth showing in a pure, joyous smile.

Marlow finished counting and began her walk around the area. So far, she'd been behind a hut or tree every time. After the first time, hiding in the ragged field, Barchek had gotten better each round. She moved without making a sound and controlled her breathing well. No wonder she'd been the first Wyan Marlow heard speak English.

After the first sweep, Marlow decided Barchek had taken it to the next level. She couldn't find her anywhere. After the second sweep, Marlow was a little concerned, then she looked at the open ramp to the *Mack*. Surely Barchek knew better than to go back on the ship. Marlow had met her mom when she'd arrived that first day. They'd spent a moment of Marlow explaining she could understand them with her translator, and that she wanted to learn from them. Barchek's mom seemed relieved by the end of the conversation.

When she walked off, Marlow pictured her going to have a glass of wine and get a pedicure. *Good luck to whoever had to do that job,* thought Marlow, with a laugh to herself. Though she couldn't get over the look in the Wyan mother's eyes. Hollow would be the best definition. *And where did they live?* Marlow hadn't been by the main village yet, but it definitely wasn't in the direction she was going. She needed to work on her Wyan and see if she could get an explanation out of the mom.

Marlow stopped at the bottom of the ramp, looked up and considered calling for Barchek to come out, then she looked around. Barchek's mom was nowhere to be seen. She'd give her this one. Barchek knew it was the last game. Marlow would remind her of the importance of staying off the ship, then mention to Lana they should probably close the ramp from there on out.

Marlow went up the ramp and passed the takeoff seats. She saw nothing out of the ordinary and continued down the long hall. She checked a few rooms, growing more anxious as she went. Every room was dark. The hall was dark. Avani was quiet, which was rare, but after Marlow checked her breathing, she found her to just be asleep. When Marlow turned down the next hall, she finally saw the extra shadow she was looking for. Barchek sat outside one of the bunk doors. There were two things that gave Marlow pause, Barchek wasn't attempting to hide anymore, and there was light coming from under the door. *Why was there a light on with the door closed?* Barchek saw her when she was a few feet back. She looked up with big eyes and a finger at her lips. She pointed at the door and whispered. The translator didn't pick up the low volume. Marlow leaned in and made her whisper it again.

"He's hurting her," Barchek whispered.

Marlow tilted her head, then put her ear to the door. She didn't need a translation for what she heard next.

"Say my name, whore," came a man's voice. Marlow scrubbed

her brain for which man it was. There were only so many on Wyan.

"Thomas," came another voice, and it was unmistakably Julie, her new roommate.

Marlow's lips pulled back and her stomach turned. She wanted to tell Barchek to get the hell out of there, but she might need her. There was still a sleeping baby strapped to her chest. If she needed to—

"Louder," the man again.

"Thomas," said Julie with more force.

"Who's my little bitch?"

"I am."

There was a slapping sound and Barchek shot Marlow a concerned look. "Shit-bitch?" Barchek whispered.

Marlow nodded and would've laughed in any other circumstance.

"You want this?" asked the man.

"Yes, Thomas, yes." Julie sounded like a bad actress selling her interest in a wealthy businessman. Marlow knew who the man was and felt sick to her stomach. She had to get out of there before Avani woke up and gave them away.

Marlow grabbed Barchek's arm and put a finger to her lips, waving her to follow. Barchek protested but Marlow waved a hand to signal no worries. "Game."

Barchek's head tilted at her. "Game?" she asked.

Marlow nodded then pulled her down the hall away from whatever the hell was going on in that room.

When they reached the bottom of the ramp, Marlow reminded Barchek to never go into the ship again. She asked again if Julie was okay and if she was hurt. Marlow repeated the "game" explanation. It was the best she could do with the limited vocabulary. Barchek accepted it the best she could be expected to, and Marlow said her goodbyes.

The walk back to their village gave her plenty of time to contemplate.

~ * ~

"You're on tail duty," whispered Walters.

"I am goddamn not," said Marlin.

He looked at Zane with pleading eyes to put a stop to the whole situation.

Zane held up a machete in a shaking hand. "I will gladly switch."

"No, no," said Marlin. "I'm saying, isn't there another way?"

"You wanna eat," said Walters, "you gotta hunt."

"Fish." Marlin motioned toward the ocean.

"Fish ain't gonna feed the whole village."

"Oh, Jesus."

"Okay, positions." Walters left the two of them to step to the other side of a mound in the dune.

They all watched a small hole in the sand grow bigger. There was a flickering tongue, then a jaw that looked like it belonged in Jurassic Park. Its eyes were fixed straight ahead on the blue, razor-finned fish. The dragon, as Walters called it, didn't see the humans flanking it. It wasn't used to being hunted. The long, moss-colored body slid out of its sand-home. Zane and Marlin grew more amazed by the second as the ten-foot-long monster emerged from the small hole in the sand. It tested the fish with a whack from its front foot, then planted the foot on the fish's head, ripping off the razored fin, tossing it like an unwanted chicken bone.

Zane was so entranced; he barely saw Walters waving him in. Marlin gave him a gentle push and he stumbled forward. He was at the side of the dragon, only a few feet away when it turned, spreading its jaws wide, showing its teeth.

"Oh shit," said Zane. He took a weak swing to keep the beast back. It lunged once. Zane swung again. The dragon caught his pattern and met the blade with its claws, knocking it out of Zane's hand. It lunged again. This time Zane had no defense. The jaws came toward his face, wide enough to fit Zane's head in. The dragon got itself high off the ground when it stopped midair. Its jaws shut as it fell to the sand. Its head snapped to look back at Marlin, tugging on its tail with all he had. The green beast flipped around, taking Marlin down as he lost his grip. It opened its mouth again to go after Marlin when Walters stabbed down with his machete, striking it between the eyes and into its lower jaw. Walters pushed hard, like he planned to pin the dragon to the ground, but the ground was sand. The beast shook him off. The machete remained like a cocktail stick slick with blood.

The dragon was making an awful screeching sound at them, turning in circles to confirm it was surrounded. It swung its tail and Zane jumped it, grabbing his machete from the sand.

"Just distract it," said Walters.

Zane swung the blade, striking the dragon in the nose while it fought back, shaking its head to try to dislodge the other machete. It pawed at its head as Walters jumped on its back.

"Marlin, get the back." Walters rode the dragon like a bucking bronco.

"What am I...?"

"Just sit on it," Walters screamed.

Marlin stood rooted to the ground, so Zane ran around the back, jumping on with all his weight. Walters held the blade with two hands. He gave a firm yank back like he was forcing a car into first gear. There was the sickening sound of tearing flesh, but the result was immediate. Zane and Walters felt the body go limp and drop to the sand. They sat for a few seconds, breathing hard, making sure it really was over. Marlin watched from a few feet back.

"Is it...?" asked Marlin.

Walters was drenched in dragon blood, laughing like a psychopath. "Woo. We're eating good tonight."

Chapter Nine

Walters walked into the camp with a huge smile. His clothes were covered in dried blood. Zane urged him to wash up, but he said it would ruin his grand entrance. They carried their dragon, tied to a log with fishing line, over their shoulders, while Marlin trailed behind with the remains of the blue razor-fin.

Williams looked over from a discussion with Arjen and started clapping. A few joined in, as Percy ran up to examine the dragon.

"Holy shit. You actually caught one."

"Not just caught," said Walters.

"Can we please set this down?" asked Zane.

"Right."

Walters led them to the circle of log seats and dropped the dragon in the middle. He looked around to spot Admani watching from the door to the lab, then he called out, "Now, someone start a fire, we're having dragon tonight."

He walked tall toward his hut. Lana fell in next to him.

"Did you get bit?"

Walters shook his head. "Nope."

"Good, 'cause we don't know if those are poisonous." She examined his face. "What's this?"

Walters wiped at his cheek and grimaced. "From the fish."

She nodded and walked back toward the group.

Walters eyed Admani as he reached his hut. "I should probably get changed before dinner. Still up for that walk later?"

She blinked a few times. "Sure. If you are."

"I'm prime." He tucked in the hut, closed the door and collapsed on the floor.

Zane lay next to the seats, across from their catch, as Isolde and Percy stacked logs for the fire.

"All right there?" Ice asked Zane.

"Just beat. Have you *been* down to the dunes yet? We had to lug that monster all the way up."

Ice wrinkled her face into a forced smile. "Oh, but you looked so tough doing it. Walters especially with all the blood."

"Shut it." Zane laughed with her.

Marlin sat down on one of the wooden seats next to where Zane lay. He was still holding the fish by the cut piece of line.

"That is the last time I let Walters take me fishing. I thought that was supposed to be peaceful."

"It was anything but," said Zane. "But at least we're fed."

His heart was slowing down, and it felt good to just stare up at the trees for a minute.

"Well, count me out next time."

Captain Williams stood next to Marlin with a long knife. "Mind if I do the honors?" He reached out a hand and Marlin gladly gave him the fish.

"Watch for the fins. They're sharp."

Marlow sat down next to Marlin, watching Zane with Avani on her lap.

"That's your big strong daddy. Yes, it is."

"Please don't," said Zane.

"What? I'm just talking."

"I'm just..." Zane propped himself up on his elbows. "I'm still not sure how I feel about all that."

Marlow's face tightened. "What does *that* mean?"

Marlin stood up. "Let me go see if Williams needs help." And promptly removed himself from the conversation.

Marlow, expectant, stared at Zane.

He sighed. "Just being a dad. I never said...*you* never planned on..."

Marlow softened. "I know, but once she was here, everything changed, Zane. Can't you see that?"

"I can. For *you*, but for me..."

"I get it." She sighed. "I just feel like the whole plan, everything we set out to do in the Belt, *for* the Belt, fell through, and now I'm the one left with the child. Everybody else gets to say, 'not my problem, you're the mom.' But I'm over here by myself. I have no clue how to raise a child. I figured it out the best I could while you all slept. Now, I could just use some help."

"I mean," said Zane, "I can—"

"Earthlings?" Marlin walked back over. "I couldn't help but hear. was trying not to, but Marlow, if you need help with Avani, let me help."

"What?"

"I'm saying, let me take her off your hands once in a while." He sighed and looked around. "I'm useless out here otherwise. If that wasn't clear before today...well, Zane can tell you."

"You're not useless, Marlin," said Zane. "I was just as scared."

"But you still got the job done." Marlin shifted from foot to foot. "There's no 'Panel here. I'm not a hunter. I'm not a scientist. I can do a little gathering but besides that, I'm useless."

"You're not—" started Marlow.

"Just let me help. Give this guy a break. He's too young—hell, you're both too young to be raising a child already."

"Not a lot of choice," said Marlow, "given our conditions."

"I know," Marlin looked off to the sky, "but let me give you a little chance, a little of your freedom back. You deserve that much."

They finished the fire and roasted the dragon in sections. They used salt and wild herbs the Wyans helped them collect for seasoning. The overall smell was odd. Williams skinned the beast, and its greasy insides dripped into the fire to make smoke that moved the birds from the trees. A couple mercows stood at the edge of the human's village, watching.

No one was sure where to start, so Captain Williams and Percy chopped off hunks to pass around. The meat wasn't half bad for thos‹ who had been eating solids for more than a week. The rest went light o‹ it. Marlow gagged down a few pieces before she decided to grab som‹ more fruit from the morning.

"Hold on," said Lana, between bites. "Where's Walters? He'‹ going to be pissed we started without him."

Williams waved a hand, holding a bone with loose meat swinging "Ah, we saved him the head. He'll probably want the brain or the heart a‹ is the tradition."

"There is no tradition."

"Yes, there is," said Percy. "Remember when Ken caught tha‹ mercow? He ate the heart before we even cooked it."

"Yes," said Lana, "but mercow tastes terrible, they're a bugger t‹ catch, and Ken's no longer with us."

"All the more reason to carry on the tradition with a new animal."

Lana scoffed and turned back to her hunk of meat.

"I'll check on him," said Marlin. "I've had enough anyway."

He stepped down the slight decline to the huts. Before anyon‹ could strike up a conversation, Marlin was calling for help.

Admani and Julie were the first ones there. Walters lay just insid‹ the doorway, still in his blood-covered clothes.

"He's breathing but his pulse is racing." Julie squatted next to him

"Let's get him to the lab," said Admani.

The rest of the group joined them and helped carry Walters ont‹ an exam table in the lab.

"Get him some water," Julie said to anyone listening.

Admani stripped off his shirt and wiped him down, revealing ‹ gash on his left breast.

"I think he's been poisoned."

Julie rubbed a wet rag on his head. Walters blinked at her.

"Can't see right."

"Just try to stay calm," she said.

Admani leaned close to Julie. "Can you get me a blood sample?"‹

Julie nodded and reached for a needle, extracted some blood, the‹

inserted it into a machine to read. It was a painstaking two minutes while Admani tried to keep Walters calm.

Walters blinked and mumbled but not much he said was coherent. Julie pulled the blood sample out and held it up to Admani. They read the machine's screen together.

"Okay," said Admani. "It's definitely some kind of poison. I think I have the tools here to create the antivenom. I'll need some of the dragon's venom to do it though. Is there any left?"

Williams shook his head. "We cooked it. Everything but the skin."

Admani shook her head. "Then we need more."

"*More?*" asked Williams.

"More."

"Oh, Jesus," said Marlin.

"Come on," said Zane. "Grab the machetes."

"No, no, we can't..." Marlin looked at the hitch in each breath Walters took. "Damnit."

Zane headed off, joined by Ice, Percy, and Arjen. Marlin watched them, sighed and followed.

Admani and Julie rotated wet rags and vital checks while others stood by nervously watching. After Zane's group disappeared into the forest, Lana huffed and took off out of the lab. Marlow was pacing outside with Avani.

"Where're you headed?" asked Marlow.

"To the *Mack*," said Lana. "Gonna check the med bay for anything we may have missed."

"Didn't we clean it out on the first day?"

"Yes, but I've gotta do something. I can't stand around anymore."

"I'll come with," said Marlow.

"As long as you keep up." She motioned at Avani.

"I will."

They took the path between the mountains at a slow jog. After Lana's initial rebuff, she seemed happy to have the company.

"I just can't lose another person." Lana let out a sick laugh. "Not like they grow on trees around here."

"No, they sure don't," said Marlow.

"I should've followed him into his hut. I should've checked on him before the meal."

"You didn't know. He said he was good."

"Walters is a loose cannon. He's been more neurotic since Ken died. If I would've thought about it before all this, I would've had Arjen convince a belt psychiatrist to come with us. We could probably all use one."

"What about them?" asked Marlow. "What if the psychiatrist couldn't cope with life out here either?"

"Then maybe we're all just fucked, Marlow."

They came to the clearing, seeing the giant ship parked at the end of it. Lana had little hope, but she picked up her pace. She was first to the ramp when she heard Marlow scream. She turned to see a Wyan rolling on its back honking out a laugh.

"Barchek," yelled Marlow. "You scared the shit out of me."

"Shit-bitch," said Barchek. "Game?"

"No, no game. Um...friend is hurt."

Barchek tilted her head. Lana was frozen at the stairs when Barchek's mom came out looking concerned. She mumbled something and Marlow had to tuck back in her earpiece and have her repeat it.

"What's wrong?" asked Barchek's mom.

Marlow looked to Lana and she came back to join them. She explained in the Wyan language about Walters and his injury. She didn't know the word for the dragon. Barchek and her mom didn't seem to understand it.

"I can see?" Barchek's mom—whose name was Cannie, Marlow learned—asked them.

"Do you think you can help?" Lana asked.

Cannie put her hands out, palms up. "I can try."

Marlow agreed to lead them back to the village while Lana did a quick sweep of the *Mack*. She promised to catch up as soon as she could.

When they reached the village not much had changed. More of the viewers were pacing outside the lab rather than in. Marlow took Cannie and Barchek to the fire where the skin of the dragon was laid out. Williams planned to make it into a tough leather.

Cannie picked up strips of it, examining the hide. When Marlow showed her the cooked skull, she got the picture. Cannie grunted a word that the translator didn't pick up. Marlow shook her head and pointed at her ear. Cannie tried again.

"Lana said poison," said Cannie. Marlow nodded. "No poison."

Marlow pointed to the lab. "But he's sick."

Cannie squinted and Barchek translated "sick" for her. Cannie nodded but pointed at the skull. "Not from this."

Marlow fought a squirming Avani who was tired of riding in her pack. "Then what?"

"Cunt, cunt," said Barchek on the other side of the firepit.

Marlow stepped over, once again hoping the child did not mean what she said.

Barchek was pointing at the blue razor-fin sitting in a pile of fish bones.

"Yes," said Cannie. "Those are poisonous. Did your friend—"

Marlow was already running to the lab.

"It's the fish. It's the fish."

Chapter Ten

Admani and Julie administered the antivenom while the camp waited on the results. Cannie and Barchek waited with Marlow while Peter went to call off the dragon hunt.

Lana paced, holding her head and cursing at herself. When she'd learned of the true origin of the poison she was incensed. He'd told her the cut on his face was just from the fish, but she'd failed to see past the great danger of the dragon to notice the threat a little fish could be.

Williams and Davis stood to the side of the burnt-out fire, deep in discussion. Marlow didn't like the way Williams' eyes shifted to her. She wanted to strike up a real conversation with the Wyans, but each sentence with Cannie ended short without her understanding much. Marlow needed her to initiate so her translator could help her out. Barchek waited respectfully for a few minutes before asking for another game of hide-and-seek.

Finally, a minute before the dragon hunters appeared at the trees, Admani walked out and shook her head.

"He's unconscious. We got his heart rate down. We won't know if the antivenom worked just yet. If we would've known earlier...it's just had time to move. Thankfully, it's a slow-moving poison, but we don't know all the damage it's done."

Peter stepped out of the trees with the dragon hunters. They looked defeated and relieved at the same time. When they were caught up to speed on the full situation, the group sat around the coals of the fire, waiting for further word.

Barchek was completely impatient at that point and Cannie

signaled Marlow they'd be heading back. She gave her best wishes for Walters and was regretful she couldn't have done more. Marlow and Lana hanked her as they walked away. Williams was at their side as soon as he Wyans were out of earshot.

"Interesting, isn't it?" His baritone voice made Marlow's skin crawl.

"What's that?" asked Lana.

He leaned on a tree and continued, "They're vegetarian, aren't hey?"

Lana just nodded. It was a known fact all Wyans were.

"How do they know so much about venomous animals? What business do they have hunting those dragons or catching fish?"

Lana frowned at him. "They could've come across them down by the water."

Williams straightened up. "They *could've,* but to know, confidently, that the dragons are not poisonous, but the fish is?"

Lana turned to look him straight in the face. "What are you getting at with this?"

Williams didn't back down. "There's a reason they don't live with the rest of them."

"Yes, because the Night Chasers destroyed their village and killed most of them, along with Barchek's father."

"I've heard the story." Williams' voice was getting more commanding. "The other survivors moved into the main village up the road. Why not them?"

"I'm not their shrink, but they're probably emotionally attached."

"I think they're sneaking around the ship. Especially the little one."

Marlow's mind lit up like a light bulb. She could hear his voice repeating in her head, *"Say my name, whore."* Captain Thomas Williams was wondering if Barchek was going to turn him in for his escapades with Julie.

Lana looked confused. "What does that have to do with their knowledge of venomous fish?"

"They're plotting something back there. I wouldn't be surprised if they were part of what happened to Walters."

"They were nowhere near him," said Marlow.

"Shut your mouth, sympathizer."

"Williams," said Lana. "Keep it civil."

He took a step back. "Forgive me. It just seems like the young mother here has struck up quite a friendship with the girl and yet could not warn us about what happened to Walters."

Lana was about to rebuke him when Marlow stopped her.

"No, I wasn't able to stop Walters from getting himself poisoned, but thankfully Lana and I got the Wyans here to help us try to save him. Still, you're right, Williams, we really should do something about Barchek going on the ship. Maybe we should lock it up. Make it so only Lana has the code, so no one else can get in without her allowing it."

Marlow stared hard at him, waiting to see if he'd budge. Lana looked at both of them like they were crazy.

Williams tried to read the Earthling, then said, "That would be a bit hasty. Situations like today have proven it prudent for us to still have access to the *Mack*. I have a better idea. We go right to the source and we ask."

"What are you saying?" asked Lana.

"I'm saying we get some answers about what else they know that they're not telling us."

"You want to interrogate a child?"

Williams pursed his lips. "I want to know everything I can about our enemies."

"The Wyans are not our enemies, remember that? We are working together with them to end their suffering and live in peace."

Williams pointed a finger in Lana's face. "*Rule* in peace. Don't forget that." He turned on a heel and walked to his hut.

Lana watched him go, then met Marlow's eyes and growled. "Ah, I just can't right now."

Marlow considered telling her what she'd heard on the *Mack*, but decided against it. Lana headed to the lab to check on Walters, and

Marlow had a second to think before Honey the duck was swung into her face by a chubby-armed baby.

~ * ~

The village settled down for a rest period. Admani and Julie took shifts watching Walters' vitals.

Zane had just found his way to his bunk in the dark hut when the light from the door blinded him, then it was dark again.

Zane laid down. "Done wandering, Ice?"

"No," came a quiet voice.

Zane rose to his elbows, feeling his body protest from the exertion that day. "Who...?"

"That was really something you did today."

"Peter?"

"First, catching the dragon and carrying it on your shoulders like a fucking warrior. That was one thing, then going back out to get another one with no hesitation...Jesus."

Zane blinked at the dark room, feeling the shadow grow closer. "What are you saying, Peter? I was just doing what needed to be done."

"I noticed." Peter finally had some of his old flair in his voice.

Zane felt Peter's hands working their way up his legs. "Peter?"

Peter's hands stopped, resting on Zane's hips. "I've been an ass. Pretty much since we landed. It wasn't fair to you. I realized you had to do what you had to do, and you just wanted me with you for support and instead..."

Zane met his hands. "It's been different from what we thought it would be. I'm sorry I pulled you away from your life on the Belt for this."

"I'm just glad that if I left the Belt, it was for you and not Mark."

Zane started giggling. "Mark would've been a mistake."

"Right?"

"So...? You just came to apologize?"

"Maybe." Peter gripped the bed and pulled himself up to mount Zane.

"Whoa." Zane felt the electricity in his hips beginning. "Baby, what about Ice? She could be back any minute."

Peter shook his head. "I caught her outside, told her we needed to talk, and she understood. We should have some time."

"Oh, God. I'm *sure* she understood. I'll be hearing it later."

Peter's hand came down to his chest and Zane groaned.

"Sorry," said Peter.

"Just sore from today."

Peter slowed to a gentle massage. "I bet. Don't worry, I'm going to take care of you."

He leaned in and kissed him in the dark, starting at his mouth, then working his way down. Zane lay back and let him work.

An hour later, Ice knocked on the door, cracking it slightly. "Is it safe?"

Zane laughed from the crook of Peter's arm. "You're good, Ice."

She slipped in and found her bunk. "Guess you've smoothed things over."

"Yes," said Peter. "Zane was about to walk me back to my hut."

"Well, don't leave on my behalf."

Peter patted Zane's arm and sat up. "No, I've gotta get back and get some sleep. These bunks were not made for two."

The boys walked out to the silent camp holding hands for the first time since they arrived on Wyan.

"So, how's Percy as a roomie?" said Zane.

"God, with the tinkering. Dude's trying to build an arsenal."

"Probably a good thing, no?"

Peter sighed but didn't reply.

Zane tried to catch his eye. "Peter?"

"Yeah...Zane, we've gotta talk."

"We have been talking."

Peter stopped them near the fire pit, still holding hands.

"What you did today was brave, manly, whatever you wanna call it, but that dragon was just a dragon living peacefully here. It wasn't trying to kill you."

"Well..." said Zane.

"I mean, it wasn't a giant, black monster coming from the frozen darkness behind those mountains."

"We're working on that. That's why your roommate is tinkering all the time. That's why the rest of us—"

"What if we didn't have to?"

"Baby..."

"I mean it. Not everyone here is happy with life on Wyan. I've been talking with Captain Davis, and—"

"Are you serious?" Zane broke their link.

"I just want us to live. I think the Belt is the best chance for that. Let us get to be a boring old couple, rather than a young, hot dead one."

He smiled at Zane, but it was not returned.

"We can't. We can't just leave everyone here. Marlow and the baby..."

"They can come with. Not that you want to be a father anyway."

"Okay, that's what it is, isn't it?"

"What?"

"That attitude. I should've seen it before."

"Before what? Before you asked me to come to this god-forsaken planet with you?"

"Maybe." Zane put his hands on his hips. "You hate it here so much. Your only goal is mutiny now."

"I just want to get us to a better place together. Is that so fucking bad, Zane?"

"If it means deserting our friends, yes."

Peter threw up his arms. "That's kind of what we did when we came here."

Zane shook his head, talking low but intense, "Are you really planning to take the *Mack*?"

"I..."

"Seriously, Peter. Are you going to take the ship? Who all is going?"

Peter shushed him. "We're still working out the details."

"We stripped that ship bare of every resource on the last trip. We took all the medical equipment. You guys wouldn't make it without...I don't know, a lot of stuff."

"If we can get the baths back up and running. I've been talking to Marlin, too. You know he doesn't like it here. It's easier and really, we only need one person awake and the rest in cryo-sleep."

"What if something mechanical fails? Who's going to fix it?"

"Davis."

"All of it? On his own? What if it's outside the ship?"

"That's how they got here in the first place."

"Because they thought they were gonna die. It was a last resort."

"We could make it. It's not any more of a risk than waiting out here to fight those *things*."

"That's what you don't see." Zane paced. "If we survive here, we can actually *survive*, beyond the current generation."

Peter scoffed. "Look who's drinking the Kool-Aid now. You gonna apply to be Lana's little lap-dog?"

Zane's face was tight. He was running over a hundred terrible things he could say now but regret later. Before he had the chance, Peter said, "Just think about it. You come with us; you'll be fucking me. You stay here, you're gonna have to start fucking women."

He continued the walk to his hut alone.

~ * ~

Julie came back to the room, tired. Marlow raised a hand to her and pointed at Avani, finally sleeping in her own little bassinet they'd made. There was a hint of light coming in the window. Marlow had pulled back the shade just enough so she could see what she was doing.

Julie nodded and went to her bunk, taking off her shoes and rubbing her feet.

Marlow came over and talked low. "Any progress?"

"Still stable. I think he'll pull through. We just won't know everything until he can talk to us again."

"I'll let you sleep. I'd just been up with Avani and got her back down. I think I'm done for the moment."

"No worries. I kinda fell asleep watching him. Admani woke me up and now I just feel weird." She rubbed her eyes. "Wanna play cards or something?"

"I could go for some cards."

"Cool, hold on. I got a new deck on our last trip and I haven't been able to play it yet. I think it's called 'You-no.'"

Marlow giggled as she saw Julie produce a deck of Uno cards. "What?"

"Uno," said Marlow. "I've played it before. It's pretty easy to learn."

Julie looked at the deck. "*Uno,* duh, sorry. Can we blame it on the lack of sleep?"

Marlow dealt out their hands and explained the rules since the deck was missing them. Otherwise, it was in good shape for surviving an apocalypse back on Earth.

"So, we haven't gotten to talk about your collection," said Marlow.

Julie looked to her stash of Earth memorabilia. There was the cowboy outfit she'd had Zane try on, some studded black bracelets, random holiday decorations, and, "Is that a big-mouthed bass?"

"Yes." Julie was a little over excited. Avani fussed and rolled over. Julie clapped a hand over her mouth. "Sorry." She got off the bunk they were using for a card table and pulled the mounted bass out of her collection. The wood plaque read, "Big Mouth Billy Bass."

"I can't believe you brought this back."

"I know. I really wish the batteries worked." She looked over at the sleeping baby. "I mean, not right now."

Marlow scrunched her face up. "What does it do when the batteries *do* work?"

"I have no idea."

"Huh." Marlow stared at the fish for another minute. "So, Lana and them were okay with you collecting this *fun* stuff rather than weapons or medicine?"

Julie scratched her head. "Well, there really wasn't much to scavenge when we went. Outside of the weapons we did find, there wasn' much left. The Earth is pretty destroyed and used up."

"Don't I know it."

"I mean, we did our research, or Lana did. We hit up a coupl facilities out in the middle of the Pacific Ocean. There was only so mucl there. The mainland we hit wasn't much better. We got enough of wha they were looking for, so I grabbed a couple fun things. I mean, we'r talking months on the *Mack* to get a few weapons, a few supplies. I needec to make it worthwhile for myself too." Julie put the bass back in its hidin; place behind her bunk. "Don't get me wrong, Lana doesn't know abou all this stuff. I think she's seen something here or there but..."

"I gotcha," said Marlow. "I won't say anything to her, o Williams, or anyone if you don't want."

Julie waved a hand. "Oh, Williams knows. He kinda helped m sneak some of it on."

"The bass?"

"Well, no..." Julie's face drooped a little and Marlow knew sh had to go in for the kill.

"What did he help with?"

"Oh, this and that. Nothing special." She picked up her hand o Uno cards. "Whose turn was it?"

Marlow looked down at her own hand but didn't pick it up. "Julie' Is something going on with you and Williams?"

Her eyes widened but she didn't look up. "What? Like what?"

"I was on the ship yesterday or...whatever day it was. I heard som things."

Julie looked at her, concerned. "What did you hear?"

"Is that, whatever is going on, consensual?"

Julie avoided Marlow's eyes again. "I mean, he's not raping m or anything. We just mess around from time to time. What were you doin; there?"

"I was playing hide-and-seek with the Wyan kid, Barchek. I reall didn't mean to eavesdrop or anything. I just heard the way he was talking to you. I wanted to make sure you were safe."

Julie's hands were at her beet-red face. "Oh, God, this is so embarrassing. He's not...he just likes to get a little, I don't know, *aggressive*, but—"

"Aggressive?"

"I mean, not at first. The first time was just like, I couldn't believe the captain of the ship was interested in me. Even if he's older, you know? And there's not a lot of options. I swear, I would have to be the last woman alive before Percy would make a move."

"I don't think that's on you."

"Anyway, I liked the attention even if the sex was a little weird, but now it's just gotten weirder."

"More aggressive?"

"*That* and the outfits. The deal was, he'd help me sneak on the stuff I wanted, the cards, the bass, whatever, and I'd have to sneak on stuff he wanted."

"Outfits?"

"Yeah, they're all like stuff little girls would wear. Cutesy dresses and skirts, bows for my hair. Knee-high socks."

Marlow felt her stomach turning but Julie was talking, and she wasn't going to stop her.

"I thought it might be fun at first, then he turned into this character. Like he was roleplaying too, but it was always some domineering figure. He'd talk down to me, like you heard, get more physical and say he needed to punish me. I never understood why, I just went along with it."

"Do you want to stop?"

"I don't know. I don't want to make him mad. I mean, out here, there are so few of us. He's the only one who cares for me."

"That's not true. I care. Lana cares. I'm know others—"

Julie put a hand on Marlow's shoulder. "That's very sweet, but you don't have to worry about me. I'm not in danger or anything."

Avani had been stirring and now broke into a fuss.

Marlow gave Julie one firm look. "Just don't feel like you have

nobody to talk to." She got up to grab Avani. "I'm here if you need me."
"Thank you, but please don't worry, and don't tell Thomas."
Marlow could barely hear her over the crying baby.

"Okay." She rocked Avani in her arms to no avail. "We'll have to try Uno another time. I'm gonna take her on a little walk. Hopefully it will calm her down."

"All right. I'll try to rest a bit."

Marlow stepped out to see the light of the, almost, never-ending day on Wyan. She thought back to her time on the Belt and wondered what Williams' dead wife, Carol, would've thought about his extracurricular activities. She wondered if they'd started before he knew Carol was dead and assumed it to likely be the case. That being said, what did marriage mean on the Belt? Marlow wasn't exactly sure of their rules after less than a year there.

There was a cool breeze hitting Marlow in the shade of the giant trees. She wrapped Avani in her blanket and kept rocking. Zane was sitting on one of the wood seats by the coals of the fire. She heard him sniff and maybe if she hadn't spent years of her life with him watching everyone they loved die, she would've mistaken it for nothing, but Marlow knew, Zane was crying. She walked over, purposely stepping on a stick, so he'd hear her. His head raised as she approached but he didn't look at her.

"Hey," she said.

"Hey."

"Everything okay?"

"Fucking Peter. Fucking relationships." He looked up at Avani. "Sorry."

Marlow smiled. "It's okay, she's not repeating anything yet." She sat next to him, bouncing Avani on her knee. "Want to give me more details?"

Zane told her the full story from Peter visiting him to Peter walking off.

"They can't really take the ship, right?" asked Marlow.

Zane shrugged. "I mean, I hope they don't."

"Should we tell Lana?"

"If they don't want to stay..."

"Zane."

"I'm saying, we can't force them to stay."

"The ship belongs to all of us, or at least...well shit, I guess it belongs to the Belt."

"Right? Who's to stop them?"

"I don't know anymore."

Zane rubbed his eyes. They were less puffy now. "You really think this is better?"

"Than the Belt?"

He nodded.

"I mean, it's more rustic but you and I have lived in worse."

"Don't remind me."

"You miss your baths?"

"Not the baths so much. Civilization."

"I get it. It was different for you." She saw the defensive look forming on his face. "No blame, okay? I just mean, I was still secluded a lot. I had a run in with Wesley, then Rami. They're both gone. Things haven't worked out no matter where I've been. Maybe Wyan is my chance."

"Maybe they haven't worked out, but you survived, Mar. *We* survived some shit and we're still here. No matter where we are in the universe, we find a way."

"Look who's getting all inspirational on me." She put a hand on his. "Guess this means you're not taking the next ship out of here."

"Guess not. I couldn't stand to be next to Peter that long anyway. Even in cryo-sleep."

"Harsh words for someone who was just in your bed."

Zane stood up with a groan. "Relationships are fickle. If we've learned nothing else, we've learned that."

Marlow stood next to him, holding their offspring. They were both transfixed on the fog hanging over the mountains. It was like the darkness behind them was trying to billow out. They each felt shivers down their spines.

"Reminds me of Earth," said Zane, with reverence in his voice. "When we first got to the bunker."

"That's when Mom and I took to the roads. It was so thick some days. It would always be biting the back of your throat, no matter what you did."

"And my eyes always watered. Remember that? They were either dry or watering."

Marlow took a deep breath, sucking in fresh air then releasing it in a gust.

"Gotta remind ourselves it's not like that here. We can fight the fog here. We can win this time."

"Keep telling yourself that." He smiled at her. "I'm going to try to rest a bit. Night, Mar, or rest time, or whatever the hell they say here."

She bowed to him and with a smirk, said, "Have a delightful rest period, Zane. I am off to wash our offspring's britches in the lake."

Chapter Eleven

The rest period ended with good news. Walters was up and walking. Admani and Julie flanked him. They feared he'd go down and get a head injury to top things off, but he limped his way along. The left side of his face drooped like he'd had a stroke, and the only medical experts they had, came to a consensus his symptoms were not far off from that. His limp was just numbness they hoped would pass with time. His face, they weren't sure.

The group gathered by the fire pit as Walters walked up. He was greeted with cheers and a smattering of applause. He raised his hands to quiet them.

Walters' words were slurred. "I jus have wun queshun. How wus da meat?"

More cheers went up for him and his nurses promised he'd get some of the dragon meat if he'd please go lay back down. Walters acquiesced and was back to the lab within a minute. He was determined not to let the limp slow him.

Lana took Marlow aside.

"I want you to come with me to the village today."

Marlow had Avani strapped to her as she swung Honey around. "Okay, what for?"

"Relations. They need to trust us. If we're going to work together, we have to keep that bond strong. Since we've been back, they've been a bit *distant* if you will. The loss of Doth and Gow'on was bad for all of us."

"So, why me? Why not Arjen, the great diplomat?"

"Because he's a man. The women run things on Wyan. They choose their partners. They have children. They lead. Men don't speak when the women are making decisions. Arjen would not last long trying to persuade them with his smooth tongue."

Marlow was giggling. "Sorry. It shouldn't please me so much to know he's not allowed to speak in front of them, but it does."

Avani threw Honey to the ground and Lana retrieved her, patting Avani's fluffy hair as she handed the duck back.

"Are you ready?"

"I guess. Sure. What about Avani?"

"Right. We'll need someone to watch her. It'll look weak carrying her around. They usually have one of the Wits do it after their children are born."

Marlow widened her eyes and blinked a few times. "Okay. So, is that why it took a few days for Cannie to talk to me?"

"Probably. She probably thought you were one of our Wits. Though, I think the Wyans know we only have two genders."

Marlow took it all in. "Okay, let me see if Marlin is up for some babysitting."

~ * ~

As Marlow and Lana began their walk to the Wyan village, Arjen stopped them on the road. He was acting in a way Marlow had never seen before, shy.

"We'll only be gone a couple hours," said Lana.

Arjen kissed her on the cheek and pulled out a bouquet of wildflowers.

"I, uh, found these for you."

Lana smirked. "Found them, huh?"

"I thought you might like them."

"They're very beautiful, but do you mind putting them in my bunk by the window? I probably shouldn't take them with."

"Oh, right, yes. Be safe, then."

Lana continued down the path and only Marlow looked back to see Arjen still standing, watching them go.

They arrived in the village and stopped near the stone well. There were two Wits collecting water in big metal pails.

"So, how developed are they?" asked Marlow, looking around at the differing buildings.

"Early man. They're smart enough, but they haven't gotten to harnessing electricity or vehicles. They seem to be content with their evolution, if you will."

"What about you? What's your dream for them? Do you want to introduce that stuff?"

"No. I want to go backward. It sounds wrong, but I was all for the tech we had in the Belt until I got here and saw how peaceful they live. The simple life is something to be desired. Once we get through the dark time, my goal is to live like them, to rebuild the human race like we were thousands of years ago."

"Won't we just end up killing each other again? There was a lot of that before the Final War. Before technology."

"There was, but we didn't know then how it would all end up. Maybe some people did, but it was too late for most of us. The problem with the Belt is they're still holding onto all that tech and it's slowly killing them. Like fate doesn't agree with how they've cheated it. This," she motioned to the little village, "this should be our goal. We can reestablish our society here. We can get another shot, but only if we do it the right way."

"That's a big dream," said Marlow, "but who knows?"

"One step at a time. How about a tour?"

Lana took Marlow around the Wyan village. They stopped in on a food processing plant where the Wyans used large stones to grind their grains, and brute strength to move them. The next building was a sort of medical facility. Lana explained their medicine was minimal, also taken from the plants, but that they weren't prone to disease. There were only two medical personnel who covered the majority of issues.

Bruuth worked at the forge. The Wyans figured out how to mold metals into shapes. The problem for them was the focus was solely on gardening tools. Some *could* double as weapons, but it was not their intended purpose.

"Friends," Bruuth said, as the two women entered.

"Bruuth." Lana spoke in Wyan, "Good to see you doing well."

"Hey," said Marlow, not sure how much more English she should bother with.

Bruuth began a sentence, then looked at Marlow. She tapped her ear to assure him she could understand.

Bruuth smiled. "I'm working on sharp things."

"Weapons?" asked Lana.

"I think." He waved them over to take a look at what he'd made. There was a table covered in random, steel creations. One was a curved half-circle, thin enough to work like a sickle, but wide enough to be hard to brandish.

"Progress," said Lana. They talked more about better designs as Marlow looked around. Bruuth assured her he'd be working on more.

When they exited the forge, Karath, the village elder, was waiting outside with her two aides nearby.

"Lana," Karath said.

"Karath. Good words for you."

"Really?"

"This is Marlow. She is a friend."

Karath looked her over and Marlow did the same, admiring the shades of purple along her face.

"She will help?" asked Karath.

"Yes. She is one of my good leaders."

Marlow frowned at the translation. *What does that mean?*

Karath was examining her again, probing for something. "I'm glad you two are in the village. Will you join us to eat?"

Lana looked to Marlow, who nodded as the translation came through.

"We would be honored," Lana said.

The aides led Lana and Marlow to a bigger house on a hill. There were stone steps up a grassy hillside leading to the entrance. The mountains loomed in the background, starting green then fading to black and gray.

Karath's house sat perfectly along a flat patch on the hill before it dipped on every side. The view of the village was great. Marlow could see the top of the medical center, the smoke coming from the forge, and the well as it stood alone. She tapped Lana as they reached the door.

"How do I say, 'beautiful view?'"

Lana thought for a second, then grunted a few words for Marlow to repeat.

Karath smiled at her pronunciation and thanked her.

The inside of the house was furnished with a wooden bench that was likely a chair for a four-legged Wyan. There was what looked like a pile of stuffing in the corner of the room. Marlow assumed it was used like a bed as Karath went and plopped down into it. She was having a hard time not thinking of the Wyans as advanced horses.

Lana led them to the bench to sit and the aides brought them a curved, wooden bowl filled with produce. They set it between them and left the room. Marlow followed Lana's lead. There was no praying, no utensils, just digging in. It wasn't far off from life in the bunker, though it was much warmer, and the food was actually fresh.

"Our harvest has been plentiful," said Karath. "Our storehouses should remain full through the time of darkness. This is what we're working on. What about you?"

Lana finished her bite of fruit and wiped her chin. "Our people are working on weapons and traps. We will work with Bruuth to best understand the path the Night Chasers will take and try to make it difficult for them."

"You know we don't condone the violence," Karath hung her head, "but we understand it is necessary."

Lana patted Marlow. "Her and I had the same conversation on the way over. When Wyan is free from the Night Chasers, we can all live peacefully again. Until then, we must do whatever it takes to be prepared."

"I am tired," said Karath. "I didn't want to live to see another time of darkness, but it comes anyway."

"We will do our best to make sure it's the last time you will have to fear."

Karath let out a wheeze of a breath. "You don't know that. You don't know all that lives on the dark side."

Lana nodded. "It is true."

Marlow looked out the window, past the village and past the fields. "What's out there? What if we just took a trip, followed the sun out of town and just didn't come back until it was light again?"

Lana repeated Marlow's thought in Wyan for Karath to hear.

"Desert," said Karath. "Our home is here. If they destroy it, we have nothing left."

Lana echoed her sentiment. "We must protect your home." Then in English. "We had the talk about waiting it out and coming back after night was over, but it would only buy us four years. What then?" She switched back to Wyan. "We have to make our stand or there will be nothing to stand for."

"We will honor our deal," said Karath, "but the Night Chasers..." She dropped a half-eaten stalk into her bowl and laid down. "I must rest."

Lana stood and Marlow with her.

"Rest well," said Lana. "We will continue working for peace."

On the walk back, Lana tried to keep it positive.

"At least she wanted to eat with us. That's about as good of an invite as you're going to get."

"She sounds suicidal," said Marlow. "Do they ever do that?"

"Commit suicide? I don't think they do. Karath is just being honest. They don't like war. It wears on her."

"So, what is 'the deal?'" asked Marlow. "I've heard it more than once. What happens after, assuming anyone is alive?"

Lana stopped walking, leaning her hand on a black rock that continued up the side of a cliff.

"They will turn over leadership to us. To *me*, really."

Marlow's face tightened. "Meaning?"

"Meaning we'll integrate with them. We'll be part of the village."

"So, they'll be your slaves?"

"That is not—we will be part of their community. We'll reap the benefits of anyone in leadership."

"Will you have two lackeys that bring you your food? Dress you? Bathe you?"

"We'll have a better life for us and future generations. Better than the Belt, better than Earth."

"And the Wyans?"

Lana's fists were clenched. "The Wyans will get to survive."

Lana's words were punctuated by a loud sound in the distance. It was unmistakable to them both, but Marlow didn't share Lana's surprise. As they saw it rise above the trees a mile and a half away, Lana cursed the sky.

"What the fuck?"

The *Mack* took off into the atmosphere. Lana broke into a sprint back toward camp. Marlow followed.

Chapter Twelve

The village stood in awe as Marlow and Lana arrived. They'd all watched the *Mack* disappear into the sky, then counted their remaining numbers more than once.

Marlin rushed to Marlow with a crying baby in his arms.

"I was afraid..."

"What?" asked Marlow, taking Avani back and shushing her.

"We thought you defected," said Williams.

"I told you we were going to the village," said Lana. "Why would I lie?"

Williams didn't reply.

Lana looked around, counting eleven plus the baby. "Who...?"

"Peter and Davis," said Arjen. "I didn't realize they were gone. I didn't think they'd do it."

Lana was circling the area, working out her thoughts. "Abandoned us...they...didn't they think we would...?" Her eyes went wide. "What about the lab?"

Walters leaned on a wooden seat, his speech sounding better. "I was in there all morning. I would've seen them."

"So, what did they take?" asked Lana. "We didn't have much in our food stores."

Everyone looked dumbfounded.

"They're gonna die," said Lana. "The *Mack* was not ready for another trip. That was supposed to be the last."

Zane held his head in his hands, fighting back tears when Lana continued, "Who knew about this? Surely they didn't plan to go with just the two of them."

Marlow darted her eyes toward Zane but didn't speak.

"Oh, God." Marlin raised his hand. "I knew. They asked me to come, to get back to the life we had on the Belt. I thought about it, I really did, but when Marlow came over this morning and handed me Avani, I knew I couldn't do it."

"Because of the baby?" asked Lana. "That's all that stopped you? Not abandoning your friends, our mission?"

"Well, that too, but I wasn't sure I could serve a purpose out here. I thought you might be better off without me."

Lana threw her hands up. Williams stepped in.

"Why didn't you tell someone? We could've stopped them."

"What then?" Marlin asked. "We force them to take up the cause? Hide the keys to the ship and make them fight demons with us?"

"Stop them from taking the ship, you idiot," said Williams.

"We could've talked to them," said Lana. "We're down two more humans in our fight now. We're down the *Mack*."

"I'm sorry." Marlin was on the verge of tears. "I'm just scared...all the time. It's like walls closing in on me." He looked around at the group. "Doesn't anyone else feel that?"

He received a few cautious nods but no real replies.

"You have that right," said Lana. "Everyone does. It should be clear now though, for whoever is standing here, anyone who hears my voice, you live on Wyan now. You *are* a Wyan and you are sworn to protect it. The only other option is death."

She stormed off to her bunk and slammed the door.

Percy and Admani were huddled around a mounted telescope, taking turns and exchanging baffled looks.

"You really think...?" asked Admani.

"Look at it," said Percy.

Marlow and Marlin joined them.

"What is it?" asked Marlow.

"The ship. Somebody get Lana back out here, quick."

"What do you see?" asked Arjen.

"It looks like engine failure." Percy looked to Admani who confirmed.

Williams stepped over while Arjen ran to get Lana. After a brief observation, Williams chimed in, "Thrusters are burnt out. Damn fool went too hard on them getting off this rock." He shook his head as he turned the telescope back over to Percy. "Melinger's atmosphere is going to suck them in within a day if he can't correct."

Lana was out, listening to the end of his speech before taking a look herself.

"What if Davis can correct it? Could they land back here?"

"Possibly," said Williams, "but we don't want that. He'll barely have control. It'll be a crash landing if anything. They could end up in the ocean, on top of the village or worse." He looked over his shoulder. "Over those mountains. Who knows what they might stir up if that happened?"

"If Melinger sucks them in...?" Lana let her words trail off.

"Hopefully they find an ocean to break their fall."

Lana put her hands on her hips. "Give me something here."

Williams sighed. "Davis will have to check the damage himself. One-man space walk with nothing but a gay boy for support. I don't like those odds. It would be safer to strap in and pray."

"What do we know about that planet?" asked Zane, watching with red eyes.

"Not much," said Lana. "We only ever see the dark side. It's hotter than here. Life would have a much harder time there."

"So, even if they do land..."

"This is all a lot of speculation," said Williams. "There are plenty of other ways for them to die before that."

"Thank you for the optimism." Lana frowned.

"Fuck." Zane turned away, grabbing a tuft of his hair in each hand, then turned back. "We have to see what happens."

"We'll keep watch," said Percy. "You wanna take turns with me?"

"Okay."

"Me too," said Marlin. "Davis was my friend."

The group spent the better part of the day following the path of the *Mack* until it was swallowed into the blackness of Melinger. Peter and Captain Davis were gone.

Chapter Thirteen

For the next few days, clouds hung over their village. It rained off and on, echoing the dire sentiments for Davis and Peter. For some of the Belters, the rain was a new experience that had them testing the wetness on their hands before pulling back into shelter. The last rain Zane and Marlow lived through was too acidic to consume. This one was crisp, revitalizing, and had Marlin standing in the open with his shirt off. Ice convinced him to keep on his pants, reminding him they were not in the Belt bathhouses anymore. Marlow spun Avani as she blinked at each raindrop when it plunked her in the head. Soon, they had to go in to dry off and warm up. With the sun hiding for the first time since they'd landed, the temperature dropped lower than they were used to.

As the cold, gray days pressed on, and the newness wore off, the group grew restless. They stayed in their huts for too long. They didn't hunt for fresh meat and the vegetarian diet was getting to some of them.

On the third day of clouds, Walters stepped out of his hut into a slight drizzle. His limp was barely showing, though his face still drooped as if he'd aged thirty years on his left side. He didn't feel older, or tired for that matter. He'd been resting for days since the poisoning and was ready for some adventure. Walters stepped to the lab, knocking gently on the door as he could hear a baby crying a few doors down.

Admani opened it with an inquisitive look on her face. Her light-brown skin, freckles, and coffee-brown hair made Walters forget his words for a second. She'd let it settle into its natural, tight curls since they'd been on Wyan and he had no complaints.

"You okay?" asked Admani. "Need me to check your blood?"

"No, no. I'm good actually. Really good. I was hoping you'd be up for a little hike, seeing as we weren't able to take that walk the other day."

"Oh, okay. I *could* use a break. I've been staring at these walls...well, you know." She peeked her head out. "Is the weather all right?"

Walters looked over his shoulder. "It's easing up. Bring a towel anyway, though."

"Okay." She reached back into a stack of linens, wrapped a towel around a few collection tubes, then tucked them into a backpack and stepped outside with him. "Where are we going? To those springs you mentioned?"

"Yeah. You should be able to find something to study out there."

"Does anyone know we're going, just in case?"

"Yes, ma'am. I told Marlin all about it. He was planning to head up later with Percy. I figured we'd get a jump start on them."

Walters led the way to the back of their village, the side that butted up to the mountains. There was a path a few hundred feet up that went between ridges. It was tough going, but not treacherous. Walters felt his body respond to the physical activity. Half of him thought the poison made him stronger, like Spider-Man or whatever the fish version of that would be. When they reached the tallest point of their hike, still well below Ruh'la peak, Walters realized he didn't have superpowers and stopped to catch his breath. Admani was bent over as well, looking out at the camp. She could see the beginnings of the main Wyan village and parts of the wrecked one where the *Mack* had been parked a few days prior.

"This is worth it for the view," Admani said.

"Sure is," said Walters, "but the real prize is through there." He pointed to an offshoot of the path they'd been on. "Gotta crawl a bit. Hope you're not claustrophobic."

Admani made a face. "We're going through there?"

"It's only tight for a minute. I swear." He stood tall. "I'll go first."

"Okay."

Walters went ahead. The rocks hung over him like they meant to push him down the cliff, then he ducked his head, lowered to all fours, and crawled through an opening barely two feet wide. It was a fifteen-foot tunnel with little daylight, but it widened as he neared the end. When he turned around, he could see Admani peering in. He waved her on.

She took her time and when she reached the end, Walters helped her up. The path turned grassy on the side of the mountain and swept down to a craggy landscape. The edges of teal water could be seen just over a ledge of rocks. Admani pulled out a handheld telescope, held it to her eye and gasped. When they reached the bottom, she had to hold herself back from running.

"This is gorgeous," she said, dropping her backpack and pulling out her sample tubes.

Walters leaned on a rock ledge overhanging the pool. Admani tested the heat, then dipped a tube in, holding it up to admire before capping it.

"You've really gone in these?" she asked, shifting her hips.

"Yeah. Me and Percy back when. It's a bit of a trip and we had a lot of other things going on, but it's good to be back."

"Did anyone test the water first?"

"I mean, Purse and I dipped a hand in first, gave it some time and..." He cut himself short, seeing her shake her head. "What?"

Admani rolled her eyes. "I'm surprised you were still alive by the time we got here."

"Why?" He jumped up from the rock. "Is it bad?"

Admani giggled, holding up the tube. "Actually, no, the water is fine, like a strong mineral bath, nothing a Belter would be new to." She put the tube away in her bag. "I'm just saying, with this and the dragon and the *fish*. I'm surprised nothing killed you before I got here."

"I'm all here." He fought to keep the left side of his face up.

"You are, aren't you, tough guy." Admani stood for a minute before retrieving more sample tubes. "Do you think we can get some of the rock from the bottom? I'd love to bring it back to the lab."

"Give me a tube." Walters pulled off his shirt then reached his hand out.

Admani handed it over as he dropped his pants. "Didn't bring a change," he said.

"It's nothing I haven't seen."

"Right." Walters remembered the days in her care, looking up every time he heard a noise, hoping to see her face again.

He was fully nude, stepping down the slope into the hot spring. Admani watched as he gave a final thumbs up before his ass disappeared into the teal water.

She was at the edge, watching the surface for what seemed like an eternity when Walters finally popped back up like a cork. He held the tube out to her. She took it, smiled and packed it away. Then she turned back.

"You had me—" Admani stopped herself, eyes wide. "Your face."

"Oh, shit, am I drooping again?"

"No. The opposite."

Walters hands went to his face. "Is it?" He pushed his cheek up and down.

"Go back under for a few." She crouched to watch him. "As long as you can hold it."

Walters shrugged and tucked back under. After thirty seconds he came up, hand on his face. "I feel it now. Motherfucker. This is like one of those fountains of youth."

Admani was giggling at him. "I don't know about that but think about the NutrientPanel. These springs are loaded. Who knows all of what your body is absorbing?"

"I was hoping you would." Walters took handfuls of water and dumped it over his head. "You're the scientist."

"I've gotta study it more, but I don't see the harm."

"Well then," he reached out a hand, "got any ailments?"

She looked deep into the water like it was hypnotizing her. "Not that I can think of, but it looks nice and warm." She hugged herself as a breeze raised the hairs on her arm.

Walters pushed back and swam to the other side. "Then jump in."

"Okay, but I've gotta..." She pulled off her shoes, setting them next to her bag of samples. She paused before facing away and taking off her shirt.

Walters was taking in the curves of her naturally tan body. Her full head of curly hair sat just above her bare shoulders. She brushed her hands down her belly before going to work on her pants. Walters felt like he was at an old-time peep show, something a hundred years before his time he'd only seen in movies. The thing about those is they always panned away before you got the full picture. When Admani's pants and underwear dropped to her ankles, he found himself mumbling, "Jesus fucking Christ." Nudity had never been a big deal in the Belt, but it had been different with the recent crew on a new planet. Lana was a little more private. Julie was property of Williams. Walters couldn't recall the last time he'd seen a naked woman. Especially one he'd wanted to see.

Admani stepped into the spring slowly, testing the heat before going further.

"That *is* warm."

Walters tried to meet her eyes. "Sure is. You get used to it."

After a minute, the show was over, and she was submerged. Her hair lay on the water around her.

"Why did you kill the dragon?" she asked, as she got settled against the side.

He looked back at her as she stared off at the clouds hanging over the dark mountains.

"So we could eat."

"That's it?"

"I suppose to see that it could be done."

"And if it couldn't?" Admani met his eyes, probing for something he wasn't sure about.

"Try something else. I don't know. We set out to go fishing, but I got the idea and ran with it."

"That's so reckless."

"I guess. That's just how I work sometimes. Don't you ever have an impulse and just act on it?"

"Not like that. I like to plan things out, to study them and figure out how they work first. My sister is the risk taker."

"There's a first time for everything."

"Oh, don't think you're getting me on any dragon hunts."

Walters laughed. "Maybe just fishing?"

"No way. The fish is what almost did you in."

"I'm good."

She shook her head. "You're crazy, Walters." Then stood up until the water was just above her navel. "Can I look at your face?"

"Sure."

She walked until she had to swim to him, stopping where he rested against the edge. She ran warm hands down his face, one on each side for good measure.

"Smooth." Admani was too close to his face for comfort.

"What?"

"The water, it makes your skin so smooth." She held out an arm. "Feel."

Walters did and didn't want to stop. "Pretty soft I'd say."

Admani settled in next to him, and they watched the heat come off the surface of the water.

"We probably shouldn't stay in much longer," she said.

"Yeah, guess not."

Admani looked up the way they'd come. "So, Percy and Marlin..."

"Oh, right, they uh, they..."

"They're not coming, are they?"

He pursed his lips. "No."

She turned to face him. "They were probably told to stay as far away from here as they could, weren't they?"

Walters narrowed his eyes at her. "Well..."

"Good." She scooted closer. "Can I tell you a secret?"

"Yeah, sure."

"I miss the feeling of being close to someone. There's so little human touch out here, like we're all afraid of what will happen in a few months. We can't settle in."

"I miss it too," said Walters. "Hell, we don't know if this will be our last voyage. Why wait until after it's too late?"

"Right?"

She ran her wet hands through her hair, drips of the mineral water coiled down before returning to the pool. "I remember when my mom would just hold me. When I was growing up and would have a particularly hard day at school. There was so much pressure on us Belt kids, but she knew it as much as I did, the future of the human race was riding on us. One mistake and..."

Walters watched her eyes as they searched through her feelings.

"It hasn't gotten easier, though," she said. "Being here. It's probably more pressure. I miss my mom, my partner Mateo, just the community we had. It wasn't perfect but maybe we could've convinced them."

Walters rubbed his head. "Maybe. Maybe Visser would've thrown us all in the cells with the feral children and grounded our ship."

Admani gave a solemn nod. "You're probably right."

A silence hung over them, only the bubbling springs made a sound until Admani put an arm around Walters' shoulder.

"I know what you want, but after, will you just hold me for a while?"

"I...of course. Whatever you—" His words caught in his throat when he felt her hand under the water.

Walters gripped the ledge tight as her body pressed against his side, continuing to stroke. He loosened up enough for his hands to find her smooth back, caressing up and down until he felt himself release. Admani smiled as he gripped her side, then his hands relaxed and she draped her body across his, lying chest to chest as she tucked her nose into his neck.

They lay that way for another five minutes until their heads were dripping with sweat. She pulled back and looked him over.

"That was nice."

"I'd say so. Should we?"

They swam back across to their clothes, toweling off as the sun started to peek from the clouds. They dressed and started their hike back ɔ the camp.

~ * ~

The sun just started to illuminate spots in the human's camp again when Williams tossed a double-barrel shotgun into a bright patch of grass. t slid to a stop at Percy's feet.

"What do you mean it didn't make it off the ship?" yelled Williams. "What good is a goddamn gun with no ammo?"

"I thought Walters was bringing it," said Percy. "I took the guns. He took the ammo, the gunpowder. It was our deal."

"Are you sure *he* knew the deal?" Williams looked around. Where *is* Walters? Get him out here."

Percy looked sheepish. "Um..."

"I'm here, Boss." Walters emerged from the trees behind the village.

Admani was at his side, though the smile dropped from their faces when they heard Williams' tone.

"Where have you been?"

"Collecting samples," Walters replied. "What are we up in arms about?" He shot Percy a look, whose eyes told Walters enough.

"Do you recall unloading the ammo we found for those guns?"

"I was...Percy and I..." Walters caught Percy's eye again and he frowned at him. "Boss, I was planning to get it off of there, then the dragon thing happened, and they stole the ship."

"Damnit, Walters. Now the bullets are on the *Mack*, likely destroyed."

Lana came over. "All right, we get it. Is there anything else missing?"

Walters shook his head at Percy, but he couldn't hold it in.

"They're gonna know," said Percy.

"Know what?" said Lana.

"The tasers and relay equipment, too." Walters hung his head.

Williams threw up his hands, turned as if he meant to leave, then back. "You've sentenced us all. We can't even communicate now."

"Williams..." said Walters, but Williams walked off.

Lana was pacing, mumbling to herself. Arjen put a hand on her shoulder to stop her.

"Okay, okay," said Lana. "We still have some land mines from the first trip. We just can't waste any resources. We need to come up with alternatives as well, not finger pointing." She saw Admani with her bag. "Did you find anything useful?"

Admani clutched the bag, feeling her face flush. "Well, I've got to run it through the lab first." Her mind had been much more on her encounter with Walters than anything under a microscope.

"All right," said Lana. "Everyone, I need you to focus on things that can help us. We've been here a week. Everyone should be getting accustomed to life, but we can't get comfortable, not yet."

"Yes, yes," said Walters. "Impending doom. We've got it. Can' we have lunch first?" He walked to his hut as Percy retrieved the shotgun from the grass, bringing it back to the armory.

Soon, it was just Lana and Arjen. The village was silent except for a bird chirping in the distance.

"What am I doing?" Lana asked.

Arjen pulled her to him. "Trying to prevent us from going extinct."

"Maybe that's our destiny."

Arjen held her at arm's length so he could look at her. "You didn' bring us out here for that."

Lana pulled away. "No." She sighed. "I've got to go talk to Karath."

"Want me to come with?"

"No. She's going to want an explanation about the *Mack*. It's not going to be pretty."

Lana gave Arjen a quick kiss on the cheek and set off.

~ * ~

The group reconvened for dinner. Differences were set aside for hungry stomachs. Zane and Ice sat together to begin plotting out raising flightless birds they could eat. Williams chewed down a stalky root without much enthusiasm, while Walters sat by Admani, sharing food with no shame. Julie was kicked back, admiring her freshly painted nails. They were fluorescent orange, a color choice she had little say in when rummaging through the wreckage of Earth.

"What is that?" asked Lana.

Julie hid her hands. "Oh, just some nail polish."

"I'm glad our priorities are straight."

"It's been raining for three days." Julie was defensive at first, then brightened up to say, "I thought I could use a little color."

"How did it go with Karath?" asked Arjen, his blonde locks noticeably drooping.

"It didn't."

Arjen narrowed his eyes at her. "I thought you went up to meet with her."

"Bruuth met me at the edge of town and pretty much sent me away. It may have been the Wyan version of a bouncer. Though, if I'd argued, I probably could've gotten in. I think they just need more time."

"Because of the ship?" asked Zane.

"Yes. I'd promised no more trips. The promise was broken pretty much as the words left my mouth."

"Well, it's not a problem now, is it?" said Walters. "Can't take another trip if we wanted to."

No one replied. The thought of their already slim numbers shrinking, and their only means of transportation gone, was hitting hard. There weren't plans to leave Wyan, but the safety net of the *Mack*, full of their scavenged arsenal flying off, brought a bleak focus. There wouldn't be room for another mistake. The ship and the communications relay were a huge part of their strategy. Now their data-pads were useless. Their guns had minimal ammo and there was no way to get more.

Marlin pulled another batch of grenners out of the fire. They smelled like roasted potatoes and everyone had a second round of hunger hit them at once.

Percy finished his food, went to his hut, then came back out with a wind instrument resembling a clarinet. He sat off to the side of the group and started playing light melodies. It had been a long time since any of them had heard live music. Even if it was just one person, it softened the mood. No one was speaking, only listening to Percy as he followed the tune as far as he could take it. They all stared off in their own quiet reflections, hypnotized like cobras by the music.

Arjen was the first to stand, taking Lana's hand and making her slow dance with him against her will, others just watched. Over her shoulder, Arjen's face looked solemn, but content. Over his, Lana's lips were tight. Her arms lazily clasped behind his back. At the edge of the village, Barchek and Cannie stood staring from behind a tree. No one noticed them when they slipped away.

Chapter Fourteen

Zane and Isolde spent the better part of the next week building a fence to keep their birds in. Marlow dedicated her time to learning more of the Wyan language. Between Lana, Barchek, and Cannie, she was getting more fluent each day. Percy locked himself away, using Peter's bunk as an additional workstation. Walters and Admani spent their time at the beach fishing for the blue razor-fins. They set out to harvest as much poison as possible for Admani to tamper with. They found time for other things as well, both enjoying the companionship. Marlin focused on the crops. Since the Wyans rejected Lana, they'd stopped sending the Wits with breakfast. Lana assured everyone it would solve itself soon enough, but in the meantime, they needed more options.

One day, while Marlow was out in the wrecked village with Barchek, Williams entered her hut, finding Julie in a pair of parachute pants and a tank top. She was hanging a thin, rectangular piece of aluminum from the end of her bunk that was painted with a faded cactus and read, "Grand Canyon State."

"What is that?" asked Williams, startling her.

"Thomas. I didn't hear you come in." She stood up, crossing her arms over her breasts. "That's a license plate. They used to have them on cars on Earth."

"I know what it is. Why is it there, and what are you wearing?"

"It's just stuff I like. Stuff from Earth."

"Okay, okay, well, put the toys away. Marlow is out." He looked over her bunk at her stash of Earth junk. "Do you have the schoolgirl outfit?"

"Thomas..."

Williams looked back at the door. "I don't know how much time we have."

She grabbed his hand and had him sit by her on her bunk.

"I feel like things have gotten weird lately between us. Like you view me as just a body to do what you want with. I'm still a person."

"Jules." He put a hand on hers, regarding her in a sympathetic way only Captain Thomas Williams, with his thin mustache and concrete view on the universe, could. She'd always admired his unwavering confidence, even if she didn't always agree with it. "It's been intense with the whole trip back out here, the oncoming war. If I came across a little more intense, it was probably just a reflection of that. I'm sorry if I took that out on you."

"You...really?" Julie wasn't sure she'd ever heard him apologize before.

"There is immense pressure on the pilot every time that that ship takes off, then, being here, listening to the decisions Lana is making...it's been difficult. When Davis and Peter left, I felt somehow responsible for even keeping the ship open. You and I needed it for our time together, but if it led to that..."

"I don't know what to say. It's just been hard for me as well. I know it's not the same but..."

He stroked her cheek, brushing a few red hairs away before kissing along her jawline.

"It's been hard for everyone. That's why we need each other. That's why I need you."

Julie caught his hand on her thigh. "Tom..."

Williams kissed her earlobe. "I need you, Jules. You're what keeps me going each day."

"I...okay, okay." She pushed back from him. "But no outfits, no characters. Just you and me."

"It's always you and me." Williams smiled.

His mustache turned up with his lip like a raised eyebrow.

Julie ran a hand down his cheek, then stood up, giggling as she ried to remove her parachute pants.

~ * ~

Percy was pacing the firepit while Marlin and Walters loaded it and prepped it to filet fish. Percy twisted the hem of his sleeve while ticking off items on his free hand. He was mumbling until Walters called, "You short circuiting, Purse?"

"No, no, I'm just—the *bass*."

"Bass? I don't think we caught any bass. I'm not sure they even have those here. Hell, if I know though."

"No, not the..." Percy looked at the bucket of fish.

"Did I miss something?" Marlin asked.

"Only if I missed it, too," said Walters. "What the hell are you talking about?"

"Julie picked up this mounted fish thing last time we were on Earth. We didn't have any batteries to make it work, but you know her."

Walters nodded. Marlin looked confused.

"She likes junk...*memorabilia* from Earth," said Walters and Marlin nodded.

"So, I told her I'd tinker with it," said Percy. "I managed to rig it to take a solar charge and..." He shook his head and wouldn't make eye contact.

"What's it supposed to do?" asked Marlin.

"I'll show you." Percy went back to his bunk, then trotted to the firepit with the mounted bass.

Zane and Ice joined from tending to their birds past the far huts.

Percy held the board on either side, clicking the red button just below a flipper. The bass head sprung forward and started singing a distorted version of "Don't worry, be happy."

Walters burst out laughing. "That thing is great."

Percy waited for his laughter to die down, then continued,

"I thought so too, but listen." He clicked the button and again the head sprung out. The bass lips moved open and shut, but a different message played. It was the voice of a desperate man,

Honey, it's over. They've bombed the city and are shooting anyone in the streets. I couldn't wait any more for you and Dustin to get back. I can't tell you where I'm going in case someone else finds this message. I love you both, but times are different. Forget that white picket fence we talked about. We'll never see those days come back. Just try to survive. Survive a little longer and I'll do the same. Make sure Dustin wears his mask, make sure—

The audio cut out and the bass head settled back into place.

There was a long pause before Walters said, "Shit."

"Right?" said Percy.

"Earth history is awful," said Marlin.

"Tell me about it." Zane stood staring at the plastic fish.

"Did you live through that?" asked Percy.

Zane nodded, but didn't elaborate.

"Well, shit," said Walters. "Tell us about it sometime."

"Sometime."

"Have you shown Julie?" asked Ice, her arms crossed, showing tight muscles.

"No." Percy scratched his head. "She's with Williams."

"Oh."

The village was small. There were few secrets left even if people used discretion.

"Don't," said Walters. "She doesn't need to hear that. Nobody does."

"I'm sorry if—" started Percy.

"No, no, kid. No worries."

"Do you think you can get that second recording off there?" asked Zane. "I'm sure she'd love to see it works otherwise."

"I can try." Percy took the bass and disappeared back to his hut.

~ * ~

Later, after everyone had a full belly of fish and grains, Walters met Admani on the trail behind the village.

"I brought an extra towel just in case," said Walters.

"What does that even mean?" asked Admani.

"I don't know. In case we need to get out in a hurry."

Admani huffed, dragging herself up the trail. "I think everyone knows, Walters."

"Do they?"

"You may not have seen it, but the way Isolde looks at me, she knows."

"Well, so what? We're in love, big deal."

They kept walking in silence, Admani's face tight. They went over the jagged rocks, watching the reflection of the sun off the dark cliff face. When they could see the tunnel they had to crawl through, Walters said, "I thought your sister was the cold one."

Admani's head snapped back. "Excuse me?"

"I just told you I loved you back there."

"Is that what that was?"

"Yeah. The least you could do is return the favor."

"Walters...we've been intimate, it's true, but that doesn't automatically mean love. Love takes time."

"We've had time."

"It's only been a couple weeks."

"I like being around you. It's not just your body. I like the way you think. The way your face scrunches up when you're trying to solve a problem and the way it opens back up when you get an idea." Walters meant to continue when she interrupted.

"That's all very sweet. I like being around you, too. I just don't know if I can call that love."

Walters's face twitched as he turned away to look down on the village. He spoke in a quiet, gruff voice.

"There are eleven of us, you know? If we can't find love at the end of all this, what's the fucking point?"

Admani pushed her tight curls out of her face. "Survival. Sometimes that's all it is."

Walters would've replied. He had a great rebuke filled with all kinds of choice words, but he heard something then. Admani did too. The path curved to the tunnel on the right, but if you veered left along a tight shelf, there was a stone pillar fifty yards away. It looked too shapely to be naturally occurring. Below it was a Wyan, bent on four knees, the palms of its hand splayed out on the dirt, and its head lowered in reverence.

"Is that...?" said Admani.

Walters squinted. "It's the kid's mom."

"Cannie. You're right. What is she doing?"

"Looks like she's worshiping that pillar. You think it's some kind of god to them?"

"Could just be an altar." She pulled out her little telescope and looked through it. "Oh, God."

"What is it?"

Admani handed off the telescope and Walters got a look.

"Is that blood?" There were traces of red smears across the rock.

Admani nodded, her lips curling back. "You think that's part of the ritual?"

"Likely. Religious weirdos always find a way to justify doing sick shit. You took history in the Belt, didn't you?"

"Oh yeah. That class was torture to me. Genital mutilation, drinking stuff they pretend is blood. I wonder if they all do it here."

Walters shook his head. "Not that we've noticed. Maybe this is her own thing. Might be why she's an outcast."

"Think we should check on her? That's a lot of blood."

"I'm not stepping into her voodoo. Let's just go to the spring and..."

He paused. The sentence came out of his mouth automatically, even though he was still dwelling on their conversation from a minute before. Was he good with it if she didn't love him back? He wasn't sure, and he couldn't decide at that moment, but their trip to the spring was about to be much more business-like than planned. "What do you—" He stopped himself when Cannie pushed herself off the ground.

Admani and Walters ducked down behind a boulder. Cannie gave a final bow to the pillar, then tucked into the trees beyond it. Walters slapped the boulder.

"Let's go."

"Go? You want to go to the altar?"

"I wanna see what the hell she was doing."

He started off, but Admani lagged. "I don't know."

"Come on; you've gotta be curious."

"I am, but what if she sees us?"

"I'll protect you from the notoriously docile Wyan."

Admani frowned. "Okay, but let's go slow."

They took the lower path, hugging the edge as they approached the pillar. There was a trail of blood droplets leading away from it and a smattering underneath. The pillar itself was painted with blood. There was more space around it for them to stand. The pillar was a smoothed-out rock, but had deep gashes along the sides.

Admani hovered over the blood painting on the rock with her fingers, careful not to touch it.

"Does this look like a figure to you?"

"Looks like a damn Wyan," said Walters. "I don't think my voodoo theory is that far off."

"Could be a lot of reasons."

Walters gave her a look. "Painting someone on some altar in the mountains with your own blood...I don't care what planet we're on, that's some voodoo shit."

"Fair enough. We'll only know if we ask her."

"You're the one who wanted—"

Admani put up a hand to stop him. "I know. Let's just go a little further. I still don't want to run into her. Especially not after seeing this."

"Okay, I'll go first."

Walters led them under the branches to the thinner trees that grew on the side of the mountain. The circular leaves waved at them as they passed under. There was an uncommon darkness in their canopy. The layers of growth spread out to block the sun as if they were grown for that very purpose. Admani whispered in Walters' ear, "I don't like this."

"Got a queasy feeling myself," he replied, reaching back his hand that Admani took. "Look."

Cannie was ahead, brushing a carpet of leaves across the ground. She kicked back a few fresh ones, took one more look at her work, then continued down the trail.

Admani and Walters shared a look. He held a finger to his lips, and they waited until she was out of sight. There was minimal light on the forest floor as they brushed the leaves away. An unnaturally shaped piece of wood covered the ground below, like it was meant for a roof. Walters got his fingers around it and pulled it back. The wooden piece opened like a door. There were six dirt steps going into the ground where it was too dark to see.

"Is that a room?" asked Walters.

"Looks like a bunker." Admani bent over, not getting too close.

Walters picked up a stick and slapped the first stair. "Hello?"

"You're not thinking...?"

Walters smirked. "I sure am."

"It's pitch-black. We don't have a light. We don't know how far it goes."

He was already on the third step down, poking the stick out ahead of him. "Just keep a watch."

When Walters hit the bottom, he looked back and raised a thumb to her before disappearing into the black.

Chapter Fifteen

Breakfast was underway after a rest period. Everyone sat with bowls of roots and forest berries that Julie and Marlin harvested. Avani tried to pluck one from Marlow's hand, but she tossed it into her mouth and held out the open, juice-stained palm to the baby. Avani's eyes went wide at the magic trick, grabbing Marlow's thumb in one hand and pinky in the other.

Arjen sat with Lana, laughing about something. Julie held the Big-Mouthed Bass in her lap, begging everyone to let her press it one more time. Percy winked at Marlin as it only played, "Don't worry, be happy," now. Zane and Ice discussed some morning herb collecting. With each bird they selected and cooked, they got better. It was becoming a nightly event at Ice and Zane's Village Café, as some of the group called it.

When Walters and Admani came in from the back of the village, everyone turned, and a wave of silence swept through.

Walters caught his breath, then spoke. "You're not going to believe this."

His hands were on his legs.

"Busy night, Walters?" asked Captain Williams.

Others in the group chuckled.

Walters ignored him. He didn't have anything like that to brag about, but he did have something to say.

"You were right, Williams. That Cannie is up to something."

"What?" Williams' smirk dropped.

"Yep. She's not the innocent single mother she's been showing us."

"Hold on," said Marlow. "You don't know anything about her."

Walters motioned to Admani and she opened her bag. Walters reached in and pulled out a strange, white, ring-shaped object. It was about the size of a frisbee and looked to be made of some sort of plastic.

"I know *this*."

"Careful," said Admani.

"What the hell is that?" Lana stood up and approached him with caution.

"Might have to ask Cannie. She had it stashed in her secret bunker in the mountains."

The group was getting into an uproar when Arjen raised his hands and called out, "Everyone sit. Let them tell their story. We need to hear the whole thing."

Marlow and Zane looked at Arjen. It was the first sign of leadership from him since they'd landed. Like he'd been out of his element the entire time and finally had enough.

Williams and Admani gave the details of their night in the mountains, the stone pillar/altar, the bunker, and Cannie's role in it all. Marlow sat in disbelief, but couldn't defend what they'd seen. She wanted to. Nothing felt right about Cannie, Barchek's mom, being some kind of voodoo killer or whatever they were claiming.

Williams was ready to lead the riot into the wrecked village and string her up. Arjen blocked the way until they could discuss a real plan.

"We don't know where she got this *thing*," said Lana. "We don't even know what it does."

"It's tech unlike anything we made in the Belt," said Williams. "That is enough for me."

Percy was next to Walters. "Can I?"

Lana nodded and Walters handed the object to him. Percy felt the smooth, plastic-like coating and gripped a spot that seemed like it was made for a hand.

"What does it do?" asked Marlin.

"I don't...I'll have to study it for a bit," said Percy. "Is that okay?"

Lana nodded. "Just be careful."

"Enough talk," said Williams. "If we go now, we can still catch her by surprise."

"We can't just go marching in there," said Lana. "No matter your position, we'll spook her, and she'll run."

"Then we send a party to block each path she could take."

"No. We're not treating her like a criminal. We haven't witnessed her do anything wrong, no matter what they found. We don't know where this object came from. There's no way *she* made it."

"Agreed," said Marlin.

"Oh, what, are you a sympathizer now?" said Walters.

"She saved your life," said Marlow. "Did you forget that?"

Walters went to reply when Williams held a hand to stop him.

"The fish was very convenient. We can all agree on that."

"No, we ca—" started Marlow when Lana cut her off.

"We'll put it to a vote. This is not a dictatorship. All in favor of splitting up and blocking every path, show your hands."

The hands of Willams and Walters both shot up. Admani's slowly joined. Isolde shot her sister a look and Admani shrugged.

"We don't know how dangerous she is. You didn't see the blood on the altar."

Lana continued the vote. "All in favor of sending Marlow and me to *talk* with her?"

Her hand went first, followed by Marlow, Marlin, Arjen, and Zane.

Ice, Percy, and Julie just watched it all unfold as Williams and Walters protested the vote.

"Don't empathize with these beasts," said Williams. "She knows she can tell you lies and you'll eat them up."

"Just stop it, Williams," said Lana. "We're going."

"I should go too," said Walters. "I found the relic."

Lana shook her head. "You know Wyan women don't respond well to men."

"Then Admani."

Admani stood, neutral. "If you think..."

"Yes," said Williams. "I can agree to that."

"Okay." Lana gave a firm nod.

She nodded at Arjen to handle things while she was gone. She grabbed Marlow's elbow and pulled. Marlow turned to Marlin, kissed Avani and handed her off. She fussed at him as he made faces to distract her, trying not to watch her mother and show the fear in his eyes.

The ladies headed down the tight path to the wrecked village to confront Cannie.

~ * ~

Barchek lay in the brown rectangle of grass where the *Mack* had been parked, munching on a root and humming the melody to, "Hit me with your best shot," that Marlow taught her. She heard footsteps in the distance and turned to see her friend coming with the stone-faced lady and the light-brown lady. She dropped the root and pushed herself up. *Could they play hide and seek with all four of them?* Barchek hoped they would find a way. *Or tag. Tag could be fun.* She knew she was faster than the other two. Marlow without the baby would be tough, but the more she looked at their faces, the more her smile faded. They weren't coming to play. Barchek did a mental inventory of all the things she'd done wrong recently and wondered if they'd seen her spying on their village.

"Barchek," called Marlow.

She came up and put out her arms. Barchek hugged her, the concerns she had washed away.

"Play? Tag?" Barchek motioned a gray hand at Lana and Admani.

"Sorry." Marlow shook her head. "We need to talk to your mom. Is she around?"

Barchek spoke in a mixture of Wyan and English in her reply. Only Marlow understood the full sentence. "She's down at the water taking a bath."

"Okay." Marlow hesitated.

"Come on." Barchek took off toward the ocean.

The three ladies followed. They crossed through the forest, trying to keep up with the energetic Wyan girl. She darted around trees, crunched sticks and leapt over rocks, while the others did what they could to follow. When they reached the sand dunes, Barchek was waiting for them.

"Race?" Barchek asked the three out of breath women.

Marlow laughed and looked at the other two. Admani shook her head.

"I'll walk," said Lana. "Is she even down there?"

Barchek pointed to a spot in the water as Cannie rose up, rubbing water off her head.

Marlow took a deep breath and made eyes at Barchek.

"On the count of three. Okay?"

Barchek nodded and planted a foot in the ground, staring down the dune, focused.

"Marlow," said Lana. "It's hardly the time—"

"One," Marlow began and Barchek counted with her. "Two..." Marlow took off running before they got to three.

Barchek yelled, "Cunt," and took off after her.

They shot down the dunes, with Marlow in an early lead but going too fast. Her head got in front of her and she tripped into the smooth sand. Barchek caught up to her and tucked her body into a ball, rolling down the dune. Marlow got up and jogged to catch her. At the bottom, they were both laughing.

"You finally used cunt in the right context," said Marlow. "At least, I think you did. I'm not sure if I'm proud of that or not."

Cannie joined them from the water.

"The water is nice?" Marlow asked in Wyan.

"Refreshing," said Cannie. "You brought friends?"

"They want to talk."

Cannie nodded as Lana and Admani finished their descent.

"Beautiful sky," Lana greeted.

"And you," said Cannie.

Lana explained, with help from Admani, what they'd seen in the mountains and the bunker. She left out the item they'd recovered from the bunker.

"Barchek's father," said Cannie. "Balowg died there. I go to remember him."

Admani listened through her translator. "But the blood," she said. "Is that part of remembering?"

Lana translated and Cannie nodded.

"During the last time of darkness. He was killed there while me and Barchek hid in the underground. We listened to him die, but we did not help. My blood is my shame. Is that what you want to know?"

"Jesus." Admani put a hand to her mouth and turned away.

"I understand," said Lana. "Will you tell us one more thing?"

"If I must."

"We found a white object in the bunker." Lana motioned to show the size and shape. "Where did you get it?"

Cannie narrowed her eyes. "Stay out of the underground. That is for me and Barchek."

She turned, grabbed Barchek's arm and started toward the dune.

"Wait." Lana started to follow.

"Leave us alone."

"You have to understand. Our whole village knows about the white object. They want to know where it came from. If I do not tell them, they will come ask. Please."

"Then you are bad leader."

Marlow stepped in front of Cannie. "Please, Cannie. Just give us something. Maybe we can help."

"We like you, Marlow, but there is no help. The Night Chasers come, and you will die. Just like the owners of that object you found."

With that, she took off in a full sprint up the sand, her four legs propelling her at speeds the humans couldn't try to match.

"Barchek?" said Marlow.

Barchek shook her head. "I don't remember. It was dark and scary. We hid."

She ran after her mother.

"The owners of the object," Admani repeated for only those left on the beach. "Who are they?"

Lana watched the Wyans as they neared the top of the dune. "I don't know, but I know who to ask."

She started up the hill. Marlow followed. Admani huffed. Her legs felt like rubber and she needed sleep. She took her time getting back to the village.

~ * ~

Bruuth was happy to join them for a meal before the rest period. He sat with the group around the fire, eating cooked grenners and his usual root diet. Ice selected a large land-bird, the size of a dog. It didn't go quietly, but toasted up nicely on the rotisserie. The herbs they'd selected wafted through the village and hungry stomachs rumbled.

"Toss me one of them," Walters said to Zane, who passed him a grenner for an appetizer.

Bruuth watched Ice turn the bird as Zane, Walters, and Marlin stared with hungry eyes.

"I don't understand your ways," said Bruuth in his best English.

"We don't always either." Percy bit into a grenner. He'd decided to become vegetarian after the third bird-filled meal in a row.

"Bruuth," said Lana, in Wyan. "We've learned some things we need your help with."

"Okay. I am no help with birds."

She smiled. "No, not that. Do you know, was there someone here before us?"

"Someone?"

"Someone maybe like us with funny tools?"

Bruuth stared into the fire. "We don't like to talk about the times of darkness."

"I understand, but you saw other..." Lana was at a loss for the Wyan word.

"Luak," said Marlow.

"Luak?" said Bruuth. "Yes."

Lana looked at Marlow.

"Roughly translates to alien," said Marlow.

She turned to Bruuth and switched to Wyan. "Were there luaks here? Before the last time of dark?"

Bruuth nodded. "They came from Melinger." He pointed toward the black shadow in the sky.

"Like us?" asked Lana. "In a flying vessel?"

"Yes."

"Did they leave?"

"No. They were killed. We tried to warn them, but I don't think they understood us."

"By the Night Chasers?"

"Please don't tell Karath I told you this." Bruuth stood up, dropping his food as he did. "I must go."

"Bruuth, please." Lana followed him to the rocks. "We need to know anything you can tell us."

"That's all I know. I must go."

He trotted down the path to the main village. Lana watched him go. Williams came and stood by her.

"Told you these horses were up to something."

"They're afraid. Who knows what the last group was? Maybe they were here to conquer them. They might have just gotten lucky. The Wyans were pretty wary of us at first."

"I remember," Williams put a hand on her shoulder, "but you took the time to get to know them. To learn their language. We're this far because of that."

Lana shot him a look. "That's the nicest thing you've ever said to me. Something wrong with you?"

Williams chuckled. "Can't be the wine speaking because we don't have any of that. No, I think all of this has me a little shook. I realize how small we are." He looked out at the perfect skies. "You know, at one time, people on Earth thought we were God's chosen ones."

"You don't agree?"

"The further we get from Earth, the clearer it becomes that we are all just fighting to survive our blip in time."

"Well, our blip's not over."

Williams squeezed her shoulder. "Not if you have anything to say about it, huh?"

Lana gave a firm nod and left him standing under the lone star of Wyan.

Part II

Chapter One

Two months passed on Wyan. The sun was starting to hang lower later in the day, giving a clearer passing of time before rising again. The shadows hit the middle of the mountains behind the Wyan village. They were only a week away from the time of darkness. Everything, from the *Mack* finding the wormhole, to meeting the Wyans, to coming back to the Belt after three years, was culminating with this final war.

Marlow stood, perched on a mountain ledge at the height of day. Below her was a thirty-foot plummet to jagged rocks. She'd never felt more alive. Mist rolled off the raging waterfall next to her. The view was the best she'd seen on Wyan. It had become her place to think over the last month. Zane was with her, laid back on a rock, shielding his eyes from the sun. They'd escaped the village for the chance to get a little peace. Tensions were high as the days drew near. The Wyans held firm that the Night Chasers did not come until the final shadow fell, but no one could convince Lana of that.

"This is so nice," said Zane. "The running water, the birds. I have to bring Percy here."

Marlow sat, feeling the warmth of the dark rock below her. "You'd better hurry. Time's short, remember?"

"Don't start that shit up here, Mar. That's why we came."

"I'm just kidding. But if you're going to bring Percy to *my* secret spot, please tell me first."

"Secret spot? This is a waterfall. Anyone can find a waterfall."

"I'm saying, we don't need a repeat of that time I came back from my doctor's appointment."

"That was—you were supposed to be gone for a while. Peter surprised me and—"

"You were in *our* bed. The one we shared."

"Well, things are different now. Percy is *not* Peter."

"I know. I like him, too."

"You liked Peter."

"At first."

Marlow looked out. She couldn't see the dark spot they knew as Melinger, but it was always out there in her mind. "I wonder sometimes..."

"I do, too." Zane propped himself on his elbows. "You'd think we would've heard something by now though."

"Yeah, but they took all the communication relays with them, so outside of a carrier pigeon that can survive the vacuum of space..."

There was a loud splashing further up the stream. The Earthlings turned to see Barchek happily interrupting their silence.

"She's found us," said Marlow.

Barchek came over and lowered down for a hug from Marlow, then looked at Zane.

"Earth? Earth too, right?"

"Yes, I'm from Earth," said Zane, then to Marlow, "What have you been teaching her?"

"All kinds of things. Barchek, who's your favorite singer?"

"Pat Benatar," Barchek replied.

Zane sat all the way up. "I knew it. I knew I heard her singing, 'Love is a Battlefield' the other day."

Marlow was doubled over laughing.

"Glad you're focused on the important things," said Zane.

"Better than curse words."

"Yes. I still don't know what a 'shit-bitch' is."

"Shit-bitch." Barchek pointed at him.

"It's me?"

"No," said Marlow. "Barchek, don't call Zane a shit-bitch. You're going to make him sad."

"Or just confused," said Zane.

"Friend." Barchek pointed again.

"Thanks," said Marlow. "Much better."

"Game?"

"I'm up for one. Zane?"

"What are we talking?"

"Freeze tag." Barchek's eyes were wide with excitement.

"Okay, but away from the waterfall," said Marlow.

They spent the better part of the next hour freeze-tagging their way back down the path and through the forest. At one point, Zane was caught by Marlow, frozen standing up with a hand on a nearby tree. Marlow made her move at Barchek, who dodged at the last second. Marlow stepped on some loose leaves and slid to her butt, laughing as she looked up.

"What are you...?" Zane asked, as the young Wyan went barreling toward him. She ducked at the last second and went under his legs, trying to make it through as Zane toppled forward, holding onto Barchek's back with his head toward her rear. She galloped around with him hanging off her.

Marlow was laughing too much to stand up and attempt to freeze either of them. "She's trying to unfreeze you."

"I was happy frozen."

"What's all that noise?" Arjen stepped through an opening in the trees. He helped Marlow up and laughed as Zane finally fell off Barchek's back with a thump. He lay on his back, taking deep breaths.

"I think I'm done with freeze tag."

"Good," said Arjen. "They are plotting out the mines and trip wires. We only have a few, so we have to make them count and we can't leave any markers that may tip off the Night Chasers. Follow me. I want you all to see where they'll be buried."

Barchek pulled Zane out of the dirt and they continued through the forest. Percy, Lana, and Williams walked the trails ahead, talking and pointing while Karath looked on with her aids.

"They come through here," Karath spoke, as the rest of the group approached. "These two trees would make a good place for your weapons."

"Bombs," Percy said in English.

Karath ignored him, then pointed up to a ledge higher up. "There, whatever you must do, that is the path to the village."

"We only have three. We'll cover as much as we can."

"It may only take one," said Williams. "If others witness their friends getting blown to bits, they may think twice."

Karath echoed his sentiment in Wyan. "The Night Chasers are violent but not stupid. If they see their kin destroyed, they likely will give up."

"I wish we had the ammo still," said Lana. "The tasers and the relays. I'd feel a lot better."

"We have the rounds still in them," said Williams.

"If they even work." Percy fiddled with one of the mines as he spoke. "We haven't tested them since we first found them."

"We'll have to make do," said Arjen. "We'll be holed up with Bruuth in the forge. If the time comes, everyone knows their role."

Marlow explained to Barchek over and over about the trip wires and made a mental note to remind Cannie as well, then she headed back to the village to relieve Marlin of babysitting duty.

Chapter Two

The night before total darkness came. The sun dipped lower than they'd ever seen it. Everyone questioned if the Night Chasers would wait one more day. It would catch the Wyan village by surprise, but if Karath's intel was correct, they'd only be hastening their trip to the grave.

The planet was quiet. More than ever, it felt like every living thing on the sunny side of Wyan was preparing for the invasion. The human village moved their dinner to the beach where the waves had an orange glow swimming across them. The sunset had a mesmerizing effect on a group that was unaccustomed to it. It sat on the edge of the horizon, threatening to leave them in total darkness, but by the time their meal was over—the best bird yet—it was starting to rise again.

"Everyone get some rest," said Lana. "We have roughly eight hours of daylight. Make any final preparations and meet by the well in the Wyan village."

There were mumbles of agreement as people started pairing off and leaving the beach in different directions. Lana and Arjen went one way, holding hands. Zane and Percy went another. Then Julie and Williams. At last, Admani rose and patted Ice on the shoulder. Walters waited down the beach.

"Really?" said Ice.

Admani shrugged. "Better than being alone." She hugged herself against the breeze and went to him.

Soon there was just Isolde, Marlin, Marlow, and Avani.

"Guess we're missing out on the fuck fest," said Marlow.

Ice snorted out a laugh.

112

Marlin picked loose meat off a bone and tossed it in the fire. "Ah, I never get invited to those, anyway."

"I'm beginning to think I'm asexual," said Ice.

"I've found men repulsive since I had Avani," said Marlow. "Just the thought of...well, you know."

"Listen to us." Marlin stared off at the water. "I mean, I'm getting older, but you? You're still two young, lovely ladies. Don't give up like I did." He laughed at his own comment.

"Please don't tell us there are plenty of fish in the sea," said Ice. "Because there are not."

"And they're poisonous," said Marlow.

"Good point." Marlin winked.

The silence hung for a few minutes, the three of them having deeper thoughts than sexual encounters. Within a week, their life on Wyan would be drastically different. The repopulation plan would have to go into effect. The oncoming threat of the Night Chasers would be over and the real integration with the Wyans would begin.

Would it be that smooth? wondered Marlow. *Would they just bow to their new leaders?* That still didn't feel right, but to Lana's point, it was better than being wiped out. If the integration didn't go smoothly, where were they? Out in deep space, unwelcome guests with no way out. Marlow didn't miss the Belt, the stale, recycled air, the vast universe looming from the edge of every TechBubble. She didn't miss Robin Visser and his phony smile, or the men who took her, killed Rami and Honey, and had Avani cut from her womb. She didn't miss any of that, but it was a little frightening to think that once again, they were it. They could begin repopulating, but all it took was one sickness that they couldn't cure, one change in climate they couldn't overcome. They'd left so much technology, so much advancement behind for the chance to start new, but humans were running out of chances. Maybe they would save the Wyans only to go extinct themselves, so the Wyans could tell stories of the stupid humans who came on their metal beasts to wipe out the Night Chasers, only to die of the common cold.

If her entire life hadn't been teetering on extinction, Marlow would've feared the coming days, but she was an old hand at cheating death. As she bounced Avani on her knee, she knew she had one goal left. It was the same goal her own mother had: to keep her daughter alive as long as she was able to do so. Give her the best life she could. Beyond that, she couldn't predict much, only that the next few days would determine how difficult those goals would be.

Everyone else had paired off so they could push these thoughts out for a few moments of pleasure. Marlow took all the pleasure she could from the toothless smile she received for only just existing, for being there when Avani opened her eyes.

Marlin finally broke the silence. "Anyone for some cards?"

"I knew you were gonna say that," said Marlow.

"Come on. We're not getting lucky. Let's at least play a few hands before we call it a day."

Marlow looked over. "Ice?"

"Okay, but I'm probably going to lose."

Marlow spread out a blanket for Avani near the warmth of the fire so she could practice rolling from front to back. She placed Honey just out of reach to give her something to work for. They took turns between hands encouraging her as her eyes were bugged out with determination. Soon after, they doused the fire and headed back to the village for one last rest.

Chapter Three

The humans stepped out, hut by hut, and marched to the well for one final meeting. They were bundled in their warmest clothes as the temperatures would drop considerably when the sun disappeared. They'd blocked all paths to the Wyan village with trees, rocks, and carved out spears on the other side. Any overzealous Night Chaser would impale itself if it crossed the barricades. The landmines were set, the trip wires in place. Percy and Walters set up motion sensor alarms at each entrance. If anyone made it over, they'd be alerted immediately, then the team would be ready with the poison-tipped arrows made from the blue razor-fins. The few guns they had were held by Williams, Lana, and Isolde. The rest had been brushing up on their bow skills as the days drew near.

They met Bruuth's team of the most able-bodied men. They carried an array of steel weapons. Other Wyans perched on rooftops with rocks and spears.

Karath stood with her aids as the teams greeted.

"Let this be our final battle for peace." She received cheers from the crowd. "The night will be long, but we will keep the fires burning." She motioned for Lana to join her. "We have accepted this group of humans from another land. They will fight for our village and we will fight with them." She turned over the floor to Lana.

Lana could see the fear in the eyes of the Wyans. Fear and uncertainty.

"Good friends. We know that war is not your way. We don't desire it, either, but you are good people. You deserve to live without threat of violence and death. We *will* deliver you from that. We will fight for you so we can all inhabit together in peace." She received no cheers, only blank, mistrusting stares.

"Tough crowd," muttered Walters.

"To your assignments," said Karath, and the Wyans scattered at her command.

She turned to the humans and Bruuth, as his team slinked away into their hiding places.

"We will keep to our word as you keep to yours. Bruuth will stay with your team in the forge. The storehouse is prepared for those with the child."

"Thank you," said Lana.

"See you when the sun shines again."

"Hopefully before."

Lana turned to the group, holding their weapons, nerves on edge. "We keep at it until they are all dead, then we celebrate. If everything goes according to plan, they will never make it to the village."

She watched the sun edging its way down the mountain. Karath's house on the hill was the first to be struck with shadow. The streets were silent, but for the errant clank of a weapon, though the distant hills had come alive with a low growling, a scraping of claws on rock. Lana picked up her speech. "Okay, one last time: attack team one, covering the western entrance, is led by Williams. With him are Walters, Percy, and Zane. Attack team two covering the eastern entrance is led by me. I have Isolde, Arjen, and Bruuth. We will camp at opposite sides of the forge. Emergency team in the storehouse will be Marlow, Julie, Admani, and Marlin. Your job is to keep Avani quiet and stay underground. In case of emergency, we will call for backup. Otherwise, stay hidden. Each team leader has a radio. We don't know how long the batteries will last, but we had no other options. Keep the chatter to a minimum. Is everyone clear?"

There were nods and quiet agreement all around.

Marlow looked at Zane with a determined face. He came over and kissed her on the forehead, then bent to Avani, strapped to her chest, and kissed her dark hair.

"See you soon."

The group split to their respective camps. There were bonfires burning in choice places around town. The forge was near the middle of the village and had large doors on either side. Lana's team perched at the east entrance with Williams's at the west. They held their weapons tight and prepared for darkness.

Marlow's group passed the food processing plant—the largest building in the village—to the storehouse nearby. There were cellar doors leading down to the vast underground. Admani carried a torch to light their way. It smelled of earth, crop dust, and stale air. The room was fifty by fifty feet and the walls were packed with food. There were bundles of hay they used for seats and a stand for the torch. The smoke was already adding to the smells, but no one wanted to put out their only light. They sat in silence for a while until the inevitable darkness came.

"At least we won't run out of food," said Marlin.

"If we can find it," said Marlow. "What's that?"

There was a green glow coming from a few feet to her left.

"New Kids on the Block?" asked Admani.

"Yeah." Julie ran a hand down her glow-in-the-dark shirt. "I can't believe it still works. I set it in the sun like all day." She tied her coat around her waist to let her shirt shine.

Admani shook her head. "I'm going to light a candle. It won't be much, but it will be something."

"Works for me," said Marlow. "Avani is ready to roll some more."

Marlin spread out a blanket as Marlow unstrapped the baby from her.

"Before you ask," said Julie, "I did bring my Uno cards."

"Okay," said Marlin, "but I don't think I'm going to be up for cards until this is all over."

"Oh, come on. Lana and Williams have got this covered."

"But we're the backup team. We have to be ready if—"

"*Emergency* backup team. Plus, we'll hear the explosions long before they'd get to the village. If they even do."

~ * ~

Hours later, the teams in the forge grew antsy.

"It's so quiet out there." Walters tucked his head back in. "All I can hear are the fires crackling."

"I almost liked the growling better," said Percy.

Lana turned to Bruuth. "Is this normal?"

He tightened his grip on a sword-like weapon he'd made. "None of this is normal. We always hid in the past. We are very new to fighting."

Lana patted his shoulder. "It will all be for the better."

"I hope."

They waited longer, half of the group pacing the long room. Percy stayed at one window and Zane at the other.

"Hey Williams," said Walters. "If I wussed out like Marlin, could I get babysitting duty, too?"

Williams laughed a deep belly laugh.

"Everyone is playing a part," said Lana. "Not everyone can be a dragon slayer like you."

"Gonna be more than that after tonight." Walters took a lap around the room, dragging the barrel of his rifle across the floor.

"Could you...?" Percy said. "Trying to listen."

Walters picked up the rifle. "My bad, Purse." He spun the rifle instead. "Anyone want to share details about what they did last night?" He received no reply. "Okay. Wanna hear mine?"

"No," came a raspy whisper from Percy. "Be quiet."

He narrowed his eyes at the fire down the path toward the food processing plant. The shadows danced like demons, everything did in his state of mind. It was hypnotic. He had to look away. "I see jack shit over here. Zane?"

Zane strained his eyes for some sign of movement, but came up empty. "Nothing."

Lana feared the silence. They should've heard an explosion by now. Shouldn't they have? She continued to pace.

~ * ~

In the cellar, Marlin was crunching down a root vegetable as Marlow cut her eyes to her sleeping baby, then back to him.

"Eating already?"

He stopped mid-bite. "Sorry. Nervous habit."

"You just started eating solids less than six months ago and you already have a nervous habit?"

He shrugged. "I did it with baths. Same idea really."

She sighed. "I'm sorry. I just can't handle being down here when everything is happening out there."

Marlin put a hand on her shoulder. "You're a fighter, Little Earthling, but you're also a mother now. It is no less commendable to be here protecting her."

"But there's four of us..."

"We're not completely out of it. If they need something, they'll call."

Marlow listened to him, flaring her nostrils out, then back in. She stood up and found her way to the cellar door, putting an ear to it. After a minute, she felt Admani's hand on her back.

"Anything?"

"Worse, nothing."

"Well, we'll just have to—"

Marlow cut her off. "We should check on them."

Admani grabbed her arm. "You have the radio. Do not open that door."

Marlow unclipped the radio off the waist of her pants and pressed the button.

"Lana? Williams? Anyone there?"

"This is Lana, everything okay down there?"

"Just quiet. Do you see anything?"

"Not yet. Just stay calm. We'll let you know when we hear it."

Marlow stared at the radio as it cut off.

"You good?" asked Admani.

"I guess. Do you...? Listen." Marlow's ear was back at the door.

Admani's eyeroll couldn't be seen in the dark. "Mar..."

"Listen," Marlow repeated.

Admani sighed, brushed the hair from over her ear and put it on the door. At first there was nothing, then she *felt* it.

"Footsteps," said Admani. "Probably just the Wyans."

"They shouldn't be patrolling," Marlow whispered.

"Maybe they're restless."

But then they heard a low growling, something they'd never heard out of a Wyan. Admani fell back first, a little too quick and hit the ground with a thud. Marlow looked at the door as if it would burst open at any second. When nothing happened, she went down the stairs.

"What *was* that?" asked Admani, as Marlow helped her up.

"What we've been waiting for."

Chapter Four

Lana didn't need the warning over the radio. The west alarm was ringing. Before Williams could give the command to check it out, the east alarm went off.

"They're flanking us?" asked Percy.

"We don't know that," said Lana. "Something else could've tripped it."

"What about the mines? Why didn't they go off?"

"Maybe because they're old," said Walters. "We don't goddamn know, and we don't have time to debate." He grabbed his rifle and headed for the door.

"Hold on," said Lana. "Stick to the plan."

"Stay silent." Walters was at the door. "Two at a time. Purse?"

"Coming." Percy grabbed some poison-tipped arrows and a bow. They opened the door and stepped into the street.

"Ice?" said Lana.

Isolde grabbed a spear and followed Lana out. Arjen, Zane, Williams, and Bruuth remained, eyes peeled as their companions disappeared past the swirling fires.

Lana and Ice slid along the side of the medical facility. It was the last building before the straight path to the eastern entrance. There was little light from the fire hitting the log barricade. The wooden spears, planted on the landing side, were particularly shaded, though they were empty. The ladies hoped to find a few impaled Night Chasers to finish off, then do a quick study of them.

"Think the sounds scared them?" asked Ice, looking around.

"Where are the Wyans?" They stood shoulder to shoulder, making sure nothing was waiting to pounce but the village was silent. A few minutes ago, the alarm rang for its programmed five seconds, then stopped. Once again, nothing felt right.

"I don't know," said Lana. "There should be half of Bruuth's team here to back us up."

At the western entrance, Walters and Percy were also perplexed. Walters had his rifle trained at the barricade while Percy scanned the area.

"This doesn't seem right," said Walters.

"No," Percy whispered, "You think they're over there? Waiting?" He motioned at the wall of logs and spikes.

Walters shrugged. "One way to find out." He headed to the side that was tight against a tree.

"That's not what I meant. We should wait for more backup. They should be here soon, right?"

Walters looked back. "Just cover me."

"You have the gun."

Walters hoofed himself up the first log, careful not to impale himself on the spears. "With your bow and arrow, Robin Hood. Don't let me down."

"Oh, Jesus." Percy pulled back the bowstring, training an arrow just over Walters' head where he knew any second a giant, clawed hand would reach over and take it clean off.

Soon Walters was on top of the barricade, his gun scanning the dark forest behind it. Percy was at the bottom watching.

"Anything?"

"Nope." Walters turned as if he meant to start his climb down, but froze when he heard screams from the center of town.

"Oh, shit," said Percy. "Come on."

The group at the forge heard the Night Chasers before they saw them. There were loud thumps on the roof, pounding hard and fast, then it gave way. Splintered chunks of wood fell around the group. They were split down the middle as furry, black bodies swarmed like eight-foot-tall locusts. Arjen froze for a second when he saw the monster before him.

It was on all fours like a giant wolf but had two arms up front like the Wyans. Its teeth were a rotting yellow, jagged and sporadic in its mouth. The arms reached for Arjen with two-inch claws on the end of each finger.

He broke his daze just in time to raise his spear, thrusting it at the crooked neck of the beast. It caught lower, near the shoulder and the Night Chaser growled at him, gripping the spear, trying to shake Arjen off it.

Arjen held strong until it took a swipe at his face. He ducked but lost his grip, hitting the ground as the Night Chaser wrestled the spear out of its flesh.

Arjen didn't waste time watching. He reached back for another weapon, finding a gardening tool and raising it. He saw Bruuth then, pushing a fallen board off himself and swinging one of his makeshift swords straight into the Night Chaser's back. The sword stuck deep as the beast writhed in pain.

Arjen stepped forward and clubbed it in the head with the crop shucker, then he found his spear on the ground. He dropped the tool and used two hands to thrust the spear through the beast's neck. It toppled over, trying to pull at the wooden handle but failing. It gasped in wretched, bloody breaths until it stopped.

During the struggle, Arjen heard Williams' rifle fire twice and Zane yelling. The collapsed roof blocked them in. Arjen yanked the eastern door open and Bruuth followed, slowed by his disbelief in what was happening.

"We'll head around and cut them off," said Arjen. Williams cried out as Arjen finished his sentence. By the time Arjen and Bruuth made it around the forge building, there was nothing but rubble from the collapsed roof to see. Zane and Williams were gone.

In the food cellar, Marlow, Admani, Julie, and Marlin huddled together. Avani was strapped to Marlow's chest, fussing. Marlow tried to shush her, but her own heart was racing. They'd heard only static through the radios, but the gunfire and screaming told them it had begun topside.

"Do we just wait?" asked Admani. "They're supposed to call, right?"

"I don't think they can call," said Marlin.

"Fuck." Marlow squeezed her fists until they turned white.

The lone candle burned between them, the whites of everyone's eyes showing.

Don't worry, be happy, sang the big-mouthed bass somewhere in the distance.

The other three turned to Julie with wide eyes.

"Percy hooked it up with a motion sensor," said Julie.

"Where is it?" asked Marlow.

"Right outside the door."

Within ten seconds, the cellar door swung open. Long, black legs pushed down the stairs, sniffing around at the variety of smells. It was drawn to a green glow ten feet forward and pounced on the New Kids on the Block shirt, tearing it to pieces. There was a fluttering of feet and a muffled cry just behind it.

Admani went first, followed by Marlow, Julie with just her coat now, and Marlin. Stomps in the dirt could be heard just behind them as they emerged, one at a time. The three women and the baby made it topside, then Marlin was almost there when a ragged handful of claws came out of the dark and sunk into his shoulder. He cried out with so much fear and pain it sounded like he'd lost his voice. Marlin's hand reached for anything he could, first catching Julie's shoulder before slipping back. He found the handle to the cellar door, putting it in a death grip within his right fist. A second black hand stuck into his side, pulling him down as his shoulder joint popped trying to hold on. The cellar door betrayed him and swung to its peak. Marlow tried to stop it, but it slipped through her fingers as it slammed shut. Marlin's screams were short-lived.

Everything happened within a few seconds and the group from the food cellar were stuck with the aftermath.

Marlow looked at the door, knowing Marlin was dead. Knowing if they waited any longer, the door would swing back open and the Night Chaser would be after them.

"Run." She gritted her teeth. "Just run."

"Where?" asked Julie.

Marlow looked back, seeing a shadow crossing the grass near the food processing plant.

"Just go," Marlow said, and took off.

Avani was into a full cry and she couldn't wait with the living siren attached to her. She darted between buildings, not looking back. She hated herself for it, but she was in survival mode. After thirty seconds, she reached the forge to find it caved in on itself with only the corpse of a Night Chaser remaining. She continued toward the well. A wave of relief hit her as she saw Arjen and Bruuth, armed with a sword and spear.

"Hey," she yelled, and they rushed to her. "What happened?"

"They ambushed us," said Arjen. "They bypassed every defense. Something's wrong."

"Where can we go?"

"Is the cellar compromised?"

Marlow pursed her lips, then nodded.

"Then out of town," Arjen said.

"What about everyone else?"

"We'll regroup later. Come on." He waved her and Bruuth on and they went to the eastern wall.

Arjen looked around wildly. "This is where Lana and Ice were supposed to be. Where are they?"

Bruuth pointed to a spattering of blood in the dirt. "This?"

Arjen nodded. "Let's get her over. Maybe they went this way, too."

They helped Marlow climb, then Arjen followed. When it was Bruuth's turn, he turned back to the village and his face sunk.

"I must stay."

"I understand," said Arjen. "We'll see you again when the light shines."

Bruuth bowed, held his sword up and charged back to the village.

On the western wall, Percy and Walters were locked into a fight with a Night Chaser. It had gray streaks through its dark fur as it lunged at Percy. He dodged to the left, countering with an arrow that missed just over its head. Walters fired a shot into its hip. The beast flinched, surprised at the bite of the bullet. It dragged the bad leg behind it and continued.

Percy broke off one of the spears from the barricade and threw it like a javelin. The Night Chaser ducked just low enough for it to pass over, then it raised back up just in time to catch a second shot from the rifle into the side of its face. It was flailing wildly with one hand to its face and the other swinging around, trying to make purchase with either of the humans. They ducked away and ran back toward the forge.

When they found it empty, they continued to the well. Zane came out from the nearest building when they arrived.

"Thank God. Where's everyone else?"

"Your guess is as good as ours," said Walters.

"Where's Williams?" asked Percy.

"They got him," said Zane. "After they came through the ceiling I—"

He stopped when they spotted two Night Chasers coming down from Karath's house on the hill.

"Let's go," said Percy.

"No." Walters raised the gun. "We can't keep running." He aimed and clicked the empty barrel. "Shit."

He turned the stock around and held the barrel like a baseball bat. Percy queued up an arrow. Walters took the first swing, cracking one of the Night Chasers across the arm as it shielded its head. The other broke off to run at Percy and Zane. Percy fired his last arrow into the dirt just in front of it, then threw the bow at it for good measure. Zane raised his spear. In the background, Walters was overtaken, the rifle torn from his hands as he disappeared under the beast. Zane thrust his spear into the shoulder of the Night Chaser. It turned its attention from Percy and grabbed Zane across the chest. Its thick claws tore through his clothes, into his skin and pulled him close.

"No," yelled Percy.

He struck the Night Chaser across the face with the bucket from the well. There was a clanging sound and it dropped Zane. Percy grabbed his arm and pulled him away. Their backsides hit the well as another

Night Chaser growled behind them.

"Shit, shit, shit." Percy reached across the well, grabbing the rope, and spinning it around Zane's wrist.

"What the—" said Zane, as the Night Chaser he'd speared lunged at them.

Percy pushed Zane into the opening, and he swung down, smashing into the side of the stones. The rope was dropping him fast when Percy grabbed the other end, dodging the Night Chaser as he did. The rope dragged down his hands, setting fire to his palms. He lowered Zane hand over hand as fast as he could when the claws wrapped around his leg.

Zane felt his momentum stop. He was halfway down, twenty feet from the bottom when the rope tugged him back up, then released completely. He felt his stomach in his throat as he dropped to the water below.

~ * ~

Across the eastern wall, Marlow and Arjen ran, ducking through the rocks into the path to their village. They didn't see the Night Chaser on the ledge above. It stalked them until the right moment came. It landed between them and body-checked Arjen into the dark rocks. When his head connected, the world went black and he slumped to the dirt.

Marlow continued running, wanting to turn back, to help Arjen but she had to protect Avani before everything else. She tucked between a narrow passage and hoped it would be enough to slow the bigger-bodied monster behind her, then she heard the clicking of claws on rock. They were getting closer by the second. Marlow pushed her body until her legs felt like flames, then she felt hands wrap around her shoulders. She was lifted off the ground and tucked under the beast's arm. The clicking of its claws slowed to a mid-tempo rhythm. Marlow kicked and screamed, fighting to keep the sharp tips on its fingers from reaching the package strapped to her chest. She kept waiting for its teeth to sink into the back of her neck and finish the job, but the Night Chaser continued toward the human village, carrying her like a child throwing a tantrum. She felt the claws in her arms, scraping the surface, drawing blood but doing little damage, as if it didn't mean to hurt her. She wiggled a hand down to her pants pocket and found what she was looking for. *Aim for the heart,* was what Admani said when they made the poison-tipped arrows, only, Marlow knew she wouldn't be firing a bow with Avani on her chest. She'd pocketed a couple darts for an emergency.

She worked the dart to her other hand. The angle would be awkward, but if she craned her shoulder just right...

Marlow popped the protective cap off and slammed the dart into the Night Chaser's chest. It grunted and swatted her hand away like a fly. The dart hung for another few seconds before the monster brushed it off, then tightened its grip on her. She felt her joints popping and let out a groan of her own. Avani screamed in protest as she was smashed between Marlow's arms and chest. The rank smell from the beast made them both gag.

As they reached the opening, she could see the firepit glowing with embers by their huts. A dark figure headed toward the lab, and the Night Chaser that carried her raised a hand. The other figure tucked in without noticing them as her captor stumbled a little. It shook its head to clear its thoughts, took a step and went down to its front knees. Marlow didn't wait. She slipped back out of its arms. It opened its mouth to call for help when a rock the size of Avani slammed down onto its head. It collapsed the rest of the way. Arjen gave it one more hit with the rock for good measure. There was a sick, cracking sound as he let go, then he grabbed Marlow's arm.

"Are you okay?"

"Yeah. You?"

"Good enough. Through the forest, quick."

They ducked behind the lab as the other Night Chaser came out to find its companion dead.

Marlow and Arjen did their best to quiet Avani as they ran toward the wrecked village.

Chapter Five

Embers crackled and snapped just behind the row of captives. The screams and gunshots ceased hours ago. The line of black figures before them joked with each other, standing tall on their hind legs. A few had to limp into the meeting and a few never made it. These facts would not be forgotten over the next couple of minutes.

Walters leaned over to Lana, each of their hands bound behind them by a line of rope that made a human chain.

"Why aren't we dead?" he whispered.

"Give it time," Lana replied.

In the line next to them were Admani, Julie, and Williams. There were tears running down Julie's cheeks as she fought outright sobs. She'd looked up to Williams for a calming, reassuring look, but found only terror.

The largest of the Night Chasers stepped forward. He had a thick jaw and most of his teeth. The others were missing at least a few teeth each. One was missing the side of his face where Walters shot him. He was the gray-streaked Night Chaser and he eyed Walters with his good side.

The largest opened his mouth and spoke a rugged version of the Wyan language. The last months leading to this day had found most of the humans to be fluent in Wyan, but it was still shocking to hear the ruthless beasts communicating much the same as their daytime neighbors.

"If you are useful, you get to live."

The accent didn't change the words. He was answering Walters' question whether he knew it or not.

A silence hung over the humans. They couldn't bring themselves to trust the monsters they'd just seen tearing apart their companions. The Night Chasers still talked and laughed with each other. Finally, Lana replied in Wyan,

"What do you want with us?"

The big one looked at her with piercing eyes. "You'll know..." The rest of his sentence was unintelligible to them. He continued on, "...with our uprising. The...will be ours again."

Lana scrunched her face, trying to understand his message.

"You want the village?" asked Lana.

The big one smiled. "Not the village, the..." He repeated the word he'd said earlier, widening his arms as he did. *Hilan.*

"*City?*" Lana used the English word to what was left of her team. "What city?"

"Biral," called the gray-haired one to the leader, obviously not interested in Lana's questions. "First me."

"Are you able, Urun?" Biral asked.

Urun choked out a laugh, then his hand shot back to his face and he groaned. He shook a handful of blood onto the ground and limped forward toward the chain of humans, stopping in front of Walters. A sickening smile crossed his mutilated face.

"Hold on," said Lana. "I thought—"

Biral cut her off. "Not him."

Urun took more blood from his face and rubbed it across Walters' cheek. There was a low growl in Urun's throat.

"What? Tough guy," said Walters. "Want to kiss me?" There was a sharp inhale as Urun's clawed hand dove deep into Walters' guts.

"No," Admani yelled.

Urun held the claws in place as Walters poured blood between their feet.

Walters spoke English now. "Needed me tied up to—"

He groaned as Urun twisted before yanking his hand back out. Walters' head hung. He was dying on his feet. Lana and Admani wanted to support him, to help hold his body up but their hands were tied. All they could do was slow his fall as his legs gave out. He was face first in a puddle of his own blood at the feet of the Night Chaser he'd shot earlier defending the Wyan village.

Urun stepped back, content with his revenge and fell in line.

Biral seemed unamused at the sidetracking. "Which one is the leader?" He pointed at the humans. "I hope not him."

"Me," said Lana.

"Good. Tell me why the rest of you should not join your companion." He motioned to Walters, whose quick, sharp breaths had stopped.

Lana found herself searching for words. The night had not gone at all to plan. The Night Chasers had not been the big, dumb, feral beasts they'd been advertised to be. They saw through every trap and set off the border alarms to split the team up for easier pickings. The Wyans had not been there for support. They would all be killed, if not already, soon. Lana's team should've been dead, and she knew it. For all intents and purposes, she'd failed, only, for some reason, some of them were still alive and it was her job to keep it that way as long as she could.

"They are medics," she finally blurted out. "The two females. Your group could use that."

Biral squinted at her, trying to decide if he accepted her reasoning.

"Maybe." He looked at Williams. "Him?"

Williams had opposed Lana every step of the way. Half of her hated him for it and the other half wondered how things would've been different if he were in charge. Either way, she didn't want him to suffer the same fate as Walters.

"He's the captain of our vessel."

Immediately, she wanted to take back her comment. They had no ship. She wasn't sure how else to explain what kind of *vessel* she was talking about in the Wyan language. She may as well have told them Williams was the Prince of Wales.

Biral's eyes widened as his head snapped to examine Williams.

"*Flying* vessel?" Biral asked.

Williams looked to Lana who nodded at him.

"Yes," said Williams. "I fly the vessel."

Great, thought Lana. *Now we just have to convince them that this invisible vessel was stolen. That's why we have no proof.*

Only Biral didn't have any further questions. He smiled at his group and gave a command, "Take them with us. Leave the dead."

Walters was cut loose, Admani and Julie were linked together, and the two groups were on the move.

~ * ~

Arjen groaned as Marlow checked the bandage on his head. They hadn't had time to address the bleeding as they escaped the Night Chasers, and he began feeling dizzy halfway to the bunker. He was laid out in the woods as she tried to keep Avani from crying when Cannie came across them. She'd helped Marlow get him underground. That was hours ago. Cannie was back out, scouting the aftermath, leaving Marlow and Arjen, while Barchek played with Avani. They had only candlelight and a wind-up flashlight to see. The bunker in the woods was much smaller than the food storehouse Marlow was in before. Still, they were safe for the moment. The trees concealed them. Someone would have to know the location to come looking.

Avani bounced happily on Barchek's belly, as she held her by the armpits, lowering her down to push off again.

"Okay." Marlow pushed her palms towards the ground. "Give it a little rest. She's getting too loud."

Avani's giggles had turned to squeals as Barchek made bigger faces with each bounce. She caught the baby and hugged her close. Marlow smiled as she finished checking out Arjen's head. They sat waiting on Cannie to return.

For the first time since their meeting, Barchek hadn't asked Marlow to play. Cannie drilled her well on what they needed to do to survive in the bunker until daylight came within the week. Until then, they were close to fresh streams if their water supplies ran low. They had food, but they weren't planning on two adult humans and a baby.

"We are young," Barchek sang softly to Avani. "Heartache to heartache, we stand..."

"You sure the bleeding stopped?" asked Arjen. "I swear she's singing, 'Love is a battlefield.'"

"Hah-hah," said Marlow. "I taught her."

"Just thought I'd descended to Hell, what with the underground, the fire and the song."

"Good to see you're feeling better."

"Yeah, guess that means it's not a concussion."

He watched Barchek playing with Avani in the dirt floor of the bunker as she started the second verse. "Seriously, Marlow, how much of that song does she know?"

"Most of it, and a few others. Julie let me borrow a working Walkman she scavenged. Apparently Pat Benatar's greatest hits will survive anything."

The conversation lulled at the mention of Julie. They couldn't keep up with the jokes, knowing the rest of their team was likely slaughtered. Avani's laughs and Barchek's singing gave them momentary amnesia from their surroundings. For Marlow, it was too real being back in a bunker, losing those she loved again. This time she had a possibly concussed man and alien child as support, never mind her own baby.

Marlow broke the silence. "Do you think they're all dead?"

Arjen's face tightened. "It's...I don't wanna think..." His voice caught.

It took no time for the weight of the situation to hit them like a falling building. If their group was dead, if they were the last living humans on Wyan, what happened next? Even if they survived the rest of the darkness...

There was no time for tears as the trapdoor swung open. Cannie's head appeared, but she didn't come down the stairs. There was fear in her eyes.

"I've found the dark woman. She's hurt bad. Bring your supplies."

Arjen jumped up too quick, stumbling and using the wall for support. "Ice? Where is she?"

Marlow helped steady him.

"Up by the waterfall," said Cannie.

"What about the Night Chasers?" asked Marlow.

Cannie paused, contemplating her answer. "It is clear, but we must hurry."

Marlow grabbed the few supplies she had to bandage wounds then looked back at Barchek.

"Shit."

"Shit-bitch?"

Marlow looked to Arjen for confirmation and he nodded.

"Can you watch Avani for a few minutes?" Marlow asked.

Barchek gave a thumbs up.

"Keep her happy," Marlow said. "If she starts crying..."

Arjen grabbed her arm before she could come up with more instructions. "Let's go. She'll be fine for a few. We have to help Ice."

They left the bunker, closing it up and brushing a few leaves across it. Marlow hoped it would be enough.

~ * ~

A half hour before Marlow left the bunker in search of Ice, the Night Chasers, eight in all, led the surviving humans through the hills. They connected with a pathway that seemed impassable until two of the bigger Night Chasers stepped forward and pushed a rock to the side. It revealed a ledge, leading along the outer edge of the mountainside.

There was a little starlight, but something else was illuminating the path. Glowing crystal shards were stuck in the hillside like darts in a dartboard. The blue glow was weak but enough to show the footholds you'd need to survive the ledges.

Biral, the leader, went first, hugging the cliff and shimmying sideways. His fur black and shining with the blue light. He was followed by two more Night Chasers, the third holding onto the rope that led to Lana. He tugged and she stumbled forward toward the edge.

"Come."

"My hands." Lana showed the knot behind her back.

He raised the rope, looped it twice around his wrist and tugged again. "You won't fall."

"Okay, okay. Just let me..."

She inched to the edge, her feet sideways, belly against the rocks. There was just enough room for her shoes. Another inch and her heels would be hanging. Lana looked back at Admani and motioned for her to mimic her steps. The rope tied from her hands to Admani and down the line. They'd doctored the line to remove Walters. Admani's legs wouldn't stop shaking. Julie behind her was worse. Lana could hear Williams reassuring them, that they'd make it, that he wouldn't let them fall. Soon, they were all teetering on the edge. The Night Chasers fell in behind, one holding the other end of the rope and the rest following. Urun was behind the rope holder, struggling with the bullet in his hip. The path coiled around the side of the mountain, the fall becoming more and more treacherous as they went. Admani whimpered as her face scraped the rocks, drawing blood, but she didn't dare to pull her head back. A slight breeze felt like a gale in their precarious position. They ducked under a low hanging shelf of black rock, the Night Chasers barely clearing it. As the humans made it out, they could finally see the ledge widening again twenty feet ahead.

There was a groan as Urun made his last push from under the ledge, then the cracking of loose rock. He cried out, reaching forward to catch the hind leg of the Night Chaser ahead of him. Williams felt the rope go tight as the Night Chaser tried to hold on. Urun called for help, but the one behind him offered none.

"Don't lose them," called back Biral.

The Night Chaser on the other end of the rope kicked back, striking Urun in the caved in part of his face. He roared in pain, letting go of his grip, his momentum carrying him off the ledge in a slow arc. He picked up speed, cracking his back on a ledge a few feet down, then plummeting to his death below. The Night Chaser at the end of the rope regained his footing, loosening his pull on Williams. They continued like it was nothing but a brief hiccup in their journey.

When the path opened again, everyone let out a breath as if they'd been holding it the entire way across the ledge.

The darkness closed in again. Only the face of a neighboring planet they didn't know the name of gave them light. The glowing crystals were gone from this part of the trail, but the Night Chasers picked up their speed. It felt like a mile of stumbling in the darkness. The rope was the only thing keeping the humans from eating dirt every ten steps or so. They strained against each other each time one would lose their footing. Their ties tightened on their wrists digging deeper into their skin and cutting off their circulation. Lana wanted to yell for them to stop. To at least slow down and to loosen their binds, but after witnessing their disregard for their own man, she didn't think they'd get much sympathy.

Biral finally slowed as they reached a drop-off. There was light coming from below, some of it orange, some blue. As the humans made it to the edge, they saw a small village, built like a slum in a ditch. Makeshift roofs hung on questionable supports. There was a fire near an open, common area. Black figures were huddled around it with cloths over their heads, passing items back and forth. The whole area was the size of a football field. The ground looked like clay. There were roughly placed rocks for stairs in and out. The left side of the village tucked into a hillside overhang, as if they'd burrowed it out. The right leveled out back onto flat land in the distance.

Biral stood at the edge of the stairs, looking at the scattered clan below. "We've returned," he yelled, "and we have the luaks." He and another Night Chaser pulled the rope to line up their hostage marionette for the village to see.

There were cheers from some, others came running up the stairs. One, a small creature about the size of Barchek came up to sniff Lana. Biral kicked him away.

When Biral saw he had most of the village's attention, thirty or so gathered in the common area, he raised his arms.

"They are going to help us get back to Hilan."

More throaty cheers went up. When it got quiet again, one called out, "Let's eat them." There were yells and wicked laughs in the group below.

Biral did not seem amused. "First the city, then you will have all the food you need." He grabbed the rope, pulling the human chain with him towards the stairs, then muttered to one of the Night Chasers next to him. "Unless they can't help us."

Lana wanted to turn back and reassure the group they'd be okay, but she felt her chest start heaving. She was having a panic attack.

Chapter Six

"She's not going to survive here," said Marlow. "She lost too much blood."

Isolde's mangled body lay between Marlow and Arjen in the bunker. They'd found her unconscious, wrapped her wounds tighter and carried her in. She was shivering spastically. She'd used strips of her clothes to tie off her wounds, but the bare skin in the cold and the loss of blood caught up to her. Cannie wrapped her in a blanket as they discussed their options.

"Blood transfusion?" Arjen asked.

"Do we know her type?" Marlow replied. "Do we have any medical supplies to do that?"

He shook his head in defeat. "No, and without Julie or Admani, I wouldn't dare."

"What then? There's gotta be something back at the lab."

"We didn't exactly have a blood bank there."

Cannie was whispering with Barchek. She spoke for her mother in English.

"She says your lab was destroyed."

"Shit," said Marlow.

"We've gotta do something for her," said Arjen.

"Hold on. Remember when Walters' face stopped sagging?"

"Yeah, when he was out with Admani."

"He said it was the springs that did it. His body absorbed the nutrients like crazy because of the hagfish DNA we've all been injected with. Ice needs nutrients. We can't exactly feed her. Maybe that would help."

"That sounds like our only decent option. But where are those springs?"

"Just down the path from here and through that tunnel."

"Oh, God, we're gonna be sitting ducks out there." Arjen looked at the flickering candlelight, thinking back on Ice checking in on him to make sure he was eating. She was always looking out for him and their team on gathering missions, even if she didn't verbalize it. If the roles were reversed, she'd be hauling his ass to the springs. "We have to try. Ice would for us."

"It's true." Marlow looked to Barchek and Cannie. "We need to save our friend. We think the springs might be our only option. Can you watch Avani one more time?"

They nodded in agreement. "Should I...?" Cannie motioned towards the door.

"No. You've helped a lot already. Arjen and I can carry her."

"Be safe. Be fast," said Cannie.

They grabbed Isolde and took her back into the dark forest.

~ * ~

Lana held the bars of their makeshift prison. It was a random grouping of thin boards jammed into the cliffside, reinforced with rocks. She watched the Night Chasers. They were much like the Wyans. They had three genders, with the Wits, if that's what they were called on this side of Wyan, watching the children, only the women didn't seem to be in charge.

Biral was the biggest and called the shots. The group with him did what they wanted around the village, taking food out of the hands of others and eating it in front of them, going in any dwelling they pleased. It was survival of the fittest on this side of the planet and Lana wondered what that meant for them.

She heard Williams whispering as he looked through an opening in the boards next to her.

"We could break these down. A couple kicks and—"

"Then what?" She cut him off. "Find out which one of those beasts will maul us first?"

"We would catch them by surprise. They must sleep at some point."

"Even so, do you know the way in this pitch-black landscape? Who's to say we wouldn't find another group of them out in the dark that wasn't as friendly?"

Williams' voice got sharper, keeping his volume low. "We are not going to roll over and die. Not after all we've done."

Lana turned to him. "I agree, but we are not going to provoke them. We saw what happened to Walters."

Admani was just behind them, watching the looks they were getting from afar. "I don't think they are worried about keeping us in." A ragged, thin female looked their way and Admani lowered her voice. "I think they are trying to keep the rest of them out."

Lana felt a shiver go up her spine. She tightened her coat and stepped back from the bars.

~ * ~

Marlow and Arjen carried Ice's shivering body into the cold. They were hitting the junction where they could turn to do the thousand-foot climb down to their village or enter the rock tunnel that Walters had shown Admani back in easier days.

They stopped at the mouth, knowing they'd have to drag her, trying to decide how that would work, then they heard trotting footsteps.

Marlow and Arjen squinted to see a black shadow on the trail they'd just come down.

"Shit, shit, shit," said Marlow. "Get her in."

Arjen felt his veins freeze up as he dragged his long-time travelling companion into the tunnel. He banged the back of his head on a low-hanging rock and felt the world spin. Fresh blood trickled out of his bandage as Marlow looked up and yelled at him.

"Come on, Arjen. Don't sleep now."

Arjen blinked away the stars, ducked his head and pulled. Marlow pushed Isolde's legs and soon they were both in the tunnel with Arjen. The skidding of feet could be heard just behind them at the junction.

"Yes," came a growling voice. A Night Chaser stalked up to the edge of the tunnel as Arjen and Marlow continued dragging their friend deeper. They hoped it would get too tight for the beast to follow.

"Who do you have?" the voice slurred.

Marlow looked back to see his jaw hanging looser than it should. She trained the flashlight at his eyes and he covered them.

"If you come in here, you die."

The Night Chaser laughed at her and lunged forward. It was tight but he was gaining ground, his jagged and broken claws pulling him forward. Marlow found a loose rock, tucked into a sitting position to keep her feet out of his reach and waited.

"Give me the dark woman," he said. "I'll leave you."

"Go jump off a mountain."

He twisted his shoulder free and swiped a hand at her. Marlow anticipated his move, dodged her head back, pinned his hand to the tunnel wall and smashed it with the rock. He tried to pull his arm back, but she crushed his wrist with her feet, using her back as leverage on the other wall. His body was wedged from his attack and he couldn't free his other arm. She smashed every bone in his hand until he finally pulled back his arm with a pop and a scream.

"Come out and fight me," he said. "You cannot hide in there." He backed out slowly until he was on all fours at the entrance. His injured hand pulled to his chest, supporting it at the elbow.

Arjen whispered to Marlow, "Is there another way over here?"

He was looking at the end of the tunnel, not far away.

"Let's find out."

They dragged Ice to the end. When it widened, Marlow looked back.

"I don't see him. Let's stay back just in case."

Within the minute, the Night Chaser dropped in front of the other entrance, laughing.

"You're trapped. Leave the woman and go back to your village."

They scrambled back to the center of the tunnel. They couldn't stay out in the cold much longer. Ice's breathing was sharp. Her color was getting pale. Arjen took a turn winding the flashlight so they could keep track of the Night Chaser.

"Should we make a break back for the bunker?" asked Marlow.

"Ice will die."

"If we leave her out here much longer, she'll die. If we take her down to the springs, we'll be sitting out in the open for him to find us. I don't think we can win. We left all our weapons back in the Wyan village."

"We won't make it to the bunker. Not with Ice, and we'll risk leading him there."

Marlow took the light from him. "Can you carry her to the springs on your own?"

"I...probably. What are you saying?"

"I'll take the light, use it to distract him and get back to the bunker. You take Ice. If you can get her better at all, it's worth it."

Arjen rubbed his hands back through his hair. "Not if you die."

On cue, the Night Chaser landed back on the other side, blocking the way back to the bunker.

"Give me the woman."

"She kicked your rear, didn't she?" said Marlow.

She didn't know better Wyan insults. Barchek hadn't taught her them.

The Night Chaser just growled at her. "You will be next—ah!"

His sentence was interrupted as he toppled over on his side, landing on his bad arm. There was the familiar honking laugh from Barchek, then scurrying feet.

"Barchek, no," Marlow yelled.

"Fuck," said Arjen.

Marlow crawled out of the tunnel as fast as she could. The Night Chaser was already on his feet, chasing the young Wyan. Marlow emerged, hitting them with the flashlight as Barchek ran down a separate trail, away from the tunnel, away from the bunker.

"What are you...?" said Marlow. "Oh no. Stop! Stop, Barchek!" She watched, frozen in place as Barchek was heading down the dark path towards the trip wire. She had a solid lead on the Night Chaser but was about to be blown to bits.

"Mine!" yelled Marlow, using the English word. Barchek didn't slow. If anything, she kicked it into another gear. She had the potential to lose the bigger beast chasing her, but not if she blew herself up.

When Barchek was a few feet away, she jumped as high as her legs would send her over the tripwire and onto the path on the other side. She tucked into a roll like she had on the sand dunes. The Night Chaser was gaining ground, but didn't see the tripwire. He slowed the slightest bit, confused by her jump, but the darkness gave him no sign of the oncoming danger. When he caught the wire, Percy's final fireworks went off. The beast's midsection exploded into chunks of flesh and bone. The tunnel shook. Barchek stopped her roll and looked back at the spectacle as blood rained down.

"Cunt."

Barchek trotted back up the hill, avoiding the gore the best she could. They didn't have time to talk. Marlow thanked Barchek and sent her back to the bunker as they finally made it through the tunnel. Marlow and Arjen struggled down the hill before stopping to unwrap the blanket from Ice.

"We should start slow," said Marlow. "Too much heat and she'll go into shock."

Arjen nodded as they lowered her feet first, stopping at her knees. Ice lolled over into Arjen's chest as he held her, waiting for the warmth to bring her back to life. Her breathing was sporadic, but her shivers were slowing. They held her waist deep. Marlow splashed some water on her torso, trying to prepare her skin. She looked like an old scarecrow, an arm out each direction with an unconvincing head.

When they reached chest level, Ice's eyes shot open.

"It's warm," she muttered.

"Good warm?" asked Arjen. "Are you with us again?"

Her eyes found him, swiveling on a lethargic neck. "I think I pissed myself."

Arjen smiled. "That's okay. Can we lower you more?"

"I don't think I'm ready to swim."

"I'll be with you."

He had Marlow hold Ice up while he submerged himself in front of her. Arjen put an arm around her waist and slowly lowered her to a sitting position with the water stopping at her collar bone.

"This stings like a mother," said Ice.

"I'm sure it does but you're awake now," said Arjen. "It's progress, right?"

"I guess."

"Care to tell us what happened?"

"Fight." She rolled her head back to rest on the edge. "Big sucker."

"Did you break his jaw?" asked Marlow.

She managed a half smile. "I caught him pretty good with a kick. It's how I got away."

"What about Lana?" asked Arjen. "Were you with her when...?"

"I...no. They split us up. Two of them. She didn't have time to fire the gun. The next thing I knew, the village was overrun. I doubled back to look for you." She nodded at Marlow. "Marlin, he..."

"I know."

"At that point, I figured it was time to get out of town. Nothing went right. We failed. We failed them." Ice began to cry. Arjen pulled her into a hug. They sat, soaking in the nutrients as Marlow kept watch. When Ice was able to sit on her own, Arjen sat beside her and said, "We're hiding out with Cannie and Barchek until we know more. Until we see the bodies..."

"Okay." Ice moved each of her limbs with winces and groans. "Give me another minute if it's clear still."

"Yeah." Marlow looked at hills, blanketed with shadows but despite a few tricks of the eye, none of them were moving.

For the moment.

~ * ~

They arrived back at the small bunker with no resistance. It was overcrowded with all of them inside at once, but the door was still able to close. Avani was excited to see Marlow and smacked Barchek two or three times in the face to show it. It didn't take long for the air to get heavy. The humans were out of place once again. The village that was supposed to be their safe haven had fallen. The group that was supposed to be their companions for the coming years were likely wiped out. They were hiding out in the bunker of an outcast and her daughter, but if anyone knew what they were feeling, Cannie did.

She looked at them with sad eyes. "Now that we're all together, I have to tell you a story."

Chapter Seven

The time of darkness was approaching nearly four years ago. Barchek's father, Balowg, survived the previous one before Barchek was born, but didn't want to see her go through it. Each time it had gotten worse. He knew soon they couldn't meet the demands of the Night Chasers and what then? He proposed a plan that was quickly shot down. He wanted to catch and kill a Night Chaser, then string it up as a warning that there would be opposition, that the Wyans would not bow to their oppressors anymore. It was the only type of message they'd understand, he'd told everyone. The rest of the Wyans were too afraid of the consequences, of the steps it would take to stand up to the Night Chasers and what would happen if it didn't work.

Balowg knew their numbers outweighed the Night Chasers, but it would not be long before they didn't. They had to act before it was too late. His village's representative, Latey, finally agreed to back his plan as long as they didn't kill the Night Chaser. They would capture a Night Chaser and put it on display for the rest to see when they came for their offering.

Of the three villages, each was required to offer up a Wyan for each night of darkness. If the offerings were there, no further questions were asked. They were taken back to the Night Chaser village and never heard from again.

Balowg lost his sister in the last time of darkness and couldn't bear to lose another loved one, or anyone in the village for that matter. He knew his plan wasn't foolproof, so he dug out the bunker as a backup. Only Cannie and Barchek knew about it. Trapping the Night Chaser would be harder, but he had a plan for that as well.

One day, Balowg brought a team of two other male Wyans and Cannie up to Ruh'la peak. They crossed to the darkness and laid in wait for a Night Chaser to stray too far from their village. It took time and patience, but finally they spotted one further down the mountain, hunting a type of mole.

Cannie made herself known and lured him in. Wyans were never so devious and deceptive, but Balowg reminded them it would all be worth it in the end. When Cannie led the Night Chaser to the cave they were hiding in, the Wyans jumped him, tying his mouth and limbs and carrying him back to their village.

Balowg kept the Night Chaser in the bunker as the time of darkness grew closer.

Then there was the flying vessel. It flew overhead like a giant bird. The Wyans knew it couldn't be a bird but had no idea what it was. The beings that came out of it were even stranger. They stood on only two feet and were porous. They were white like rock or seafoam. Their faces were friendly enough, but the Wyans stuck to themselves.

Balowg had other ideas. After a full day and rest period, he befriended them. They were called Pelosins. They were there to study the land, to live in peace. Their language was strange. They seemed to be always listening, but never understanding. He wanted to recruit the Pelosins in their fight for freedom from the Night Chasers, but the rest of his village opposed it and he ran out of time. They shared as much as they could with each other, but Balowg had to go through with his original plan. He warned them of the time of darkness and went to his bunker. If the plan worked, he would reconvene with them after and learn more of their ways.

The Night Chaser was enraged. Balowg couldn't get him into position like he was. He used the wing of a blue razor-fin and slit it down his left arm. Barchek stayed in the bunker while Balowg and one of the other Wyans strapped the Night Chaser to a tall, smooth rock. The poison took effect and his left side was close to paralyzed.

All of Balowg and Cannie's village were there to meet the Night

Chasers when they arrived, to show them what they'd done to the one they captured and what would happen to the rest of them if they crossed the line. Balowg sent Cannie to the bunker to stay with Barchek, knowing his plan wasn't perfect.

Cannie didn't see where it went wrong, only that the confrontation ended with the full ranks of the Night Chasers storming their village, destroying and killing everything in sight. Balowg didn't come back and Cannie didn't leave the bunker. He'd told her to stay, that if things took a turn, it was the only safe place. When it cleared up, he'd come for them. Days passed and no one came. When the first sunlight showed, Cannie shot out of the bunker, down the path and found the remains of Balowg's corpse tied to the stone where the Night Chaser should've been. She wept for what must have been an hour until she felt Barchek hugging her back. She covered the child's eyes and took her down to the village to see what remained.

Cannie and Barchek were shunned for Balowg's actions. The rest of their village had been destroyed and most of their neighbors killed. They lived in the ruins as a constant reminder. The fields still produced enough with a little upkeep. In the rubble, she found the white relic left by the Pelosins. She stashed it in the bunker as a memory of them, as well. Their flying vessel was gone.

When Cannie's story came to a stopping point, Arjen shared a look with Ice and Marlow. They'd heard a much different side from Lana and no mention of the Pelosins until Walters found the relic.

"I don't know where to start," said Marlow. "That's terrible. So, the other village won't accept you because Balowg tried to protect them?"

"Yes, but he failed. He brought death on us all."

"But he tried. He tried to do something instead of just letting them have their way."

"Just like us?" said Ice. "That worked out well, didn't it?"

"What should we have done?" asked Marlow. "Just hide out? Watch them die and come back when it's over?"

"What about not coming here? Ever thought of that? This was all a terrible mistake. Now Admani, Lana, Zane..."

"Wait," said Cannie. "I haven't finished."

"There's more to your story?" asked Arjen.

"There is today. When I was scouting, I saw the Night Chasers. A group of them were returning. They had some of your friends."

"What?" said Arjen. "What do you mean? When were you going to—"

Marlow cut him off. "Let her finish." Then to Cannie, "Who was with them? Zane?"

Cannie shook her head and described them the best she could.

"Admani," said Ice. "She's still out there."

"And Lana," said Arjen. "If they haven't eaten her."

"We have to go before it's too late." Marlow was ready to move.

"Go?" said Cannie. "No. You will die."

"But they are our friends," said Marlow. "The last of our kind."

Cannie contemplated her words. "You will all die, then."

Marlow sighed. "What if it was Balowg? What if he was alive out there?"

Cannie looked away and walked over to a crate of food. She reached a hand behind it and produced the white Pelosin relic. She turned it over a few times, then handed it to Marlow.

"You should take it with if you go."

Marlow smiled as she gripped the relic. "You stole it back, huh?"

Cannie met her grin. "It was mine."

"Can you tell us how to use it?"

Cannie shook her head. "I hoped you would know."

Marlow shrugged and turned to Arjen and Ice.

"Sounds like suicide," said Arjen, "but I can't sit here knowing Lana and others are out there."

"I know," said Marlow, "but Avani..."

"I can't tell you..." started Arjen.

Marlow's face was tight, looking at the perfect child she was contemplating leaving behind. "I can't let you go alone."

"But she's your daughter. I understand."

Marlow held Avani tight, squeezing her chubby cheeks against her face. "Balowg was right, though. If we don't do something now, it will just happen again. Just before Avani's fifth birthday, then what?"

"Yes, but..."

"I'll be here with Avani," said Ice. "I can get around enough."

"Are you sure you're okay?" asked Marlow.

Ice gave a thumbs up. "That mineral bath worked wonders, and I've got Barchek to watch out for me, right?"

Barchek leaned her head over and smiled.

"Just promise me you'll be careful," said Ice.

"We will," Marlow assured her.

"And bring back my sister."

"We will," said Arjen.

"I'll show you the way," said Cannie "but I will not stay with."

Arjen put a hand on her shoulder. "Thank you."

Marlow was hugging Avani as tears welled up.

"You don't have to do this," said Arjen.

Marlow just shook her head at him. He let her have her last moment with Avani in silence.

They packed up a few supplies, tucking the relic into a bag at last, just in case. Cannie dressed Arjen in some dry clothes, roughly tailored to fit him. Marlow said another heart-wrenching goodbye to Avani, then left her in the care of Ice and Barchek. Arjen and Cannie waited.

They went down the path to the mountainside their companions travelled just hours earlier.

Chapter Eight

Admani was slipping in and out of consciousness, huddled against the rest of the group for warmth. The physical and emotional strain she'd been through was far greater than anything she'd ever experienced in her life. Especially life on the Belt. She was bored, if anything, growing up in the Belt. Her work was interesting, to a point, but there was only so far she could go with artificial everything. Wyan was supposed to be her great exploration. To prove to her sister that she was just as tough. That the lab hadn't made her soft. Only, she knew it had. At least compared to Isolde. Their mother told her so on more than one occasion. Admani sat on the cold clay floor of the Night Chasers' makeshift prison and silently wept. She wept for her mother, back in the Belt, expecting her daughters to be off exploring new lands, doing great things. Instead, they'd both become food for the locals. If Admani could be granted one wish, it would be to get a message to Kaia. She'd tell her it wasn't her mother's high expectations that drove her away. It was her desire to make her proud. So, she could show her how much the hard work had paid off.

Admani was jarred from her reflection by a clanging on the bars. There was a smaller Night Chaser staring at them. Admani was afraid it was hungry.

"Medic," it said.

Julie raised her head from Admani's shoulder and shook it. "Don't," she said. "I c-can't."

"What do you need with a medic?" Lana asked in fluent Wyan.

"Are you the medic?" Its face was against the bars, sniffing as if it can tell someone's knowledge base by smell.

"I am," said Admani. "What do you want?"

Julie gasped next to her, equally afraid for her counterpart.

151

"Come with me. Biral said I could use you."

None of the humans liked that translation, *use you*. It could mean so many things. Still, Admani stood. Julie held onto her hand from the floor.

"Is someone hurt?" Admani asked.

The Night Chaser slammed its hands on the bars. "Now."

Admani flinched, then slowly approached the bars. Lana was by her side.

"Sit down. Just her," it said.

There was enough light on its face to tell it was a Wit, or the Night Chaser version of that. They'd never heard a Wit exert authority like that. Lana gave a nod to Admani and she returned it, going to the bars to meet the Wit.

It pulled them open, grabbed Admani's arm to yank her through before slamming the bars back in place, then they were off into the village. Lana, Williams, and Julie watched until she was out of sight.

A few minutes later, Julie and Williams were back against the wall sitting. She was sobbing into his shoulder as he tried to comfort her. He didn't have any consoling words left. He was stroking her red braid, taking as much comfort as he was giving.

"More company," said Lana, standing near the bars as Biral approached.

"Leader." He pointed at Lana. "Come."

"What is this about?"

"Just talk."

She looked around. There were a few stray Night Chasers, but it looked like Biral had come alone. She hoped that was a good sign as he opened the bars and took her with him.

Lana looked back to Williams and Julie. "I'll do what I can," she said in English.

Biral led her by the arm up the other set of stairs, out of the slum and further into the darkness.

They walked through a cool breeze. Lana trying to hug herself against the cold. Biral said, "Do not run," then let go of her arm.

She followed him, stumbling here and there on loose rocks. The ground smoothed out into a sandy road of sorts. There were a few cactus-like plants on the sides of their path, lit up by only the light of the distant planet. They were thriving despite the constant dark.

"Where are you taking me?" she asked, trying to keep the fear out of her voice.

"You'll see. Just over this hill."

As Biral ascended, Lana considered how futile an escape attempt would be. There was no ending she could come up with that wouldn't end in her death and possible torture along the way. She followed him, grunting her way up a boulder. She saw light, lots of it. There was a glowing beacon in the distance, blue and tall, like a tower of some sort. Only, the more she looked, the more she realized it was too large to be a tower, it had to be...

"Hilan?" she asked.

Biral grunted an agreement. "*My* Hilan. Before I was banished."

There was a silence between them. Lana wanted to ask so many questions. The first being, why was she still alive? Also, why was he showing her this city?

Finally, Biral continued, "All of us have been banished. Locked out of our Hilan."

Lana felt like he was opening up to her, so she asked, "For what?"

"There was a great disagreement." Biral's face turned sour. "I worked under Kaman. He controls everything in Hilan. I wanted to bring in new ideas, ways we could prosper, and he saw it as a challenge to his rule." Biral turned his dark eyes toward her, able to pick apart every feature on her face in the low light. "It *was* a challenge. In turn, my supporters were banished or killed, one at a time until there were just a few of us. I knew they were saving me for last, so I snuck out while I still could." He shook his head, looking back toward the glowing city. "He thinks he can keep me from my house. My people."

So, you want to storm the castle gates? Lana thought. *Take back what's yours?*

"You want to go back?" she asked.

"Yes, but the guards are many and the walls are tall."

"Okay..." Lana saw where he was going with it. "I don't have a...a flying vessel. Mine was stolen."

It's not something she could lie about at this point, but she braced for impact. For Biral to say, "Then you are useless to me," and kill her on the spot, but instead, he said, "I do, and you're going to fly it for me and take back my Hilan."

~ * ~

The inside of the rickety huts in the village were not much different from the outside, makeshift junk thrown together to resemble dwellings. The one Admani was in had two rooms split by boards with a tarp between them. The Wit led her to a boy that looked a little younger than Barchek. He was laid on his side, feet dangling, and arms holding his stomach. The Wit looked at her. After its commanding display at the jail, its eyes gave away its helplessness.

"He's sick. Help him."

"Okay." Admani looked him over but didn't move. "Sick how?"

"It's been days. If he dies while I watch him, I will die too."

Admani was afraid that was all the help she was going to get. She leaned in and asked the boy to explain his symptoms, gently pushing on his stomach as he cried out. After a lot of back and forth, the best she could tell is he had some kind of bacterial infection. Without being able to run any blood tests back in the lab, she could only make her best guess.

She turned to the caretaker, nervously standing by.

"I need..."

Admani didn't know the word for antibiotics. They probably didn't have one, but she'd studied some mushrooms on Wyan that had all the properties she needed. "Mushrooms..." she said, wondering if the word was the same from the other side of the mountains.

The Wit tilted its head at her. She put her hand low to the ground.

"Little, brown...plants. Grow from the ground."

The Wit seemed to get her gist and soon they were off, leaving the

154

sick boy behind to go mushroom hunting in the dark.

~ * ~

Arjen and Marlow crossed the mountain ledge slowly, knowing one slip would be all it took. Cannie's directions were to look for the watchful eyes, three stars in the northern sky. Two flanked like eyes with the middle one sinking down like a nose. When they hit solid land again, the stars would be overhead, leading them to the Night Chaser's village. That was the extent of what Cannie knew, though she'd never been herself.

Marlow loosed a glowing crystal shard from the mountain side. It looked like it had been jammed in for their journey.

"This will be less obvious than the flashlight."

"Right." Arjen patted a backpack with their food, water, and the alien relic. The flashlight was on top in case they found a place they'd dare to use it. The blue glow from the crystal was weak, barely enough to give them a few feet of vision but better than tripping on every rock along the way.

Soon they saw lights from the village coming into view. The stars led them right to it. Now they had to decide how they were going to find their friends and escape alive.

They stayed a hundred yards back, watching for movement. There was plenty to see. Night Chasers coming and going, carrying food or sticks for the fire. There was too much activity.

"Think that's where they are?" asked Marlow.

"Gotta be," said Arjen, "but we can't get anywhere near there until things calm down." He was pacing behind a cactus, popping his head out then back behind the quills. "Lana..."

Marlow grabbed his arm to stop him. "This is not a suicide mission. We've gotta be smart. If we're found, there's no help coming."

"I know, but—" He cut himself off when they saw a pair of Night Chasers coming away from the village straight in their direction. "Under the rock."

Without another word, they slipped underneath a rock hanging off the remains of the mountain. It formed a small cave and, most importantly, shrouded them in total darkness. They watched from their bellies as the Night Chasers crunched dirt under their feet, stopping just short of the cactus. They were arguing about something. When Arjen and Marlow started picking up the translation, their blood froze.

"...our reward? If Biral fails, we get nothing."

"Then we take it anyway. Here or there."

"I don't want to wait. I'm hungry now."

The other Night Chaser looked around. "Sometimes the bogars live around here. See, tracks?" He kicked dirt under the rock and caught Marlow in the eyes. She couldn't help but bring her hands to her eyes, scraping her elbows across the ground.

One Night Chaser looked at the other. "Hey, I think you're right. There's one under there now."

"You're going to get bit, Morlan."

"Then I'll pull it out by its teeth. I don't care, I'm hungry."

A furry, clawed hand slammed down a few seconds later, just short of Marlow's face. She was blinking away dirt as tears streamed down her cheeks. She tried to scoot back, but her heels caught the edge of the cave. The hand patted left, then right. She feared it would come forward and tear her skin into strips of meat. As it raised to do so, it was pinned back to the ground by a dart. Arjen's fist was white, twisting and dragging the tip down the Night Chaser's hand until it was free.

Morlan yelled out curses, crying in pain and pulling his hand back, as the other Night Chaser laughed his guts out.

"What did I say?" He was bent over as Morlan looked at the cave with rage.

"You going to try again?"

Morlan snorted. "If only just to kill it."

He took a couple steps to the left, then the right, then lowered his head down. Even in the utter darkness, Marlow feared he could see them. She closed her eyes for good measure. Morlan's eyes crossed for a second. He stood up and stumbled a bit. "Thinks it can..." He held a hand to his head to steady it.

"Going to get it or not?"

Morlan shook his head clear, dropped to his belly and began to crawl into the cave.

Marlow wasn't worried about being heard anymore. She slid over against Arjen as the giant head of the Night Chaser turned sideways and tucked in. His eyes blinked, focusing in the dark. They were getting wider and wider, either from the surprise of seeing Marlow and Arjen down there, or for another reason they could only hope for. Morlan's nose was going as he swept a hand toward them. It hit Marlow's shoulder and she flinched, not from pain but the sheer weight of it. The only place left for her to go was out from under the rock. Arjen reached over her and slapped the hand off. It landed limp in the dirt. They couldn't see Morlan's eyes in the dark, as they hung in their sockets, not closing, just losing their focus. Soon, they heard his partner calling,

"Morlan? You all right?"

Marlow gripped Arjen's hand. They were trying to control their breathing. If they came out, the other Night Chaser would be on them. If they stayed, they were company to a quickly, cooling corpse.

"Hey, hey," the Night Chaser said.

Morlan's body slid out of the cave as if it was floating on to a better place. Marlow and Arjen got the slightest bit of light to see the dart had taken its full effect. Morlan rolled over with a thump. His partner stared, confused, first at his condition, then at the entry to the cave. He made no move to inspect the cave further. He looked back at Morlan, now questioning what to do with his corpse. The Night Chaser looked around to see if he was being watched, kicked Morlan a couple times, then trotted off toward the village. Marlow and Arjen exchanged confused looks as they slowly crawled out. The cool air of the constant night bit their skin as they examined Morlan.

"That was our last dart," said Marlow.

"Seemed like a good use," replied Arjen.

"Did you hear what they said? It sounds like our people are being kept alive for something. We've gotta get down there."

"We're not going to get this lucky again. All it took was for that other Night Chaser to see what kind of animal was really in that cave. Who's to say he's not coming back here to avenge his friend's death?"

"Wait." Marlow looked toward the village. "Is that...?"

"Admani," said Arjen. "I'd know that hair anywhere."

The Night Chaser they'd just watched leave his friend was quickly approaching her as she hit the top of the stairs to the village exit.

"Shit," said Marlow. "We have to help her."

She went to run when Arjen caught her shoulder.

"Wait. We can't..."

Admani kept her head down and passed the Night Chaser. He eyed her for a few seconds before taking the stairs.

Marlow was jumping and waving her arms, still fifty yards away, trying to get Admani's attention.

"Why doesn't she run?" asked Arjen.

They watched Admani bend down to her haunches and start searching the ground. Then they saw a smaller Night Chaser next to her. It tapped her on the shoulder and Admani got up, following it to the right and out of sight.

"What do they have them doing?" asked Arjen.

Marlow was bouncing on her toes. "Let's go find out."

"Okay, but we stay in the dark."

Marlow and Arjen grabbed hands and took off into the shadows.

Chapter Nine

The Night Chasers' side of the planet was like a constant horror show. The wrecked village, the fires, the beasts that inhabited it. Even the lights from the distant city struck Lana with fear. The ominous tower was no comfort knowing what lived inside. As they walked further from the village but not nearer to the city, Lana feared they were being dragged out into the desert to be shot. The plodding steps of Biral were accompanied by the dragging scrapes of a Wit he'd picked up from the village. They'd gone back for Captain Williams, leaving Julie alone in the cell. Lana tried to give her as much strength through the last look they exchanged, but she had little to give.

Biral led them, followed by Lana, Williams, and the Wit trailing behind. The village lights were barely in view when Biral stopped.

"We're here." He turned to smile at his followers.

"Here?" Lana tried to see anything but desert and death.

"There." Biral pointed, the faint glow giving a hazy outline of something big ahead. "My flying vessel."

Lana stumbled forward and it came into view. A ship, smaller than the *Mack* but as big as a grocery store, sitting in the middle of the deserted, dark land.

"Oh my god."

Thoughts sprang alive in her head. She looked at Williams who seemed to be having the same revelations.

"Where...?"

Biral stood, proud, as if he'd built the thing. "Impressive? Can you make it fly?"

The humans climbed down the slight decline, touching the exterior.

"We can try." Lana tried to hold back her excitement.

Biral didn't know what he'd just given them access to. "Show me."

"Do you have a crystal so I can see better?" Lana asked.

Biral nodded at the Wit and it handed over a small crystal shard from its bag. Lana and Williams circled the ship, looking for markings, for anything to tell them where it had come from. There were no major identifying marks, only smooth, white material.

"It's like the relic," Lana whispered in English.

"It's got to be the same," said Williams, "but how did it get over here?"

"There's the door." Lana pointed at the crystal. "Let's go find out."

There was a ramp stuck in the sand leading in. The ship was dark from there. The blue glow of the crystal gave way to another scene of horror. Dried blood streaked the walls of the walkway. There were spots on the ground with old footprints in them. Night Chaser footprints.

"What happened here?" asked Lana.

"I think it's pretty clear," said Williams.

The clanging sound on the ramp behind them made them jump. Biral and the Wit were there watching.

"They wouldn't fly us," said Biral. "I hope you can do better."

~ * ~

Two Night Chaser children and their Wit caretaker stood in rapt amazement as Julie made her Yo-Yo sleep. The rainbow pattern became hypnotic as it spun on the end of the string. She snapped it back up to her hand.

"Wow," said the kids in unison.

The Wit just stared.

Julie took a short bow from behind her bars.

"I know a better trick. It's called..." She paused for the Wyan word, then just used the English, "Cat's cradle. It's even better but I need more space. Can you...?" She motioned at the bars.

The kids went right at it with no hesitation, pulling at the rugged, makeshift cell door. The Wit raised a hand, grunted at them, but didn't make them stop.

Julie was surprised her trick worked so easily. She would do her best to keep their attention, wait for her opening, then—

Two Night Chasers approached the jail. One of them yelled at the kids, throwing a rock that clocked off the bars. Julie ducked, dropping the Yo-Yo from her hand as she covered her head. It swung from the string around her middle finger.

"Leave the alien," said the bigger of the two Night Chasers.

He was missing all his front teeth. His companion was shorter, mainly because he was hunched over from some sort of injury or deformity.

They shooed away Julie's audience and she was left standing with nothing but the Yo-Yo. Her short window of hope was gone. The Night Chasers talked amongst themselves, only eyeing her occasionally like an animal.

"Biral won't know," said Toothless. "We can blame the children. They were going to let her out anyway."

Hunchback snorted. "He'll find out and it will be your skin."

"He has the others. Why does he need this one too? She's not important."

Hunchback raised his hands and backed away from the bars. "You do what you want. I can't stop you."

Toothless stuck his snout through the bars. Julie slinked back as far as she could, her back against the wall. He sniffed the air.

"Come closer."

Julie shook her head, her eyes at the floor. "Please leave me alone."

"You do tricks. Show me a trick."

Julie didn't respond. She wished she had anything to protect herself with. All the stupid gathering trips and she passed up dull knives for a Big-Mouthed Bass and baseball bats for a license plate and card games. She'd give anything to have the dullest of knives right then.

She jumped at the slam on the bars.

"Hey, show me a trick before I come in and make you."

Julie wound the string around the Yo-Yo with a shaky hand, hoping her next trick wouldn't be her last.

~ * ~

"One more of these," said Admani, raising a mushroom to the Wit and dropping it in its hands. They were full from her harvest. Admani was unsure if any of them truly contained the antibiotics that would fight the infection. She made her best guess in the darkness, biding her time for something she could've never planned for. When she saw Marlow and Arjen circling them, she felt her insides tighten up. The initial instinct was to run as fast as she could to the arms of her friends. They'd disappear and figure the rest out from there, but her second thought was the voice of reason. The Wit might chase them, but it was much more likely to call for reinforcements. Either way, their chance of saving the rest of their party was out the window if the Wit turned them in. Admani could only hope the Wit didn't spot them the way she had.

Their circle tightened, Marlow staying low in the shadows on one side, Arjen on the other. The Wit motioned for Admani to follow it back to the village. She saw Arjen appear behind it, only a few feet back, directly in the path to the village.

"Wait." Admani caught its attention. She pointed at the handful of mushrooms. "Does that one have—?"

Her words stopped as Arjen brought a rock down on the spine of the Wit. It grunted and stumbled forward, dropping the load of mushrooms as Marlow ran from the other side with a rock of her own, targeting its head.

"Stop." Admani raised her hands and stepped between them. Marlow pulled up.

"What? Why?"

Admani grabbed the arm of the Wit.

"It's helping take care of a sick child. It hasn't harmed me."

Arjen stood, still holding his rock. "We need to kill it and get out of here. If we act quickly—"

"No. I can't let you do that."

She was torn on her decision, but bludgeoning the poor caretaker to death just didn't feel right.

"Then what?" Marlow took a step closer.

The Wit tugged to free its arm, but Admani tightened her grip.

"Deal?" said Admani.

The Wit looked between the three humans, trying to put together what it was seeing.

"What deal?" it asked.

"Take the..." Admani motioned at the mushrooms strewn about the ground. She wasn't sure of the Wyan word for them. "They should help the boy. Don't tell anyone you saw us or..." She stepped away to show Marlow and Arjen holding their rocks.

The Wit looked between them, weighing its options.

"If Biral finds out..."

Admani shrugged. "If you want to help the boy..."

The Wit nodded slowly. "Okay." It bent down to collect the mushrooms, then paused and in a quiet voice, said, "Will these kill him?"

"No. They should help fight the sickness he has. From the studies I've done...I can't promise more."

The Wit observed her for another few seconds, then finished collecting the mushrooms and stood.

Admani put a hand on its furry arm. "Two each period until they are gone."

The Wit nodded.

"We just want to live," said Admani. "Same as you."

The Wit looked in the direction of the village. "Then don't come back."

"Our friends."

163

The Wit looked solemn as it turned toward the village and started walking. "Leave while you can. Even if I don't tell, they will know soon."

When it was out of earshot, Marlow dropped her rock and caught Admani into a hug.

"I'm so glad you're alive," said Marlow.

"Same here," said Admani. "I thought everyone else...how did you get here? Were you taken?"

Marlow shook her head. "We ran from the village when it all went down. We hid out with Cannie and Barchek. Ice is with them."

Admani held a hand to her chest and let out a long breath when she heard her sister's name, then fear came to her eyes. "Avani?"

"She's with them in the bunker. Ice is hurt, but should be okay."

Admani gripped her hands.

Arjen joined them. "Is everyone else, okay?"

"They killed Walters." Admani pursed her lips and shook her head. "The damn fool couldn't keep his mouth shut."

They gave her a minute to compose herself. "Lana, Williams, Julie, and I were locked in a makeshift jail. They pulled me out to help with a sick child, but they were keeping us alive."

"For what?" asked Arjen.

"I don't know."

"So, what do we do from here?" asked Marlow.

"We can't go back into the village. The Wit wasn't lying about that. There are Night Chasers everywhere. We need a better plan."

"I'd say wait for night," said Marlow, "but, it's always night around here. I wonder when they sleep."

"It's hard to tell so far."

Arjen looked beyond the village. "What's that?"

Admani squinted at the lights of the tower. "It must be their city. The leader kept talking about it. From what we could tell, the ones in the village are disgraced from the main city. They were banished for some reason and they want to go back, to take it over."

"So, another place full of Night Chasers?" said Marlow. "No thanks."

"Hold on." Arjen pointed further to the right of the village. "Did you see that flash?"

"Lights." Marlow followed his gaze.

"Any clue what's over there?" asked Arjen.

"No." Admani looked back at the village entrance where the Wit disappeared down the stairs. "But it's worth a look in case we're about to get double-crossed."

Arjen picked up his rock, Marlow followed suit and they were on their way once again.

Chapter Ten

"That did something." Lana patted Williams on the shoulder as he sat in the seat of the ship, hitting alien buttons and panels. There were dim lights around the cabin coming on.

Biral growled happily behind them. "Now make it fly."

"Not that easy," said Williams, in English. "This is all completely foreign. I'm just as likely to hit a self-destruct sequence as I am to start the engines. If they even work."

Biral looked at the back of his head with anger. Lana held up her hands to calm him and translated.

"He doesn't want to break it. It hasn't flown in years. We have to be careful."

Biral seemed to accept her reply and went back to pacing the lit cabin of the alien ship.

Lana wondered what the species was like that the Night Chasers killed. Did they have any weapons she could find and use? There was a corridor now lit up that she'd very much like to explore. If nothing else, maybe she could find a room to lock her and Williams in, but they would kill the rest of her team then. The stakes were very clear. They needed a one-hundred-percent victory or nothing.

Williams was obviously on the same page with her. "I need the rest of my team."

Biral watched him get out of the seat and stand face to face with him.

"You fly the vessel." Biral pointed a sharp claw straight into Williams's chest.

"Yes," said Williams, "but this is not my vessel. I need help. Together we—"

Biral struck him in the chest with a quick punch. Williams flew back into the control panel, slammed his head on a low hanging monitor and hit the ground in a heap. Lana rushed to his side, helping Williams into a sitting position as he held his hand to his head. He felt blood, but couldn't focus on doing anything about it. The room was spinning.

"Please," said Lana. "He's not lying. We work as a team. You think one of us can fly this vessel by themselves?"

Biral narrowed his eyes at her, towering over them with the Wit at his side.

"You're the leader. He flies the vessel. Why do you need more?"

"Because all of this..." Lana motioned around at the flickering panels, "is new to us. Together we can get it working, but we need everyone."

Biral considered her request as the Wit whispered something in his ear.

"If I bring your team, this will fly?"

Lana nodded. "Yes."

"Pick one and we will go get them."

"One? We need the whole—"

"One, and one stays in case you try something."

A hostage, thought Lana. The Night Chasers were far from feral beasts. They might be smarter than the Wyans. Maybe she'd picked the wrong side all along.

Lana helped Williams to his feet. "It has to be Admani," she whispered but Williams shook his head.

"Julie."

Lana shot him a look, speaking in sharp English. "Don't let your emotions affect your decision-making."

"I'm not." He lowered his voice even more. "Neither of them are going to know any more than I do. This is just a chance to get them out. If we have to pick, Julie is helpless on her own."

Lana couldn't argue with the logic, but she hated where it was going. Williams didn't think he could get the ship running. He was doing nothing but stalling. Bringing Julie back just so he had a chance to say goodbye before Biral took all their heads for failing.

Their conversation was cut short by the tight grip of the Wit on their arms, dragging them along. It pushed them towards the ramp as Biral led the way.

"You can decide when we get there." Biral turned back and pointed at the Wit. "You will gather the team. Tell them it is time to take back our Hilan."

They trudged back through the cold desert toward the lights of the village. Behind a giant cactus only fifty yards away, Marlow, Arjen, and Admani hid.

"Someone's coming." Admani ducked low.

Marlow watched as the tails of the ship's flashing lights illuminated Biral, the Wit, and...

"It's Lana and Williams," said Marlow.

"Let's get them." Arjen took the first step out. Admani pulled him back.

"You think we're going to just jump their leader with rocks? We wouldn't get close in this open sand. He'd hear us and be on us in a second."

"But there's five of us and two of them. I like the odds."

"There's a ship right there. Maybe we can find something useful."

"Shh, listen," said Marlow.

They could only hear parts of the conversation across the distance. After thirty seconds, Admani turned to the other two.

"They're going back to get the medic. That's me or Julie. If I'm not there..."

"What are you saying?" Marlow held her arm.

Admani groaned. "This sounds crazy, but if I go back, I could warn them. You and Arjen can get to the ship, set a trap or something. It sounds like they plan to get it off the ground."

"You're going to walk back in there?" asked Arjen. "What if they just kill you on the spot?"

Admani was fighting back tears. "I don't know. They could. I want nothing more than to go hide out in the ship, or even run back to the Wyan side, but it's not what Ice would do, or Mom, or Walters...it's our chance to get the drop on them."

Marlow was pacing, Arjen running his hands through his hair, tugging it as he did. Biral's party was getting further and further away.

"I've got to go," said Admani. "I've got to try."

Arjen found himself unable to decide. His words tangled up inside his chest. He sounded like he was having a heart attack.

Marlow rested a hand on his shoulder. "Let's try. Arjen and I will come up with something."

Admani hugged each of them and started off to tail Biral's party back to the village.

~ * ~

Marlow came down the long corridor. The running lights gave a soft glow to it. In other times, she would've been intrigued and excited to explore an alien craft. Instead, she was frantic, looking for anything she could use to lay a trap with. Arjen was panting as he met her at the control panels.

"All I can do is fuck with the goddamn lights. Come on."

"The one open room was pretty much empty," said Marlow. "No bed, no food..." Then she had a thought. "Arjen, what the fuck are we thinking? The backpack."

"Jesus, we're idiots." He opened it up and pulled out the relic they'd gotten from Cannie. "What do you think it does?"

They explored the cabin with a new sense of purpose, finally stopping on a spot that had a circular-shaped indent. They exchanged glances and Arjen stuck it in. There was a magnetic feel as it stuck in place. Arjen pulled his hand away and the cabin lit up fully.

"Brighter lights?" he said.

"Gotta be more than that."

Arjen looked at the control panel. "We should be careful. We don't want to initiate a launch sequence."

"You think we can do that by accident?"

He shrugged and went back to examining buttons.

Marlow went to the hall. There were ceiling lights on top of the blue running lights. The one open room had claw marks across the doorjam. Marlow noticed it now had touch points inside, lit up with multicolored lights. The walls were plain and white with little décor. Marlow couldn't help herself. She was going to push every button she could until something happened.

The first one she hit raised some sort of desk from the floor. It was smooth and sleek. It looked like it had never been worked on. Underneath was a cupboard that she slid open. Inside was a relic just like the one they'd inserted into the control panel. Marlow left it where it was. The next button was on the far wall. A panel slid out from it. It was as long as she was tall from side to side and came out from the wall two feet until it hit her chest. Marlow peered in. There was a dry, foam-like substance filling the panel. She ran her hand along it, feeling the scrape on her fingertips.

"Arjen?" she called.

Within a few seconds, Arjen's head appeared in the doorway. "Find something?"

"Yeah. Come here."

He joined her at the open panel.

"What do you think this is?"

His head tilted, forehead scrunching together as he watched the foamy substance.

"Food?" He rubbed his fingers across it too, then licked them. He frowned at Marlow. "If it is food, it tastes like shit."

"You probably have to rehydrate it."

Marlow felt along the wall, hitting some of the lighted spots. A humming began and they exchanged a look.

"Are we seriously preparing food right now? We need to find some weapons, traps...anything." Arjen started for the door.

"Sorry," said Marlow. "I just...wait. Look. It's growing."

Arjen huffed. "Mar..."

"Right. We'll eat later."

She stepped back, watching the foam grow a little longer.

Arjen tapped his foot. "Weapons."

"On it."

Together, they checked the rest of the rooms, looking for anything but more living quarters. There were more tables, more panels—those ones empty of the foamy food-like substance—and a few stray objects. None of them looked threatening in any way. They went back to the main control room, standing side by side.

"There's just nothing," said Marlow in defeat.

"If we knew how to fly it..." Arjen looked at the ramp. "I'm gonna go take a look. Who knows how long they'll take?"

Arjen stepped out to the dark. He walked away from the lights of the ship, letting his eyes adjust to see further into the distance. When he hit the ramp again, he called up,

"All clear for now. If we could just—" He cut off when he saw Marlow frozen in place. There was a figure in the hall standing around five feet tall, skin porous and ivory. It raised its three-fingered hands and began speaking a gibberish of words.

Marlow gave a quick look at Arjen, then back to the creature.

"I don't...we don't understand."

The creature stopped, looked them over and started again, this time it spoke Wyan.

"Are you here to kill me?"

"No, no." Marlow crossed her hands back and forth to deny the question, then switched language. "Wait, you speak Wyan?"

"I speak the language of the beasts. Are you...alien too?"

Marlow nodded. "We are from the stars." She pointed up.

Its face widened into a strange, vicious smile. "Then you would burn."

Marlow smiled back. "It's true, but we are from far away. Is this your vessel?"

"Yes." Its face shrunk back. "It was my kind's. They are gone.

171

Did you save me?"

"Were you in that room?"

"Sleep place. I don't know the word."

"The Wyan language is limited," Arjen agreed, turning to Marlow. "Like our cryo-sleep it seems." He switched back to Wyan. "Were your people killed by the Night Chasers? The beasts?"

"Yes."

"Ours too."

They stopped their conversation when they heard growling in the distance.

Marlow looked to Arjen. He pursed his lips and addressed the creature before them.

"Will you help us fight back?"

Part III

Chapter One

Translated Pelosin ship audio recording, Day 4: Julan's screams faded quickly. Amun

could be heard pacing his room, a broken moan coming from his throat. There was the Night Chaser's heavy breathing, then the thud of a body hitting the floor. Quick steps padded up the ramp.

"Amun. No!" It was the voice of a Pelosin.

"This is our ritual," rasped a Night Chaser. "You will not steal our offering."

"Please leave us alone," the Pelosin said. "We mean no harm. Our planet—"

There was a thud and smashing sound. The Pelosin cried out.

"Father," yelled Amun.

There was a high-pitched sound that crackled in the speaker. The Night Chaser let out a yell, then stomping footsteps were heard and the sliding of a door. Pounding and more growling from the Night Chaser followed.

The engines came to life. The pounding stopped and the ground rumbled.

"What is happening?" came the Night Chaser's confused voice.

"Come on, come on," said Amun's father.

The rumbling ended and an electric whine sounded. A clanging thump followed it as the Night Chaser growled.

"Father," called Amun.

"Shoot it again," he screamed back. "While it's down."

The high-pitched sound went off again. The Night Chaser roared, but its feet slammed into a rhythm. Amun cried out in fear. The ship made a low hum and more bodies crashed. There was a faint alarm calling in the background.

"Just get in your cabin," said Amun's father.

"The ramp," said Amun.

"The weapon's no good. I'm going to try to tip it out. Just get in your cabin and hold on."

"Okay."

The cabin door slid shut and within a second, there was pounding on it.

"Come this way," called Amun's father. There was a low hum again as the ship turned. A scraping of claws was heard. "Just let go," he urged.

More scratching and clawing noises then a final grunt before Amun's father cried out, "No."

There was a sharp whine, more alarms, and the whooshing of air. Within a few seconds, a collision was heard, then more wind, and a louder booming at the end. Groaning echoed all around. The settling of loose pieces commenced, and everything was quiet, then the clink of claws began.

"Ah, please—" started Amun's father, then he was silent.

There was only the sound of claws on the floor, closer, then further away, then closer again. Sniffing, growling, grunting, and mumbling came. The clawed feet clacked down the ramp and the recording went calm.

After another minute, a door slid open. Soft padding feet sounded, accompanied by whimpering.

"Father," Amun's voice was low. There was a gasp of breath. "No, no, no." Scrambling, grunting, and the sound of powering down, followed. Feet padded away and the cabin door slid closed again.

Hoots and calls were heard outside the ramp, then the plodding of a group coming aboard.

"It flew like a bird," said a Night Chaser.

"We saw it," said another. "It crashed like a dead bird, but how?"

"One of the aliens controlled it. I saw him."

There were many conversations going before one called out,

"Quiet. Everyone, listen." It was Biral's voice. "Do you know what this means? Our city has rejected us. Locked us out, but they plan on us going under. What if we could go over?"

There were mumbles and agreements that turned into an odd variety of cheers.

"Where is the one who can control it?" asked Biral.

A sheepish voice was barely picked up. "I killed it."

"What?"

"It tried to kill me. Both of them."

"*Both?*"

"There was another." A long silence fell over the room. "In that door."

Chapter Two

Julie, Williams, and Lana huddled together on the walk back to the ship. A herd of Night Chasers surrounded them. There was excitement and fear in their voices, like kids on the way to a carnival, sizing up the giant Ferris wheel.

The humans were picking up bits and pieces of their conversations. The overall theme was they were going home. The city in the distance would be theirs again after they got the vessel in the air. They had no clue how they would make it fly, only that the three small aliens between them would figure it out or they would die trying.

The smell of the beasts created a musty cloud around them. The Belters' feet sunk into the sand, their calves burning at each step of the rapid pace the Night Chasers kept. They didn't share the excitement, the haste to reach their Trojan horse. They couldn't get much out of the ship the first round. Julie wouldn't be any more help. She was just free from the cage. Only one from their group had been left behind. When Admani exchanged places with Julie, she managed only a few words in passing: "Friends in the ship. Look for signs."

The ship's lights seemed brighter as they came into view. Though every light seemed blinding in the darkness they were in.

Biral led the group of seven Night Chasers, three Wits, and three humans to the ramp. The bridge filled up as they stacked in like cigarettes. Lana looked down the hall, the lights looked different. She shared a glance with Williams, and he narrowed his eyes. They walked over to the control panel together.

"Where do you think our sign is?" Williams put a hand on the panel, and it lit up. "That's new."

Across the screen was a navigation course showing the outline of the planet and location of the ship. There was a red bar on the right showing an alert.

"Guys?" Julie motioned toward the bottom of the monitor.

There was a message written in English in a small, freehand scrawl.

Pull the gray lever on the right, then get to the hallway, alone.

The humans exchanged looks then located the lever in unison. Lana reached out a hand when Biral's giant head loomed over them.

"How long until we can fly?"

Julie jumped, grabbed her heart and Williams pulled her close to him.

"Give us a few minutes." Lana redirected her hand to the top of the monitor, hoping to draw his attention from the message and the lever. She knew there was no way the Night Chaser could read English, though she couldn't help but worry.

Biral grunted, stomped a foot and turned away.

Lana's hand slid back to the lever, gripping as she looked to her companions for assurance.

"The path isn't clear," whispered Julie.

"We don't even know what this does," said Williams.

"We have to try," said Lana.

"Oh, God." Julie wrung her hands.

Lana spoke louder, in Wyan this time. "Julie, check the hall for the..." Then in English, "flux capacitor."

Julie gave her a confused look. Lana slapped her on the shoulder and continued in Wyan language. "Now, and take Williams. He might have to help you lift it."

Williams nodded and grabbed Julie's arm.

"Right," he said. "I'll make sure you don't break it." He motioned toward the panel. "Once we plug it in, we should be able to fly." His Wyan wasn't great, but his acting was worse. Lana tried not to think about it.

Julie went with him, not resisting. Just as they reached the entry to the hall, Lana pulled the gray lever. A whirring sound could be heard. There was a horrible screeching as the ramp tried to raise. It had been damaged during its crash landing those years ago. It seemed to right itself and began closing. The Night Chasers watched it with fascination as Lana did her best to slink between them toward the hall. Julie and Williams stood watching just beyond the last Night Chaser.

"Excuse me," Lana tried to get around him, but he closed the gap, blocking her way. "I need to—" He caught her with a big hand to her chest.

"Where are you going?" he asked.

"I just need to help them." Lana looked back to see Biral take notice. "Just let me by."

The Night Chaser doubled down. "You're supposed to fly the vessel. Over there."

Biral was approaching when a blast of heat came down the hall and struck the Night Chaser in the face. He pulled back his hands to cover himself.

"Ah. It burns. It burns."

Lana lowered her stance and lunged a shoulder into his chest, knocking him from the hall entrance. Julie and Williams were heading down to an open door as an ivory creature stepped out, wielding a handheld weapon. Lana stopped just past the room that had been forced open when she saw the creature, then she felt a hand around her waist. She looked to see Arjen coming from the adjacent room. He also held a weapon and fired it into Biral's chest. Julie and Williams were joined by Marlow who sent a second shot into the side of Biral's face.

The group filled the small hall as the Night Chasers backed away.

"Somebody want to explain this?" asked Lana.

"Maybe later." Arjen gave her a quick peck on the cheek while keeping his weapon trained on the beasts. "For now, the alien back there is Amun. He's on our side and we're about to make a deal. Also, I'm glad you're alive."

Arjen and Marlow stepped to the front of the hall, shoulder to shoulder with Amun behind them. They kept their weapons up. Lana whispered to Arjen,

"Can you kill them with those?"

"Don't think so, but they don't know that. More importantly, we don't want them dead."

"What?"

"Just listen." Arjen switched to Wyan. "We have a disagreement. We want to work it out. Everyone stay back, bring your leader."

There was grumbling as Biral pushed away from his team. He was ten feet back while the rest were against the closed ramp.

"Do you think you can order me?" asked Biral, in a low growl.

"No, but you want your lives back. We need energy for the flying vessel. The city has both."

"What?" asked Lana, under her breath.

"The vessel already flies," said Biral. "We have seen it."

Arjen shook his head. "That was much time ago. It needs more energy. We need the blue crystals from the city."

"But we need to fly to get into the city. They guard the entrance. They would see us coming."

Arjen motioned for Amun and he walked to the monitor with the map, keeping his weapon raised.

"There is energy here." Amun zoomed into the backside of the Night Chaser city. "The views we got show enough energy to power the vessel one hundred times. If we can get a piece of the blue crystal, just this big..." He separated his hands to mime a two-foot-by-two-foot square. "We could fly anywhere we wanted."

Biral frowned at Amun, like he wanted to ask where he'd been hiding all that time but didn't want to look ignorant.

Arjen continued their pitch. "We wouldn't have to take on the whole city. We just need the crystal, then we come back, and we can fly. Do you think you can lead us there?"

There was a rising of crowd noise from the rest of the Night Chasers, telling Biral not to trust them. He raised his hands for quiet.

"We help you. You help us, then what?"

Arjen shrugged. "You get your city back and you leave the Wyans and us alone."

Biral nodded, turned back to his group and smiled at them. Arjen could already smell the double-cross. Biral addressed the humans,

"We will work together. You stay to your deal and us to ours, then you are free."

"Okay," said Arjen. "You must honor our agreement. If any one of us is hurt, we will not fly." He stepped out to meet the beast eye to eye. Biral rose a foot over Arjen's head even on all fours. Arjen didn't falter. "That includes Admani. We need her back from the village."

Biral gritted his teeth. "We are not taking a large group into the city. We will be seen and hunted down."

"Some of us will stay to prepare the ship, but we need all our people."

Biral huffed. "We go back to the village, get your friend and those going will continue. The path through the mountains is that way. We won't be seen until we reach the back of the city. We will have to be quick."

Arjen turned to the group. "I'll get Admani and go. I'll need her to help harvest that crystal. We don't know how difficult that will be."

"You're not going alone," said Lana.

"Lana..." Arjen said, as she stepped to his side.

"She's right." Marlow looked down at the weapon in her hand, then held it out to Lana. "Take this. You'll probably need it."

"But you...?"

Marlow waved a hand. "Amun has his. We'll be on the ship. We'll close the door."

The group met at the hallway's entrance and huddled. Lana spoke, "The crystal will really power this thing?"

After a quiet translation, Amun nodded and pointed down the hall. "Get the crystal. The vessel will do the rest, then we can fly away."

"Okay," said Lana. "We'll get it and meet you all back here." She switched to English. "Then...God only knows. Just don't stop thinking. We have to be one step ahead or we'll be dead."

"Let's go." Biral slammed a hand on the ramp.

Amun stepped over, pulled the lever and the ship opened. Arjen and Lana followed.

~ * ~

An hour later, the ship door was closed. Marlow, Williams, Julie, and Amun sat in a circle around the control panel. They spoke the only language they all knew, the native one. Amun told them of arriving from the dying planet Pelosia, of the big hopes they all had when they landed and met the Wyans. He told them how the rest of his kind had been killed by the Night Chasers and how he only survived by the sacrifice of his father. The panel in his room locked him into a form of dehydrated sleep, though his brain stayed active. For almost four years, he listened to the Night Chasers come and go, trying to find a way to make his ship fly again, not knowing he'd taken one key and hid it in the floor and the other had been left on the light side of the world. In his sleep, he was able to hide as they ripped open his door. The power was off except for emergency support, so they were unable to access the panel he slept in. Four long years of waiting, wondering when he would finally die. He could stay dehydrated for many years, but if the humans hadn't brought the key, he would've never been released. It would've been an eternal prison of solitude.

It felt good to be moving, communicating again, but Amun still felt the solitude. His only hope was the small team they'd left on Melinger when they first arrived. The team he and his father were supposed to pick up, to bring to the new land. Instead, they'd abandoned them. If they could get the ship flying again, it would be his chance to find out if he was the last of his race.

"I'm sorry," said Marlow. "I once thought that I was one of the last of my kind, then I found others. Maybe it will be the same for you."

Amun forced a wide smile. He was hairless and featureless, minus his eyes and mouth. Like a mannequin from a horror movie.

"Assuming this all works." Williams changed the subject. "We get the crystal that you think will power this...vessel. We load up the Night

Chasers and drop them in their old city, then we fly back to where? The Wyans are dead."

"You don't know that," said Marlow.

He switched to English. "I know the damn monsters raided the place and we didn't exactly put up a fight. The only reason we're alive is because they want us to fly this thing into their next battle. After that, how long until we're expendable?"

"What are you suggesting?" asked Marlow.

"If we can get this old bird in the air, we need to leave."

"It's not our ship. We're helping him. He's helping us. If anything, we will go to Melinger to search for Peter and Davis."

Williams let out an inadvertent laugh. "Those traitors are long dead. Who knows though? If they got the reverse thrusters to work, the *Mack* might be salvageable."

"Glad to see you're thinking about what's important."

Amun stood. "I need food."

"Me too," said Julie, standing with him. "Do you have any?"

"Follow me." He tried to form his Wyan words. "Do you like..." Then in Pelosin, "Dried thistle weed?"

Julie didn't understand but nodded anyway. "Sounds good. I was about to eat my shoes."

Chapter Three

The village was raucous with excitement. They stoked the fire until it was full of hot coals. Admani watched from behind the bars. She wondered what it was they were planning to cook and hoped it wasn't her. A Night Chaser she recognized from their original capturing approached two women with a bundle. He held it up high for the gathering crowd to see and one of the women pulled the fabric away from it.

Admani felt sick. It was a naked body, pale and lifeless. As they turned it and began strapping the arms and legs over a pole so they could roast it, Admani felt her empty stomach lurch. The midsection was shredded and in other circumstances, she'd have trouble identifying a dead body alone, but this one she'd seen before, many times.

"Wal—" She stopped when she felt the bile in her throat. She had to turn away as her ex-lover's arms flopped like dead fish while they tied them to the pole.

One of the Night Chasers had taken the time to carry him back. Had they gone back after the initial trip? It didn't matter. Admani couldn't see through the tears in her eyes. Her hands covered her face, nails digging into her hairline. At that moment she didn't care anymore. The work she'd done to save that child...it didn't matter now. She wanted them all dead. If there were a bomb strapped to her chest at that moment, she would've set it off without a second thought.

It was a few minutes before Admani heard the horde of Night Chasers arriving back from the ship. She managed a look up to see Arjen and Lana amongst them. Something happened out in the desert, but she wasn't sure what.

Biral addressed the crowd, "We have an agreement with the aliens. When the time comes, be ready to take back our city. For now, we feast."

Lana and Arjen approached the cell. Admani's face was swollen from crying. She shook her head at them, trying to hold it together.

"Admani?" said Lana. "Did they hurt you? I swear to God—"

"No, no. It's him...*Walters* in the fire." They followed her trembling finger as it pointed at the roasting corpse. "They're going to eat him."

~ * ~

Lana and Arjen led Admani away from the fire and told her of the plan. They sat together on a group of rocks across from some of the makeshift houses.

"What if we just ran?" asked Admani. "Right now. We get everyone else from the ship and we run. We grab Ice and Avani, whoever else and we keep running until we find daylight."

Lana put an arm around her. "Because they would chase us down. Because we need that ship."

Admani looked at her with fragile eyes. "Are you ready to give up this dream? *Your* dream?"

Lana stared off. "I don't know. I've got to see how this all turns out first, but we've gotta have options. Without a ship, we're stuck out here."

They hugged until they heard Arjen. "Hey. Company."

The caretaker Wit was there, staring at the two ladies. Admani looked up.

"Hey."

It put a hand to its chest. "Sorry for your friend."

Admani scrunched up her face to prevent from crying again. "Yes. Thank you. How is the boy?"

"He sleeps." It scratched its head. "Are you going to the city?"

"We are."

It looked solemn. "They are not bad."

Lana joined in. "Who? The ones in the city?"

It nodded. "We were banned for a reason. Biral and his group opposed the laws. He wanted to overthrow the other leaders."

"What laws?" asked Arjen.

The Wit did a good look around, then continued, "Survival. As the city grew, we had to find resources for everyone. Biral wanted the weak, the old, and the deformed to be left to fend for themselves. If they couldn't make it, they didn't belong in the city anymore."

"Survival of the fittest," said Lana in English. Arjen nodded.

"His next plan was to punish the women who gave birth to the deformed. To kill the child. Then his worst of all, the 'final purpose' as he called it. When you're no longer able to keep up, you are eaten." The Wit paused to watch the look at their faces. "Just like your friend."

"This is who we're working with?" asked Admani.

"Just for a little bit," said Lana. "Just so we can get the ship working."

"So, what about you?" Arjen said to the Wit. "You're here because you're part of Biral's group, right?"

The Wit's face hung. "Yes. I am his caretaker."

"Biral's?" asked Lana.

"His son's."

Admani's eyes went wide. "You...we've been caring for his son?"

"Yes, and if he doesn't get better soon, Biral will end him, and I will be next."

"Jesus," said Lana, then in Wyan, "So, if we get him back into the city..."

The Wit looked grave. "He will destroy anyone in his path."

~ * ~

They walked in silence for the first mile of the journey. The path took to the side of a mountain, overlooking the city far off in the distance. There were lights from fires and the blue glow from the giant crystals behind it. It was as if the city had been built on it. Soon, they passed behind a ridge and the city was out of sight. The humans made up the middle of the party with three Night Chasers ahead and four behind. Lana spoke casually in English.

"It's not that we didn't know it all along. Did we think we were going to drop them back in the city that rejected them, and they'd be welcomed with open arms?"

Arjen groaned. "No, but it's different hearing the story."

"We're in no place in our own story to be picking sides. It's every race for themselves at this point."

"That's kinda how we got here, isn't it?" said Admani. "To this point in time."

"Listen," said Lana. "We tried to help the Wyans and we failed. Now we can only help ourselves. *He* knows that." She nodded toward Biral. "It's time we learned it."

When the humans were all but falling over from exhaustion, they set up camp. It would take the remaining of the next waking period to reach the back of the city. It was a long way around but worth the element of surprise they would have.

Arjen, Lana, and Admani shared the remaining snacks the Wit gave them before they left. It didn't suffice. They would need something much better to have energy for the rest of the trek there, much less coming back. The Night Chasers said the same in their muttered conversations to one another. Biral was driving them too hard and was hogging more of the food for himself.

Their sleep was sporadic, between their empty stomachs and the cold, never mind the fear of the Night Chasers only a few feet away. If they got hungry enough...

They were woken hours later to Biral calling for them to rise and continue. It was hard to tell the time with no sunlight, no change in scenery, just the aches setting in from the hike.

"W-what's on me?" Admani jumped up and brushed across her shoulders.

Lana and Arjen checked her coat.

"Snow," said Arjen. "Real, actual snow." He brushed some off, then licked his sleeve. "It's like ash but less ashy." He laughed as Admani frowned at him.

"I'm freezing."

"Let's just get moving," said Lana.

The Night Chasers led the way and the humans followed. It turned out that they had peaked the night before. The rest of the journey was a spiral of switchbacks until they found their way to the back of the city.

They were just two hours along when one of the Night Chasers sat down, complaining of his feet, his hunger, and anything else he could think of. He had old scars from claws going straight down the left side of his face. The marks eroded the hair growth to his jawline.

Biral regarded him with disdain. "The aliens still go, but you can't?"

Another Night Chaser with a mostly gray muzzle put a hand on Biral's shoulder. "We all could use a good meal. We need to take the time before we go much further."

Biral huffed and called over a younger Night Chaser already missing most of his teeth.

"Herum, go off trail and meet us by the caves." Biral looked the group over. "Take Durin with you."

The two Night Chasers took their orders and scrambled down a side path. Biral started on again, not looking back. The older Night Chaser bent down and pulled on the arms of the scarred one. "You'll die if you stay."

The humans tagged along.

In another hour, the main group reached a wall of caves on their right. Biral slowed and put his arms out to encourage others to do the same. The caves varied in size with each opening ranging from five to seven feet tall. They could walk right in if they wanted, or something could walk right out. There was a low growling echoing off each wall. It was a surround-sound effect that any movie theatre back on Earth would've been proud of. Arjen and Lana kept Admani between them as they held their Pelosin weapons ready.

Biral stepped out on his own, facing the caves as he spoke.

"Come out and we will talk."

The growling intensified.

"Or you can challenge me. If you win, you can have my place in the village."

A ragged chuckle began as a figure emerged from one of the center caves.

"You always were a liar."

It was a huge Night Chaser who walked with a limp. Hanging from his waist was a collection of bones tied to a blue cloth belt. When he turned, there was a reflection from the light of the planet in the sky that hit his belt and gave a silver glow.

Lana blinked a few times, her mouth hanging open. "That's a jumpsuit. It's one of ours."

"What?" asked Arjen, looking closer.

"Oh, God," said Admani, "but how?"

The bones on his belt rattled as he talked with Biral. Lana's face was frozen.

"Our team, the ones who never made it back...did they really come all the way out here?"

The beast from the cave turned toward her.

"If you're offering this, we can make a deal."

Biral looked at Lana and she stepped forward, pointing the weapon at the other Night Chaser.

"Have you killed my kind before?"

He sized her up. "Yes. Last time it was more work. Now you've come to me." He spread his arms and the bones of Lana's fallen comrades rattled again. She sent a blast directly into his throat.

"Ahh!" He bent over, hands on his neck as the fur was singed.

Biral let out a hearty laugh as two more Night Chasers came from the caves.

"Golen," said a female.

"Father," said a younger one.

Golen shook them off and looked up at Lana. "You will die for that."

"No." Biral stepped in front of her. "You won't touch her, but you will feed my group and we'll be on our way."

"Feed your—" Golen cut himself off when he heard the growling from Herum and Durin from above. They waited, ready to pounce on his family at any moment. The other caves had grown silent. No one else wanted to interfere. Golen motioned to the female and she went into the cave. His son stayed by his side, watching Lana with disdain. The female returned with an armful of roasted meat. Biral took the first bite, then tossed it back to the group. He called for more and more until Golen assured them they had cleaned him out.

The group ate their fill in front of the caves. Golen watched them, silently wishing one of them would choke on a bone. As their stomachs were filled, their spirits lifted, and they were on their way. The humans stayed between the Night Chasers. They'd each taken a few bites of the stolen food but mostly stashed it away for later. They couldn't bring themselves to eat the last of another's food in front of them. They were learning what survival of the fittest truly was and it was terrible.

Lana walked, conflicted once again. Golen and his outcasts killed almost half her group on their expedition. Maybe they'd gotten too close to the dark side, made too much noise, but they didn't deserve to die and have their bones strung up like a trophy. Still, she found her heart aching for the family, as they pillaged them for all their sustenance in that cold, desolate place. Would they be able to find more before they starved? Lana didn't know, only that they continued toward the back of the city, ready for their next theft.

Chapter Four

Marlow paced the Pelosin ship until Julie stood in her path.

"I know it's hard for you, but this is a small ship..."

"Sorry." Marlow tugged on her short, dark hair. "I just...Avani. She's just over those mountains. She hasn't been away from me at all until now. What if they can't get her to eat? What if one of the strays went back there and heard her crying?"

"Then Ice will take care of them."

"Ice is injured."

Julie put a hand on Marlow's shoulder. "She'll find a way. I can't believe I'm the one saying this, but just a little longer and we can go back. We can make it a little longer."

"But it's just a couple miles. If I was quiet—"

"You'd be caught and killed," said Williams.

He stepped away from a viewing port stroking his mustache. It was longer than Marlow had ever seen it. He must have meticulous grooming standards even on another planet. She could tell it bothered him as she joined him at the port. Just at the edge of the ship's lights was a Night Chaser. They could see the head come in and out of the shadow as it watched them impatiently.

"What is he waiting for?" asked Julie, joining them.

"Us to try to leave," said Williams. "These beasts are notoriously disloyal. If they were in the same position as us, they would've high-tailed it."

Amun walked over, his feet barely making a sound. They got quiet when they saw him.

"Sorry," Amun spoke Wyan. "Please keep talking. I'm tracking your language."

"Tracking?" asked Julie.

"I don't know the right word. My...vessel hears you and puts it in the..." He stalled, pointing at a screen. "In there."

"Can you show me?" said Marlow.

Amun nodded and swiped at the screen. The map was replaced by a three-columned form. There was writing across it in a language none of them understood.

"This," he pointed to the left column, "is my language. This," he pointed to the middle, "is Wyan, and this is yours." The right column was sporadically filled with words.

"So," said Marlow, "when you figure out a word, it goes here?"

"Me or the..."

"Computer. Just call it a computer in our language."

Amun smiled and went to swiping at the screen. "I will. Thank you. This is how I learned Wyan. I could access the computer while I slept."

Williams put an arm around Julie's shoulders and kissed her on the cheek. "Thanks." They watched Marlow, finally distracted from pacing as she talked with Amun.

~ * ~

It took the entire waking time for the group to reach the back of the city. It stood, glowing in the distance. There was a five-hundred-foot drop down a sheer cliff to the valley where the crystal began. It grew up the side of the city's black walls like a blue fungus.

The seven Night Chasers and three humans huddled behind various rocks, trying to avoid the stomach-churning view down.

"How...?" said Admani.

Gray Muzzle was within earshot of her. He pointed to a ledge filled with more switchbacks and no safety net.

"We're going to be out in the open," said Lana in Wyan.

"We'll go when they sleep." Biral was a few rocks away. He looked up at the distant planet's light. "The city should just be waking. You'll hear sounds soon. We will rest and wait until they go back down."

The group was silent, rejoicing that Biral was finally giving them a break. They'd have the entire waking time to rest before making their last move. Their bodies screamed for the break and they all took it, many falling into dreams before the city even woke.

The humans shared the last of their food and huddled together for warmth. They made a small shelter of prickly cactus leaves to cover them and block the light snow that wouldn't stop. They slept in hard spurts a couple hours at a time, each one waking with a flinch or jolt and stirring the others.

Arjen gave up a few hours prior to the city's rest period. He snuck away from the ladies to sit and watch, concealing himself from anyone who might be looking back. He thought of his father, Robin, the one who'd driven him to go. He wondered how different his life would've been had he stayed and joined the political party of the Belt. The comfort of always knowing where you'd be sleeping would've been nice, but the day to day would've killed him slowly. Instead, he sat on a cliffside with a group of monsters who could tear his head off if he looked at them wrong. Was it too late to admit their venture failed? That Lana's great plans had been too big? He didn't know. Only that they had to find a way to get the ship working and they'd go from there, one step at a time. He still had her, and that counted for something.

Arjen looked over at Lana sleeping. Her brow was knitted up. Even in sleep she was dealing with the problems of the universe. He remembered one of the messages he'd typed up on his data pad that he'd never sent. It was years ago, just before her team disappeared. He'd kicked himself for not sending it, thinking at the time it would've been that last words she read.

Saw the sunrise over Mars today. I think you'd like the view. I'd like to share it with you sometime. Maybe next trip out, let Williams lead, come aboard the Iris *with me just once. I'll approve it with my dad. What are they going to say that they aren't already saying? Send me an audio message sometime. I don't care if it takes weeks to get to me. I miss hearing your voice.*

-Arjen

Arjen heard a throat clearing nearby. He looked over to see the gray muzzled Night Chaser propped up the same as him a few rocks down. The crystal in the distance lit up the lighter hairs on his face, making him look like a child who'd just finished a blue-raspberry sucker. Arjen caught a laugh in his throat. He raised a hand in greeting. To his surprise, the Night Chaser raised one back, then slinked over to Arjen's position.

"Going to be a hard path down."

Arjen nodded, then added, "And back up."

"One thing first." He looked off and Arjen realized that was the equivalent of "first things first." Or "One thing at a time." The language barrier hadn't been nearly as bad as he planned, though he never planned on holding a conversation with the very beasts they were there to rid the planet of.

"Did you live in the city?" Arjen asked, though he knew the answer.

"Yes. Most of my life."

"Do you really plan to kill everyone inside?"

The beast laughed. "No. Only Kaman and his followers."

"Where I come from, everyone gets to..." Arjen couldn't think of a word for vote. "*Choose* what rules they agree with. Then, whichever rule has the most people who agree with it, that becomes the rule."

The Night Chaser nodded. "How does that work out?"

"Good and bad. Most choices are...already decided before we get to choose."

"Better to take then."

"Well..."

"We kill only to get what we want. What we *need*." He watched Arjen's face. "You think we're animals."

Arjen shook his head. "Animals can't talk. I think we're more alike than I ever thought possible."

"You may be right." He looked back at Biral stirring. "Just know when this is over, so is our alliance." He stood up. "I am Joran."

"Arjen."

Joran nodded and walked away.

Lana was at his side when Arjen turned back.

"What was that about?"

"Huh. I might have just made a friend."

"Well, don't get too attached." She looked back to Admani in the distance and gave her a thumbs up, then turned to Arjen. "Will you watch me while I pee?"

Arjen snorted and Lana smacked his shoulder.

"You know what I mean. Just keep an eye out."

The rest of the group awoke and prepared for the city to sleep.

Chapter Five

The path down the cliff was crawling with danger. The snow blew in short bursts, coating the narrow ledge they navigated. Some of the rocks would give a solid footing; the others were primed to dislodge and send one tumbling down with them. The Night Chasers went first, led by Biral. They could say what they wanted about his methods, but he was nothing if not brave. A leader who'd be the first to stick his nose in the fire.

Arjen, Lana, and Admani tied themselves together with small strips of cloth. If one of them fell, it would be unlikely that the other two could stop themselves from going with. That is, if the makeshift rope even held. Still, it made Admani feel better to feel the tug with each step Arjen took.

"Faster," Biral called back.

He was ahead of the group, taking steps and leaps the rest of them didn't dare. He was right, though. If they were spotted, the city would be awake by the time they reached the bottom. The humans didn't want to know what happened then.

They were three hundred feet up when the ground gave way under Herum. The claws on his feet dug into the rock wall, making a terrible scraping noise that filled the air. Durin reached back, catching Herum's hand and feeling his own body threaten to fall. Biral gripped his back, Durin cried out as his claws dug in, but he didn't lose his grip. Together, they pulled Herum to the other side. The next group took their time. The crevasse was wide, but not impassible. Herum stomped the ground to show it firm, then made room for landing. The rest of the Night Chasers went, one by one, until it was the humans' turn. Biral was already impatient and they could feel the pressure.

The gray-muzzled Joran stood on the other side, holding out a hand as Lana jumped. Her feet just caught the edge and Joran grabbed her upper arm, pulling her in. Arjen was next as they hauled him in, then Admani. She waited at the edge as Biral growled.

"We need to move."

"Sorry," said Admani.

"Get a running start," said Lana. "We'll be here to catch you."

"Not if I don't make it. What if I slip?"

"Jump or don't," said Biral. "We're going."

Lana pleaded with her eyes. Joran pushed past her and stretched out his arm a few feet across the open chasm. His feet brushed some stray rocks over the edge. They clacked down and Admani couldn't help but follow them with her eyes. Her stomach climbed into her chest and she felt her head spin. She held the wall for support.

"You've got to go now," said Joran. "I'm not staying."

"Okay, okay." She backed up, closed her eyes and refocused. Then stared straight at the outstretched hand and ran for it. Her jump was just enough to get her to Joran, then she felt her body sinking as he caught her and pulled her in.

Lana hugged her as Joran took off after his group. "No time," he said.

They followed, picking up the pace as the path widened just a little. Lana looked toward the city. They were sold out on this mission one way or another, but having a greeting party would put a serious damper on it. The only thing to see was the mesmerizing blue glow of the crystal.

The cliff face stayed sheer and unforgiving most of the way down, then the ground finally met them. There was a new sensation under their feet: grass. It was the color of the crystal, as if it had grown from it. The last fifty feet led straight to the giant crystal. It rose into the air nearly a hundred feet with a few limbs branching off. The walls of black rocks had been built right against it and there was a warmth like a distant fire. The grass surrounded it. Some even grew up on the side of the city. The blades all swayed towards the crystal, like sunflowers to the sun. The humans stood in amazement for a few seconds before the arms of Joran came in and swept them behind a rock.

Biral addressed the group. "It is clear now." He looked to Lana. "We just need to break off a piece?"

Lana mimed the size as Amun had done to them. "About like this. Let Admani break the piece. We don't know what kind of reaction it will have."

Arjen pulled a few borrowed tools they'd gotten in the village from his backpack. There was a crude hammer and a piece of long, thin metal that would work as a chisel.

Admani held one in each hand and nodded at him. Biral led the way. The entire group of ten trudged through the blue grass toward the crystal. The air was silent. The city slept. Everything slept. They ran on, only twenty feet back, when shadows blocked the light.

Biral said a Wyan curse under his breath, then louder, "Take them down."

Herum and Durin ran ahead, flanking the crystal and the figures in front of it.

"Wait," called a voice in the distance.

It was behind them. The group came to a halt, turning to see the origin of the call. The path they'd come down was completely blocked off by a horde of Night Chasers filling in each gap. One stepped to the front, walking slowly to Biral's team. The humans huddled inside, wondering where a group that large came from without them noticing.

The leader stopped ten feet from Biral with his army waiting, as the crystal behind was blocked by only four shadows. Biral took a step forward and sneered. "Kaman."

"Biral. You're not welcome here. Did you think I wouldn't guard the back as well as the front?"

Biral looked at the opposing swarm. There must have been thirty behind Kaman, and strays along the sides.

"You've brought your whole army back here. It's like you knew I was coming."

Kaman tightened his face. He had scars along his arms and chest. This wasn't his first battle.

"I have ways."

Biral scoffed. "Golen is a traitor just like me. You really think you can trust him?"

Kaman put out his arms. "Here we are. It was a good choice."

Biral smiled. "Then you haven't seen the rest of my group. Good."

Kaman hesitated for just a second, then said, "All your best are here. You wouldn't send your weakest to storm the entrance."

"You forget." Biral tapped a Night Chaser nearest to him on the back. "We have no weak in my village. I hope your daughter is somewhere safe."

Kaman couldn't hide the fear on his face as he turned to give a command. Biral didn't wait. He cried out for the group to follow and they all charged the crystal. There was mass confusion for a second. Kaman's most loyal received the initial command to check the front of the city, while the rest scrambled to close in on Biral's group.

The ones near the crystal stepped forward, not realizing it was the target. They weren't prepared for the savagery of Herum and Durin. They hit hard from the sides as the rest of Biral's group overwhelmed them through the middle. Their bodies were quickly mutilated. Herum and Durin used one of the corpses as a battering ram into the first responders. Biral and Joran fought off more from the sides. The main horde was approaching fast, still numbering in the twenties as the humans reached the base of the crystal. Arjen and Lana turned, aiming their weapons while Admani went to work with her hammer and chisel.

"I don't..." said Admani.

She felt the warmth as she picked a spot on one of the limbs. It was fifteen feet tall, jutting out diagonally from the main body. She looked over her shoulder as Biral and a few others turned back to hit the oncoming swarm. They were only ten feet away when they collided.

"I'll never get it in time," said Admani. "I don't even know what will happen."

She tested it with a hit and sparks of light shot out of the crystal. She flinched back.

"Just do it," screamed Lana, firing her weapon with an orange glow. It caught a Night Chaser in the side, spinning it around as it cried out.

Admani struck the hammer and caught a flash that put stars in her eyes. She blinked them away then closed her eyes for the next blow, barely striking the chisel as it made a metallic ringing sound and flew from her hand.

"Damn it."

Arjen blasted another Night Chaser off Herum.

He twisted its neck until it crumpled at his feet. Herum saw Admani's frustration.

"Move," he said, and she ducked out of the way as he scrambled up the crystal she was working on like he was climbing a tree. A couple opposing Night Chasers stopped at the base, looking up as Admani tucked between Arjen and Lana. They kept everyone at bay with warning shots, but it was all their weapons were capable of. If one charged them directly, there would be nothing they could do to fully stop it.

There was a cracking sound. The humans saw Herum rocking back and forth as the crystal gave way.

"Oh, God," said Lana.

"Cover your eyes," Admani said in English, and the three of them did, huddling together as the final snap sounded throughout the valley.

There were cries and screams as it lit up like daylight, then, the ones who hadn't seen the first flash were truly blinded by the next one as the crystal landed in the grass, breaking into pieces. It was like a giant flash bomb.

Herum rolled off onto his back. His entire midsection and down were burned by the crystal releasing heat and light when it broke. He screamed, turning side to side, trying to smolder the burns. The humans opened their eyes to see the entire battlefield stunned, holding their faces. Some fell to their knees, others were turned and stumbling the opposite direction they had been.

Lana knew it was their chance.

"Let's get a hunk into the bag and get the hell out of here."

Admani and Arjen followed Lana to the fallen crystal. It was glowing an angry blue now. Arjen whipped the backpack around, and they used their clothes to handle a large chunk, forcing it into the backpack and zipping most of the way closed. There were jagged shards hanging out the top as Arjen slung it back to his shoulders. Lana tugged on his arm and they ran, weaving between stumbling monsters. The grass leading to the cliff side was littered with bodies, some living and blinded, some dead from battle. Admani looked back to see Kaman spot them. He had two feet on Biral's chest, pinning him to the ground. He was shaking his head, squinting to make sure what he saw was right. He pushed off Biral and began toward them, then stopped, crying out as Biral sunk his teeth into his back foot, dragging along behind him.

The humans kept running, only fifty feet from the cliffside, as some of the further Night Chasers were coming out of their stupor. Lana caught one in the face with a blast, blinding it again as Arjen hit another in the foot, causing it to trip and take out a third. Their path was clear as they hit dirt again, approaching the climb they dreaded more than the battle. A few bodies came rumbling toward them. It was Durin and Joran, somehow, they'd broken free from the war and followed.

"Up, up, up," called Durin.

The humans went, slowly at first, getting their bearings, then picking up speed as they saw a crowd forming at the base. They scooted sideways. They didn't have time to tie themselves together. Arjen took on the new weight of the backpack in stride. The crystal was not as heavy as he'd expected, and he was happy for that. Durin was at the back of the group when they caught him from behind. He fought back, but in the end, he only succeeded in taking two over the edge with him. Joran urged them on as Durin fell to his death. They stayed ahead of the next group until they reached the chasm again. Lana fired the weapon back, but it only shot sparks. Arjen handed his over and after two blasts, it was down to heat and sparks as well. They had to cross. Joran stayed in the back as Lana jumped. She slid on her knees and turned back.

"Throw it," she said to Arjen. "You don't need the extra weight."

Arjen took off the backpack and swung it carefully at first, then gave her a countdown and let go. It hit her in the chest, and she fell back.

"Got it."

Admani looked at Arjen. "Please don't—"

Arjen shook his head. "I'm not leaving you." He got down on his knees and faced Lana across the gap. "Get a good start and push off my back."

"Oh, Jesus, Arjen."

He looked back. "We have to go. Now."

Admani's face scrunched up. "Okay." She backed up to Joran as another Night Chaser was only a few feet back.

Joran threw a rock at him and yelled, "Go."

Admani ran, planting a foot in Arjen's back and pushed off. He pushed too and she found herself flying through the air. She caught the wall first, bounced off and hit the ledge just next to Lana. Admani felt her momentum carrying her over the edge when Lana caught her by her hair. Admani's head snapped back as Lana dragged her to safety by her dark curls.

"Ow." Admani rubbed her neck.

"Sorry. It was all I could do."

Arjen landed a second later and looked back. Joran growled and swiped a clawed hand down, striking the other beast square in the jaw. Its head twisted and its body tipped over the edge. Joran looked to see more coming and he called for the humans to move. They scrambled up the path as he made his jump.

On the other side, Joran found a large, loose rock and smashed it down on the ledge. He was eroding the landing spot. Lana and Arjen gave him cover, picking up rocks and whipping them across at the Night Chasers trying to cross. Finally, one found a clearing as a rock whizzed over its head. It jumped directly at Joran. He ducked back, pushing off all four legs as the Night Chaser landed. The ground crumbled beneath it as it reached forward to grab Joran. Joran sent a precise kick straight into its nose and it fell back as the ground gave way.

Joran turned and urged the humans on again. The ground was covered in blood where he'd laid. He didn't slow as they progressed the rest of the cliff.

Finally, they reached the lookout where they'd last slept. Joran slouched against the rocks.

"We lost them." Lana looked down the cliff face.

There weren't any stragglers coming behind them anymore. The battlefield below was hard to see in detail but the bodies remaining were not moving.

"They'll be coming the other way." Joran pointed to the path they'd taken around the mountains. "You'll have to go the long way back."

"The long way?" asked Lana. "Where does it lead?"

Joran forced himself upright. The rock he'd leaned on was soaked in blood. He stumbled a few steps toward their new path and looked up at the glowing planet in the sky.

"Keep the light on your left. Go until you reach the river. It should take a full waking period at least, then follow the river with the light at your back for another period and a half. When you reach the bend, you should be able to see the city and the flying vessel."

"What about you?" asked Arjen. "Aren't you coming back to the village?"

Joran watched the path and shook his head. He ignored the question and continued his instructions. "The creatures are more active the further you get from the city. If you look bigger, they will leave you be, but watch for the eight-legged cave dwellers. One bite...just don't let them bite you." He bent his head when he finished. His breathing was becoming labored.

Arjen stepped over until they were face to face. "Thank you. Is there anything we can do for you?"

Joran wouldn't meet his eyes, the gray of his brows hung low. "I don't fear death. I knew the likely outcome. I will make a final trail for them to follow. If you go now..."

Arjen nodded to Joran, then looked to Lana and Admani.

Joran started down the path they'd come. Back toward a village he'd never make it to, then he turned.

"You aliens have something we don't. I hope you make it to your vessel and find your home."

Then he was gone, dragging himself along, leaving a trail of blood behind.

Chapter Six

Zane awoke in the pile of fluff the Wyans used as beds. He looked down at his legs and wondered if he'd ever walk again. The splints made from sticks and rope held them straight, but he worried about the healing process. If he was honest, there was much more to worry about: Marlow, Avani, and everyone else. Were they all dead? How soon before the Night Chasers would find him? He was in no position to fight back but none of them had been when the darkness came. All that preparation...Zane couldn't go down that mental path again. He'd been there countless times over the last twenty-four hours or so, since he'd been pulled from the well. It was dark and the fires were all out when he was carried to the remote cabin. He wondered how long until the sun came back, or if he'd ever see it again.

The door opened and quickly closed. Bruuth stood with a harvest of berries and grenners. Zane could barely make him out in the dark, but he could smell the food. His stomach growled. Once Bruuth had set his legs and found some painkillers, Zane's appetite came on strong.

Bruuth fed him and refilled his water dish, then helped him use the bathroom. It was demeaning, but Bruuth showed he was more than a blacksmith. He had the heart of a caretaker. He'd been the one to carry Marlow from the medical facility on the Belt after her c-section. And now he carried Zane behind the cabin so he wouldn't piss himself.

Zane couldn't make out much of their surroundings in the dark, only that the cabin was enclosed by a wall of trees. He wouldn't know which way to go even if he could walk.

When they got back in, Bruuth propped him up so he could sit.

"You see anything?" asked Zane.

"I think it is best to wait until the light returns, then we can walk free." He looked at Zane's legs. "Sorry. I did not mean..."

"I understand. I just can't handle this not knowing."

Bruuth nodded. "Yes, but you need to take care of yourself first."

Zane felt tears welling up. "I never should've left Marlow. We've always been together...this isn't right. None of this is right."

Bruuth was going to reply when they were interrupted by a knock on the door. Their heads snapped in unison, staring at the rickety entrance of the old cabin. Bruuth took a step towards it.

"Wait," said Zane, in a harsh whisper. "We don't know—"

"Be calm, friend. Night Chasers do not knock."

Chapter Seven

The snow was blinding their sense of direction. Arjen covered all but his eyes with his arm as Lana and Admani hugged the backpack, feeling the warmth of the crystal radiating through.

"How do we know this is the right way?" asked Lana, yelling over the wind.

Arjen pointed. "See that pass up ahead? That was the last landmark I saw before we lost the planet. If we get there, we can get shelter until the storm slows down."

"This is awful," said Admani. "Is this what Earth was like?"

"It is in the movies. It's a lot colder in reality."

"Let's just get there," said Lana. They'd tied themselves together again. Though they were unlikely to fall off an edge, the snow and the dark made it hard to navigate alone.

It took them a full hour to reach the top of the next pass. There were overhanging ledges for shelter from the elements. The blue glow of the crystal gave them enough light to see each other and enough warmth to survive with the minimal provisions they had.

Admani looked to Arjen and Lana and saw the fixed expression on each of them. She wished she had half the strength and determination they did.

"Do you think this is bad for us?" Lana held her hands up to the heat of the crystal. "Like, cancerous or something?"

"We don't know," said Admani. "I know so little about this thing, only that you guys freed me from the prison, told me we needed to collect it to power the ship, and forced me on this cursed journey."

"You're the scientist," said Lana. "All those samples you'd been collecting, I just thought you could help us."

"If I had *time*." Admani brushed her snowy hair out of her eyes. "Instead, I got in the middle of a war. I just watched some monster kill himself getting the thing down and now we're soaking in the rays because if we don't, we'll die."

"Do you have a better suggestion?" asked Lana, holding her hands out, palms up at the falling snow around the little ledge that had become their haven. It was silent but for the wind. The snow accumulated as if it meant to close them in completely.

"How about *not* coming to this cursed planet?" Admani kept running her hands through her hair, brushing off the moisture. "You brought us all out here to die. All these promises and where are we now?"

"We're trying to survive. If we'd stayed on the Belt, we would've died in a generation."

"At least it would've been comfortable." Admani covered her face.

Lana made sharp eyes at Arjen. He pushed his hands toward the ground, letting her know to ease up. She looked away with a huff. Admani started to cry, bringing her knees to her chest and burying her face. Arjen was left staring at the crystal, shaking his head.

Admani sniffed hard, trying to keep herself from a full-on cry.

"Be quiet," said Lana.

Arjen widened his eyes at her. "Lan—"

Lana put a finger to his lips then whispered, "Listen."

There was a thump outside of their shelter. The three survivors shared a look and fixed their eyes on the falling snow. Another thump followed and they could hear heavy, guttural breathing.

"What the fuck is that?" whispered Admani.

"Give me the hammer," said Arjen.

"It's in the backpack." Admani was frantic.

Arjen rifled through as fast as he could when he heard Admani gasp. She was scooting back when Lana raised up instinctually and hit her head on the slab of rock above.

"Shit." She stumbled back as Arjen pulled out the hammer just when a giant head poked out of the darkness. It was flat nosed, with a wide mouth and a back like furry rhinoceros. It plodded in, regarding the humans with disdain.

Arjen held his weapon while the others looked on. The beast that joined them in the shelter had no interest in fighting, only escaping the storm. It plopped down in the corner, wedged against the ceiling.

"Should we...?" asked Admani.

"No," said Lana. "I don't think it means us any harm."

"So, we just sit here?"

"Yes," said Arjen. "He needs the shelter as much as we do."

"*He?*" said Admani. "How do you know it's a he?"

Arjen smiled. "Just a guess."

The beast watched them for a while, then its eyes began drooping. Soon there was just the wind outside and the snore of the sleeping animal in the corner. Lana lay her head on Arjen's shoulder, watching it sleep.

"This is quaint," she said.

"One day..."

"One day, huh?"

"Yep. One day we'll get a real date."

Lana tightened her grip around his arm. "No way we could top this."

"You're telling me." Admani curled up around the crystal at their feet.

"We should rest," said Lana. "We have a long way to go when it clears up."

They slept around the crystal. Arjen spooned Lana and soon felt his body giving in to the exhaustion.

It was hours later when they awoke with a start. The beast in the corner was snorting and groaning. The three humans watched intently, but the light only reached so far.

"What is it doing?" asked Admani, scooting back behind the crystal.

Arjen once again held the hammer ready. "Think it's dreaming?"

"Really?" said Lana.

He nodded. "Marlow once told me that dogs on Earth would growl and act like they were running in their sleep when they would dream. She said it was sweet to watch."

"This doesn't sound sweet at all. What did they do to make them stop?"

"Pet them, I think."

"Not I," said Admani.

Lana made eyes at Arjen.

"Nope," he said. "Not real fond of animals."

Lana groaned. "As if any of us are." She reached out her hand and he set the hammer in it. "Just in case."

Lana crawled toward the beast. The ceiling was less than three feet high where it was.

"Hey buddy. Time to wake up, or at least stop—" She pulled her head back in a snap and barely missed smacking it on the rock above for a second time. "Shit. Jesus, shit." She was pushing off with her heels, dragging her butt back toward the crystal.

"What is it?" asked Arjen.

"Something's *eating* it."

"What? Is it even dead?"

"Its eyes..."

Lana made it to Arjen, and he had an arm around her when the beast's head lowered to the floor.

They saw movement across its body, then a creature with eight pointed legs crawled around it like some kind of giant, red centipede. The creature was much smaller in mass than its kill, but had made short work of the sleeping beast. It came off the carcass and planted itself sideways, guarding it from the humans. The creature faced them and hissed.

"Fuck," said Lana.

She reached for anything she could find to use as a weapon and came up with the Pelosin blaster. It couldn't project a beam anymore, but the hot light flashed anyway. The creature screeched and turned in a circle trying to clear its eyes. The legs clicked the rock like a bag of marbles hitting a tile floor. Admani covered her ears before Lana thrust the blaster into her stomach.

"Just keep it back while we get the crystal loaded," said Lana.

Admani was reluctant, but took the weapon and held it out in a shaking hand.

Lana and Arjen struggled packing the crystal in as Admani urged them on.

"Please hurry, please. It's looking at me."

The screeching enhanced and Admani threw her hands to her ears. The creature's sharp taps started toward them. Lana pulled the other weapon as Admani was frozen. There were needle-like teeth lining the inside of its mouth, now wide open and heading for Admani. Lana raised the weapon and hit the trigger just as it snapped. There was a sizzling sound as Admani screamed. The creature's head snapped back in shock, but they knew once it shook the stars from its eyes it would be ready to strike again. Arjen's hammer came down on the top of its head and it smacked the ground with its chin. They pulled Admani away as the eight legs retreated to guard its kill again. Arjen pulled on the backpack and they were out into the dark, snowy mountains.

They were twenty minutes along when Arjen said, "I don't see it back there. We need to take a break."

Lana looked to Admani, then to the path they'd taken.

"I'm fine," said Admani. "I can keep going."

"We barely got to rest," said Arjen. "Are you sure it didn't—"

"I think I'd know if it bit me."

Lana checked her face. "I still don't like this mark."

"It's just a burn from that damn gun. Not that I'm complaining but you got pretty close."

"Okay. If you think so."

The light of the distant planet showed their way, just as Joran told them. The snow left a blanket to make for soft steps. They only hoped no Night Chasers tried to follow after the storm. It would be hours until they reached the river, assuming the rest of Joran's directions had been true. What was to stop him from sending them on a wild goose chase into the mountains? What if it was just to spite the city that would want to punish them for their actions?

"We should keep going as long as we can see," said Admani.

She went on ahead as Arjen and Lana shared a look.

In a few hours, the mountain side became impassible. They searched the snow-capped cliffs for any other option.

"We should've known," said Lana. "A path for a Night Chaser might not be a path for us."

"There's gotta be another way," said Arjen. "If not, we'll make one."

"Down there." Admani pointed twenty feet down the side of the mountain. There was a clear overhang that jutted out from an opening in the rocks. It wasn't the only one. There were more openings lining the cliff.

"How do we know they connect?" asked Lana.

Admani looked them over, then frowned. "We don't, but what other way is there? We can't go back."

"Okay," said Arjen, "but let's be careful getting down there. If we miss that ledge..."

"If we make it," said Admani, "it looks like it leads all the way down."

Arjen went first, holding onto their makeshift rope as long as he could, then dropped to the ledge. The ladies followed and soon the three of them stood looking into a dark tunnel. It howled as wind passed through it. Lana hugged herself, shivering.

"Let's go. It's gotta be warmer in there."

Arjen nodded at her, then Admani. "Geez. That burn is worse than before."

Admani rubbed her cheek and winced. "Yeah. Gonna have to take a dip in the springs when we get back."

"Oh, the springs sound nice right now," said Lana.

They stepped into the tunnel, Arjen holding the backpack in front of him, top open for light, and the ladies with the Pelosin weapons out.

The rocks swirled above them, twisting and tightening around as they went. Soon there were a series of paths that led to the mountain side. Lana crawled out each one, then had to come back when she saw how high they still were. The next option was a narrow tunnel. Arjen held the crystal up to it, but they could only see so far.

"Looks like it goes in a ways."

"Again, we're without options," said Lana. "I checked all the other ways."

"Well, I hope nobody's claustrophobic." Arjen got on all fours with the backpack strapped to his chest. "I'll light the way."

The hole went straight for the first fifteen feet. The path was wide enough for them to move comfortably as long as they crawled. When it dipped down, Arjen felt his stomach flip.

"Okay, I'm going to take this slow." He led them down until he felt the backpack dragging on the ground and tightening to his stomach. "Running out of room." Sweat stung his eyes as it dripped down, though chills ran through the rest of his body. Lana bumped into him.

"Sorry. I can't see back here. What's it look like?"

"Getting tight." Arjen tried to focus on steady breaths.

"Can you see anything ahead?"

He lowered his head until the crystal heated his skin.

"Looks like it turns up. Ouch. This thing is hot."

"Let's get it off you and you can just push it ahead of us," said Lana, "then you'll have more space."

"I...I'm kinda freaking out here," said Arjen.

"Arjen. We need you right now. The only way to go is up. We've made it this far." She slipped a hand up his back and rubbed a bit. "Take some deep breaths and we'll get out of this tunnel."

Arjen breathed in, then out, feeling his neck muscles spasm. The rocks felt like they were tightening around him like a boa constrictor, slowly crushing him. He wanted to fall to the floor but the backpack wouldn't allow it. He closed his eyes, dipping a shoulder and shaking his arm, trying to free himself from the strap. Once one arm was free, he worked on the other. When the pack was loose, he took a few more deep breaths, then pushed it ahead of him. He lowered his face onto the cold stone and shivered.

"Arjen?"

Lana's voice was softer than he'd ever heard it. It called him back from the darkness he felt.

"Okay." Arjen pushed himself off the ground. He opened his eyes to the crystal and the tunnel ahead, then shoved the backpack and crawled after it. Lana and Admani followed as they turned uphill. The path narrowed, then there was an opening. The blue light gave him just enough to see they could be standing up straight again within a few minutes.

"I see it," said Arjen. "We're almost out of here. Just a little—"

Red, pointed, stick-legs clicked around just ahead. On his last push, Arjen landed the crystal just in front of the exit. The legs probed around for it.

"Shit." Arjen felt his pockets for the hammer and realized it was in the backpack. "Fuck." He made a quick lunge and caught one of the straps, pulling it away from the creature outside.

"Oh, God, Oh, God," said Lana. "What's happening?"

There were more legs at the exit, filling it with feelers. Arjen yanked the hammer free. The exit was completely blocked with the heads of the eight-legged creatures. They moved along the walls with ease, two-by-two, coming closer, following the light. Arjen felt his whole body go into shivers as he raised the hammer. "Everyone close your eyes," he yelled, as he brought it down on the edge of the crystal, shielding his face with his free hand. The blinding light shot out. It was accompanied by the screeches of the creatures. Arjen cried out as the top of his hair was torched off by the heat being thrown. He'd been too close, too concerned with shielding his eyes. He could smell some of his scalp burning and rubbed at it with his sleeve. The pain was immense, but he had to wipe it away before it got worse.

"Are you okay?" asked Lana. "What's happening? We can't see."

Arjen groaned but couldn't trust his voice to reply. The mouth of the tunnel was clear, and he knew they had to move before the creatures came back. He crawled forward, pushing the backpack ahead of him again until he reached the exit where he could stand. Arjen threw on the backpack and turned to pull Lana out.

"Your head," she said.

Arjen yanked her out, then grabbed Admani.

"Let's go," he said.

They assessed the room quickly. The walls were covered in red, even with the blue glow. Ahead was another tunnel and on the right, smaller ones. One of the creatures was skirting the edge of their group, probing at Admani's shoe. She pointed the Pelosin weapon as close as she dared and pulled the trigger. The heat and light were getting weaker than last time, but still scared it back. The quick glimpse they got when the weapon went off was enough to make their skin crawl. The walls were covered in the eight-legged creatures. The only path the humans could find had led them straight into their den.

Admani let out a sick moan. Lana grabbed her elbow and pulled. They were heading straight, the crystal as their beacon. Arjen had to duck to get into the tunnel as Lana pushed Admani behind him. Lana turned at the last second and fired the depleted weapon once more, then followed.

Arjen went as fast as he could go at a crouch in the low light.

"Do you see anything?" asked Lana. "I don't think I stopped them for good."

"It's just more—wait." Arjen kept on, ducking lower as he went. "I think I see light. We've gotta crawl the last bit."

He dropped to his knees, scraping them through his pants with no concerns for the pain and pumped as fast as he could. The wind bit him as soon as he stepped into the open, slipping on the snow and landing on his stomach. Admani's hand appeared and he scrambled to pull her through. Lana came next, headfirst on her back, kicking and screaming as she dragged her arms against the ground, trying to find traction.

"Get off me." She fired the weapon but got little out of it. The prickling legs poked and pulled at her, trying to reel her in like a fish. She felt Arjen's hands, one on her wrist and the other tightening around her fingers. He pulled her until it felt like her shoulder was going to pop out of socket. Arjen yelled, Lana screamed, and she was finally able to kick free. He pulled her into the snow. She was missing a shoe as she scrambled to her feet. Admani fired her weapon once more and they all ran on.

"Shouldn't we try to block it?" Admani asked.

"They'll just crawl out another way," said Lana. "Let's just go."

The humans ran for as long as they could, crossing slippery slopes with jagged rocks beneath. Their concern for safety was out the window, only speed mattered. Finally, Arjen pulled up, holding his chest.

"We've got to...take...a breath."

"We're like a damn...lighthouse with this thing." Lana motioned to the crystal.

"It...better...work," said Admani.

Her breaths had a hitch to them that continued after she spoke.

Lana put an arm on her shoulder. "Are you okay? You don't sound right."

Admani tightened her lips and shook her head. She sounded like she couldn't breathe fast enough.

"Just sit, rest a minute. I'll watch out."

"No...no. My heart..."

Lana widened her eyes at Arjen, then tried to get a look at Admani's face. The burn on her cheek was swelling up onto her forehead, partially closing on eye.

Lana put a hand on a clear part of Admani's face. "You're hot. Can I help you sit?"

Admani nodded and Lana wiped the snow off a nearby rock before helping her onto it. Arjen and Lana shared a look as Admani tried to control her breathing.

"I can't get...my heart to slow," Admani said, between breaths.

"Just rest a minute," said Lana. "Would some snow on your cheek help?"

Admani shrugged. She was staring at her feet, her mouth hanging open. Lana grabbed a handful of white powder and turned it into a makeshift ice pack, holding it gently against the burn. Admani moaned, then let out a long breath. The snow melted down her cheek, dripping onto the ground like tears.

"It's...it's helping," said Admani, after a minute. "I'm feeling a little better."

Lana took her hand away and held it to the crystal to warm it. She propped up next to Admani and did the same with her shoeless foot and wet sock.

Arjen was balancing a pack of snow on his forehead. His blond locks had been burned down to the scalp across the top of his head. The skin under the snow was blistered and quickly melting it.

Lana shook her head at their dismal group, then she looked up.

"Clouds are gone. We've got a little more light. You see anything, Arjen?"

Arjen took a couple steps forward until he could see over the next hill.

"I-I think I see water."

"What?" asked Lana, getting up. "Really?"

She joined him, squinting into the darkness. There was a place ahead, down the side of the mountain without standing snow. It was glassy but appeared to be moving.

"The river," said Lana. "Joran wasn't lying." She turned back to Admani. "We're almost there. You want to try to get down to the water?"

Admani forced herself up. Her cheek was already flaming again, and her head spun with the shift in posture. She grabbed Lana's arm to steady herself.

"I'm okay," said Admani. "Let's get to the river."

They followed Arjen down to the water. It was thirty feet across to the other side, though Joran never mentioned crossing it, only to follow it for...

"A day and a half." Arjen looked to his right. "Sweet fuck."

Lana gripped his shoulder. "Yes, but there shouldn't be any cave monsters at the river. At least...I hope."

Arjen hugged her as Admani joined them.

"Look clear still?" asked Arjen.

Admani nodded then put a hand on his shoulder for support.

"Still a long way. I—" She was fighting back tears.

Lana broke from Arjen. "We're going to help you, Admani. We'll get you back..." She stopped when she saw Admani's face. The despair was overwhelming to look at.

"Tell Ice that I love her. If she has a way—"

Lana gripped her elbow. "No, you're going to tell her when we get back."

Admani's lips peeled back as she brought her hand to her chest. Her hitching breaths started again. "Please find a way to tell my mother I love her." She gripped Lana's arm too tight, like she was holding on for dear life. "Tell her it wasn't her fault. She didn't drive us away."

"We...we don't..."

"Please. Don't let them eat me when I go." Admani's head shook at the thought.

Lana's mouth was agape, watching the woman fall apart in front of them.

"You should just rest," said Lana. "We'll find a place for you to lay down, then we'll—"

Admani's grip loosened. She fell to one knee. Lana tried to help her up, but she shook her arm free. Admani rose on her own. For half a second, they thought she was going to pull through, then she collapsed face down in the snow. Her breaths were ragged for another few seconds until they stopped.

"Oh, Jesus," said Lana.

She was on her knees in the snow on one side while Arjen was on the other. They turned her over and Lana put her head to Admani's chest.

"Her heart stopped."

They spent the next ten agonizing minutes trying to revive her to no avail. In the end, Lana sat weeping for yet another person who followed her to Wyan to start a better life, a better existence, and ended up dying in a far-off solar system.

Arjen stood on the lookout, trying to hold himself together. He'd known Admani since they were children. With parents in the government, it was inevitable. Something he'd never told Ice, Lana, or anyone but his brother Wesley, was when they'd shared a kiss during a day they both were stuck in the government building on Ceres helping their parents. It was his first kiss, awkward, rushed, and fun. They figured out quickly they weren't compatible beyond that moment and vowed to never tell anyone and stir up unnecessary rumors. Arjen always wondered if Ice knew all along. If he'd told Wesley...

A hug around the neck from Lana broke him from his trance.

"What should we do with her?" asked Lana. "We can't leave her for those creatures, or whatever else may find her."

Arjen looked over to the running river. "I mean, we don't have a shovel."

Lana agreed. "Okay."

They worked together to strip Admani down to her underwear, then they took her to the river. Arjen used the rope they'd made to tie a rock to her, and they watched her sink together.

Lana put on one of Admani's shoes that was too tight but better than nothing. They divided up the clothes to help for additional warmth, then were on their way.

Chapter Eight

The hunger gnawed at them over the next few hours. They had at least twelve more to go, an entire waking period walking with zero energy. The land flattened out near the river. It was the one positive thing they could take away, not climbing snowy mountain sides anymore. Admani's death weighed on them like lead in their shoes. Arjen discussed stopping to find shelter and rest, but Lana couldn't sleep without eating something. She knew the logic made no sense that she could keep walking on an empty stomach, but it was easier to keep dragging along. If they stopped, she'd have to listen to her stomach rumbling. Finally, they heard a splashing in the water. There was a small animal drinking and rubbing water over its whiskers.

Arjen motioned to Lana.

"How?" she whispered.

He raised the hammer and put a finger to his lips. He made it three steps before the animal looked up and darted off.

"Shit." Arjen watched it go.

He tucked the hammer away and shook his head.

When he turned, Lana already had the backpack on, waving him to keep walking. It was an hour before they saw another animal. This one was slightly bigger than the last, but still looked quick on its feet. Arjen and Lana stood in silence, pondering how to make it their next meal. Finally, Lana shed the backpack and unzipped it enough to light the area with the crystal. She backed away as quietly as she could, and Arjen followed suit.

It took five minutes of standing as statues while the animal approached the light, then backed away, testing its boundaries, but it was drawn to the warmth and soon couldn't resist, snuggling up against the blue block when it realized it was safe.

Arjen pulled the hammer from his pocket and gave Lana a sad look. She frowned, but nodded back. If they'd learned anything from the dark side of the planet, it was eat or be eaten. Arjen moved quietly and Lana looked away as he brought the hammer down.

They were able to get enough spark from the Pelosin weapon to help them start a fire on some cactus wood. It was weak, barely throwing enough heat to pull the grease from the meat, but they kept at it until the fire died off completely. They gagged down the gamey, unseasoned meat, sitting side by side, watching the river flow. Somewhere upstream was their fallen comrade, somewhere downstream their remaining friends. Their colonization had gone wrong. Their future hung on the hope of an alien they'd met only a few days before and the crystal that might or might not be giving them cancer.

Lana rested her head on Arjen's shoulder and let out a long breath.

"Do you ever feel like you've let down your entire species?"

Arjen laughed inadvertently. "Not usually, but you know—"

Lana wrapped a hand around to cover his mouth. "I know, I know. You support me."

Arjen pulled her hand away and kissed it. "Lana, I didn't come out here because I thought you were perfect, because you were the greatest leader."

"Thanks for the vote of—"

"I came because no matter where I found myself in the universe, I never felt at home, then you'd come back from a trip just before I'd leave and for those brief moments, everything just felt right. I knew I'd follow you into the sun if that's where you were going next. For those years you were lost, I thought I'd lost my chance to ever feel that way again. I was a hollow shell of a man."

She was taken aback by his confession. "Arjen...I know I haven't been great at showing it since you've been here, but I really couldn't have made it this far without you. I've been so wrapped up in becoming the queen or whatever they would've called me. Now I just want to make it back to the village alive."

"Did you really plan to be a queen to these people?"

"Yes." She eyed him. "Think of the legacy I'd leave, to be a queen on another planet."

"Legacy for who?"

"Humankind."

"The Belt?"

Lana stared at the water, not denying his claim. "When all else failed, they'd come, and who would they answer to?"

Arjen pulled back, feeling like there was another entity speaking through her.

"You wanted to rule the people of the Belt?"

"I wanted to provide them with better leadership, an outside opinion from the founding families. They are what got us off Earth as a species, but they don't have the foresight to prevent us from extinction."

"They were trying—"

"Stealing Marlow wasn't the answer. Short term, maybe, but long term, it's the Belt, the NutrientPanel, all of it. You can't fix that with lab tests. You just need a new location. I was going to provide that, to pave the way."

"You never planned for this to just be us, did you?"

"Arjen..." She put a hand on his arm, but he pulled away. "Listen, we were going to be the founders. The first family. Just like Dr. Ramirez and Gammen were to the Belt. We who colonized here were going to flip the script. We wouldn't answer to them anymore. If they came here, they'd answer to me. To *us*."

"Did you tell them? Before me, did you contact anyone?"

Lana couldn't hide the shame on her face. "Yes. As you know, we had other gathering trips of our own before we came back to the Belt. I contacted Oscar Ramirez. I just always got on with him best, but he pretty much told me we were in violation of the laws of the Belt and if we didn't return instantly, we would be considered dead. I think he thought he had more leverage, or just that his threat would mean more to me. If anything, it reaffirmed my desire to stay away, to build something they couldn't deny was better."

Arjen's head was spinning. They knew, Oscar at least, and never said anything, never told the loved ones that the group was alive. Had his dad known?

"But then you came back," he said.

"Yes."

"And..." Arjen waited for the final nail.

"We'd lost our exploration team. It wasn't just their skill sets. It was the pure manpower. We needed more if we were going to fight the war with the Night Chasers. We'd colonize with a select few, then others would see how well it worked and fall in line. Obviously, having more people didn't do it."

"That's why you came back? Manpower?"

"Arjen, you know I care about you. I just told you, I couldn't have done this without you."

"You used me to rally the troops. To be a pawn in your game for—"

"No."

She tried to put her hands on his shoulders, but he stood up.

"I'm glad I could help trick innocent people into coming here to be the peasants in your village."

Lana stood. "It's not like that. We saved Marlow from being a lab rat for your father. We gave people an opportunity to make a difference, to build a new life and new colony out here. To make names for themselves. This is a good planet. Things just went wrong."

Arjen hugged himself against the cold, feeling the blisters on top of his head pulsing.

"Very wrong." He turned his back, watching his breath dissipate into the air.

Lana stared at him for a few seconds, then said, "Not all of us were born into power."

Arjen blinked at that comment, but wouldn't look at her.

"I'm sorry." She watched him. "You didn't choose to be born how you were. Same as me."

Arjen had been feeling good from the first solid meal in a while, from confessing his deepest feelings to Lana. Now he wondered what happened if and when they got back. Where did he go from there? He'd come to Wyan for Lana, more than anything. Yes, there was the heart for adventure, for new places. He wanted to step out from the wing of his father, to give Marlow and Zane a better chance, but Lana was at the heart of it all.

She kept talking, trying to lighten the mood. "Think about it. What if we were born a hundred years ago? We would've lived on Earth, had boring jobs, drove cars. Probably died off in a war. Instead, we're here, making history."

Arjen turned, unconcerned with her seeing the tears of anger and sadness on his face.

"I loved you, Lana. I really did, and you used that to manipulate me. I'm not sure what to do with those feelings now."

Lana opened her hands towards him. "I *wanted* you here. That was no lie."

"Oh, fuck that. You knew how I felt. All that talk about us becoming the first couple of the new colony..."

The words, once a dream, felt dirty on his tongue.

"We can still do that. It would be a great ceremony, and—"

"No, not now we can't." Arjen started collecting the leftover meat and storing it away.

Lana was pacing next to him. "What do you want me to say?"

Arjen tossed the bones into the river. "Nothing."

They walked for another hour, both needing to cool off, then found a place to rest between two cacti, using Admani's clothes as blankets. The crystal was not the only thing separating them that rest period.

~ * ~

They awoke to more activity. Arjen's head shot up to see smaller animals like the one they'd eaten, scattering at his movement. There was a larger shadow he realized was one of the flat-nosed beasts they'd seen the first time they rested with the crystal. The warmth seemed to draw animals to it the same way Honey would find a sunny spot by the windows in his house on the Belt. Arjen hoped that meant they could tell it wasn't cancerous or radioactive. He realized Lana was watching him as he stood.

"Looks safe enough," said Arjen. "I'm going to pee, then we move?"

She agreed and soon they were back along the river's edge. A few hours in, they shared the remainder of the meat and didn't bother looking for more. The focus was getting back to the ship and seeing what the crystal could really do.

They walked for hours without rest. Once they'd gotten out of the mountains, everything felt like they were going downhill. The river gave them plenty of fresh water.

Finally, when their legs felt like they couldn't go another inch, they spotted lights in the distance. It was just in time as the river was turning. This had been the one question in the back of their minds that neither would say aloud. There was no river near the village that they saw. If they hadn't spotted the lights, they could've kept following the river indefinitely.

"It's there," said Arjen. "The village, and I think that's the ship."

He pointed to the left of the village lights. There was no shortage of excitement in his voice. They shared a brief hug, leaving their awful conversation behind for at least a few seconds.

"One more break?" Lana asked, when they broke their hug. "Then we need to game-plan."

Arjen agreed. It was going to look funny, leaving with seven Night Chasers and three humans, then only two humans returning. They found a good place to rest and plotted their final return.

Chapter Nine

"There is the very real possibility that they are all dead." Williams was propped against a wall on the bridge of the Pelosin ship while Marlow and Amun watched the windows for the thousandth time. The Night Chaser security detail became lazy, rotating out only two bodies at a time while the rest went back to the village. The ship's occupants discussed their increased chances of escape with such little attention left on them, but they knew they'd be condemning their companions to death if they left. That was assuming they were still alive. The group had been losing faith in that possibility by the hour.

"So, we just pack up and go?" asked Marlow. "What if they come back?"

"What if they don't?" asked Williams. "We have no food and little water. If you think those monsters are going to hand over theirs..."

"What if there are more around the ship?" asked Julie. "What if we open the door and they're just waiting for us? They're restless and hungry too. Their leader is gone. Who's to stop them from killing us?"

"We could use the bomb, assuming it works," said Williams.

"It should," said Amun, "but it's the only one."

"I'm not ready for that," said Marlow. "It would draw the whole village to us."

"Then let's just sit here and starve." Williams threw up his hands and marched back to the bunks.

A few hours later, Amun was the only one left watching when he noticed a group of Night Chasers marching toward the ship. They were led by one with a slight limp and rattling bones.

"Everyone," Amun called and they joined him on the bridge, watching the proceedings.

Soon the group was to the ship and out of sight. They called up to open the ramp.

"Was it them?" Marlow asked Amun, but he shook his head.

"I only saw more of the beasts."

"We should open and see," said Williams. "We can't sit here forever."

"No," said Julie.

Amun held up the last of the Pelosin weapons. "What choice do we have? Without the crystal, we are stuck."

Julie groaned at the idea of letting any Night Chasers in without their friends accompanying them, but their haven, the Pelosin ship was beginning to feel like a prison.

They all finally agreed to open the ramp. Amun held the weapon toward the opening as they heard footsteps. A Wit came up alone.

"Your friends have returned but are in the village."

"So, bring them here," said Marlow, as Amun kept the weapon trained on it.

The Wit shook its head. "She is hurt. Your leader. We need a medic."

They exchanged glances.

"Lana..." said Julie.

"What about Admani?" asked Marlow. "The one with the..." She spun her fingers around her head to signify Admani's curly hair. "She is a medic."

The Wit looked down the ramp, then back up at them. "She did not make it."

~ * ~

The village was dancing along with the flames from the bonfire at the center. As Julie, Marlow, Williams, and Amun walked down the steps—just as the initial group had when they were first captured—it looked like they were descending into hell. A couple of Night Chaser women danced around the flames as the group stopped. Most of the locals had thin cloths over their eyes, likely shielding them from the brightness of the flame.

The Night Chasers who'd escorted them from the ship turned. There were more closing off the staircase as the group of aliens huddled close, realizing how small their one weapon was.

"Where are Lana and Arjen?" asked Marlow.

The leader turned, bones clicking together as he did. By the light of the fire, they were able to see the material his belt was made from. Williams had the same revelation Lana had when she first came across Golen in the mountain caves.

"Everyone," Golen called to all in earshot. "I have very sad news. The group that went to the city will not be returning."

The dancing died down. The onlookers started mumbling. Marlow's group shot each other looks. They'd been double-crossed. There were no survivors. They didn't have time to mourn, as they would be next.

"But I have good news as well. You no longer have to live under Biral's reign. I will be your new leader. The hope of living in the city again is dead. Biral and his group tried, but it is not meant for us to go back there."

The crowd was beginning to become unruly.

Golen yelled over them. "You can go if you want." He motioned toward the path out the back of town. "I will not stop you. You already know I am not Biral. I actually make good on my word."

"What is your word?" called someone from the back of a growing mob near the exit. "Are you going to flee the village again?" There were laughs from the mob.

Golen's face was full of rage. He pointed a claw in the direction of the voice. "Biral threatened to kill my family. I had no choice, but now..." He looked around, triumphant. "He is gone. I will be your leader. The first thing I bring you is food." He turned just in time to catch a blast to the face. Amun stood, stunned at what he'd just done. Marlow whipped a rock at another behind them as Williams grabbed the weapon from the shocked Pelosin and blasted two more. Julie grabbed Amun and the aliens sprinted up the stairs as fast as they could.

As Golen scraped off his burning whiskers, he screamed for his group to chase them.

Marlow was pulling ahead and had to slow down for the others to keep up with her. She tagged alongside Amun.

"Is the bomb ready?"

"Yes, but I don't know how big it will be."

There were a group of boulders not far ahead as the first of the Night Chasers were up the stairs.

"Everyone, get behind those rocks. Amun's going to blow it."

Julie and Williams juked in the direction of the boulders as Marlow yelled at Amun, "Now."

He stopped, turned and saw two Night Chasers not twenty feet back. He raised the fusion bomb in his hand, twisted it until there was an audible click, then threw it over their heads into the village below. Marlow pulled him in as the explosion shook the ground. The closest Night Chasers went to their knees from the shock. Marlow and Amun joined Williams and Julie behind the boulder as pieces of roofs and walls flew into the air. There was screaming, then flames flooded the valley the village sat in. A hunk of rooftop smashed against the boulder and Julie screamed. Marlow waited a three count.

"Okay. Now what?"

"The ship," said Amun, using the English word.

"Why?" asked Williams. "We'll just be trapped in there again."

"He's right," said Marlow. "I know it's what's left of your home, but we'd have a better chance escaping to the mountains. We have a few friends left over there."

"They'll catch us." Julie watched the Night Chasers as they got back on their feet. More beasts were pouring out of the village, some on fire, others maimed by flying debris.

"Wait," said Amun. "Look."

They followed his gaze to the distance. There were the faint lights

228

of his ship, but an even dimmer light was moving toward it.

"No way," said Julie. "I thought they were..."

"We've gotta go," said Marlow. "We've gotta see."

They took off running while Williams stayed, aiming the weapon at the two oncoming Night Chasers. "I'll be right behind you." He blasted each of them, then followed.

~ * ~

Arjen and Lana jogged up the ramp of the ship, though their legs threatened to collapse beneath them. The bridge was empty as Arjen dropped the backpack, breathing heavily, looking around in dismay.

"They're not here...the explosion?"

"It was probably them," Lana said, "but what happened?"

"We took too long." Arjen was leaning on one of the viewing windows. "But we can't go looking for them, not like this."

"I know. We wouldn't make the walk at this point. If we knew how to power this ship, we could try to fly it over."

Arjen just gave her a look, then they heard footsteps from the hall. A familiar Wit and young Night Chaser stood.

"Hello," said the Wit. "Is Admani...?" The Wit looked around, but Lana shook her head, replying in Wyan.

"No. It's just us."

"Biral?"

Again, Lana shook her head. The Wit put its arm around the boy.

"He is alive because of Admani. I wanted to thank her."

Lana relaxed a bit as Arjen loosened his grip on the hammer.

"Do you know what..." Lana motioned towards the village. "The big sound was?"

"No. We were afraid. We hid."

"I understand."

The boy approached a window, squinting his eyes against the dark. "The village is on fire."

The rest in the room came to the windows to watch the flames in the distance.

"There," said the Wit. "They are coming, and they are being chased."

"What?" asked Lana. At that moment, they saw a blast from the Pelosin weapon, then another. Lana and Arjen could tell it was weakening just as theirs had. "How many? I see two."

"Two close but more coming," said the Wit.

"Oh, Jesus. We've got to go help them."

"With what?" asked Arjen. "The hammer?"

"We'll come up with something. Come on."

They headed down the ramp, leaving the crystal behind, hidden in one of the rooms.

~ * ~

Williams felt the weapon betraying him after his last shot. "Damn thing." He slammed it with the heel of his hand.

"They were not meant to kill," called back Amun.

"That's pretty clear."

The Night Chasers hadn't given up, but they slowed each time Williams hit them. There were burn marks all over them as they ran. The aliens were still a quarter mile from the ship and reality was setting in.

"We're going to have to turn and fight," said Williams.

Marlow called back, "Okay. Quick strikes. Don't let them get ahold of you."

"I'm not ready for this." Julie was gasping for breath.

"Then find something to throw," said Marlow. She turned and made a looping arc back toward one of the Night Chasers. Williams went for the other.

Marlow came at it fast. The Night Chaser was happy to oblige and pointed at her like a rocket. Marlow used her momentum and timed her jump just right, sending a spinning heel into his jaw. There was a cracking of teeth and the Night Chaser fell to his side. Marlow landed on her back, rolling to a standing position before feeling the ache in her foot. She limped into a fighting stance Ice taught her shortly after leaving Earth. The Night Chaser got up, regarding her with confusion, then lunged to catch her off guard. She parried his claws and sent a fist into his temple. He was dazed but only for a second, countering with two quick swings. Marlow stepped back and caught her sore foot on a rock, twisting her ankle just enough to send her sprawling to her butt. She grabbed the rock she slipped on and launched it into the Night Chaser's nose, just as he lunged again, then she rolled out of his grasp.

There was a scream from Julie. Marlow was on her feet in time to see Williams falling backward, holding his chest. Amun and Julie threw rocks but neither had much of an arm. The Night Chaser absorbed the blows and came at them. Marlow ran as her friends split paths to avoid his claws. He stopped between them, deciding which one to finish first. Williams tried to get back to his feet, then fell.

Marlow came running in and caught the Night Chaser with a flying kick to the ear. She followed it with an uppercut to his chin, then ducked back out of reach. The other Night Chaser caught up to her, grabbing her arm before she could pull away. He raised his other hand to gut her when his head twisted back. He shook his back like a dog trying to rid itself of fleas. It was enough distraction for Marlow to punch him in the throat and break loose. His head turned back with rage in his eyes before a hammer came slamming down straight between his eyes. The Night Chaser's long neck dropped so fast, Marlow barely got out from under him. She fell onto her back as Arjen came tumbling head-first next to her. Julie had Williams up and Amun helped Arjen and Marlow up. Lana was there cocking back a rock in her fist. She let it loose at the other Night Chaser, who caught it in the upper arm. He ducked down and backed up as his partner was slowly getting to his feet.

"Run away," Marlow growled in Wyan.

The two Night Chasers gathered themselves ten feet back as Lana collected another rock. Marlow, Julie, Williams, Amun, Lana, and Arjen stood together yelling insults and threats at the beasts, then there was a roar from their right.

Golen stood, bones strewn along his blue belt. His snout looked charred and he was missing the fur just under his chin.

"You." He pointed at Lana. "I should've eaten you when we first met."

"You were too busy crying," said Lana.

Golen smiled. "I'm surprised you survived the ambush. Impressive, but it doesn't matter. My friends are on their way." He looked back at the village as a trail of shadows moved alongside the flames. The other two Night Chasers regained their confidence and made a semi-circle around the aliens. "I promised the others meat and I will deliver."

Before Golen could step forward, a smaller voice sounded,

"You'll never be like my father." The boy from the ship stepped into the group. "You're weak."

Golen turned and cocked his head. "Oh, Biral's son. Who is the weak one? Me who left to save my family, or you who would side with these aliens over your own kind?"

"You're not my kind," said the boy, then out of the darkness, a figure sprang and attached itself to Golen's neck. He fell to his side with the momentum and landed with a thump. It was the Wit who tore at Golen while the other two Night Chasers came to help.

Biral's son waved the aliens on. "Come on." He took off running toward the ship.

Lana looked to the oncoming group from the village. It would only be a minute before they caught up. The humans had little chance against three more Night Chasers.

They ran. Lana looked back to see the Wit being ripped off Golen before it rebounded and jumped on the next. It was a losing battle, but it fought on while they ran. The boy was the first up the ramp, Williams and Julie were last with the Night Chasers closing in quick. Amun cranked the lever and the slow rise began. Marlow grabbed the Pelosin weapon they had left and ran to the ramp as a clawed hand gripped the side. She stuck the weapon directly onto it and pulled the trigger. There was a growl as the hand pulled away. She hit another on the other side with the same method then backed away as the ramp sealed shut.

Marlow turned to the rest of the group, dropped the weapon and caught Arjen in a hug. They fell to the ground.

"You made it. We thought..."

"I know." Arjen patted her back.

"So, Admani...?" asked Julie.

Lana shook her head. "We did all we could for her."

Marlow broke her hug with Arjen and embraced Lana. After a moment, Williams groaned. Julie was patching up his torso. She managed to stop the bleeding as he leaned against the control panel.

There was the screeching of claws coming from outside.

"Can they get through this?" Arjen asked Amun in Wyan.

Amun frowned. "I hope not."

Arjen pulled the crystal out of the backpack. "Will this do it?"

Amun basked in its glow. "You really got it."

"Yes. Please tell me this can power the ship." Arjen added in English, "And get us the hell out of here."

Amun examined the glowing blue block.

"It's a good size. Mostly good shape." He ran his hand across an edge. "What is this crack?"

Arjen frowned and answered in English. "I kinda hit it with a hammer." He raised the hammer to show Amun who got the gist.

"What? Why?"

Arjen switched back to Wyan. "I had to. We were in a bad situation. I'll tell you about it later."

"Okay. Let's get it to the...power room. What is it called?" Amun looked to Marlow.

"Engine," said Marlow in English.

The scraping continued outside, as they went to the end of the hall. After a minute, the lights went out completely. Julie cried out.

"Is that normal?" Lana called back.

"We took out the old one," said Arjen. "Give us a second."

They still had the light of the crystal to work with as Amun inserted it into the power core. He closed the door as rocks bounced off the outer windows.

The footsteps of Arjen and Amun returning could be heard in the dark but no one could see beyond their own face in the dark bridge. One of the display screens lit up with writing at the bottom. Amun moved to it, gliding his hands across. It was a long process that no one dared to rush, despite the assault of the Night Chasers. Finally, he turned and smiled.

"It's turning on."

A screeching of claws sounded outside.

"How long will that take?" asked Lana, watching out the window.

"I've never replaced a power source before, but the screen says..." He was trying to translate the time measurement. "How long does it take to walk to the village?"

"About twenty minutes," said Lana.

"Maybe two of those."

"Forty minutes?"

Amun flattened out his ivory face. "I can't rush it. The ship is changing the crystal, forming it into usable energy. If the crystal doesn't take, we could..." He mimicked an explosion.

"Right."

"They can't get in," said Julie. "Right?"

"Yes, but they can damage the ship," said Arjen.

"There's nothing we can do about it now." Marlow sat and patted the floor next to her. "I think we have a lot of catching up to do anyway."

The rest of the group agreed, some more reluctant than others.

Lana and Arjen told them about the trip to the city, meeting Golen, getting the crystal, Joran helping them escape, their venture through the eight-legged creature's cave, and Admani's death. They treaded lightly on the subject of Biral, as his son looked on. He seemed okay with the fact that Biral died fighting for the village.

Marlow, Williams, Julie, and Amun told of their time in the ship. Amun explained how his planet became uninhabitable because of a change in the star, leading his people to go in search of new land.

"So, you're it?" asked Arjen. "What about the team you left on Melinger?"

Amun looked solemn. "That was much time ago. If the ship will fly, I will search for them. It's all that is left of my kind."

Arjen put a hand out to him. "We too have friends that went to Melinger. If we can help you, we will."

Williams snorted. "They crashed if anything. There's no way..." He caught Lana's eyes. "Okay. It's worth a shot. Just don't get your hopes up. This is all *if* we can get this thing flying."

The navigation map came online. The screen lit up with the planet and relative locations of those around it.

"Wait." Lana approached the screen. "What does this mean?" She was pointing at the star.

"The light is coming back," said Amun. "On the other side of the mountains, it is..."

"Day." Marlow patted the floor next to her, urging the ship on. "Come on, baby. I need to see *my* baby."

Lana clapped her hands in excitement. "All right then, our first objective should be to regroup on the light side. If we can fly there first, then we can decide what to do in the safety of the sunlight."

Biral's son—Warc—they'd learned, was watching the monitor, trying to pick up the mixture of languages they were using. He flipped the cloth away from his eyes and squinted at the brightness of the screen.

"It will be light over there?"

"Oh, shit," said Julie, then in Wyan, "Yes."

Lana examined Warc as he covered his eyes with the cloth again.

"Did the crystal bother you?" She pointed back toward where they'd inserted it.

"No. My father said it is like our home, but the other light..." He pointed off toward the mountains. "I can't see any more if I look at it."

Williams burst into laughter. "All this time waiting on the war. We could've just brought some sunglasses and sped up the whole process."

Warc tilted his head, confused.

Lana shook her head at Williams. "I don't think it's that simple."

"They're using rags as Ray-Bans. Hell, Julie had an old pair in her hut we could've brought with us."

The Night Chasers

Lana ignored him, turning to Warc, switching to Wyan. "Is there anywhere for you to go?"

Warc thought, staring at the floor for answers before his head popped back up.

"My father had an old friend. He wanted to live alone, away from the village. I went with him once near the river."

"Okay," said Arjen, switching to English. "But how do we get him there?"

"No, no," said Williams. "We are not playing taxi. If we get this thing off the ground, we are getting out of dodge."

"Williams..." said Lana.

"I'm the pilot." He grunted to stand. "I'm already risking all our lives to fly this thing. I'm not adding a side-trip before it's even off the ground."

"You're right," said Arjen. "It wouldn't be safe."

Lana whispered to him as if Warc could understand their language. "We can't just dump him out there. They'll kill him. You heard Golen."

Amun was at the screen, following prompts as the status bar was about halfway.

"I think I can help. It's making me check each item to make sure it's working. One of the items are the engines. It's ready now, but for safety it will not turn."

"Because of the Night Chasers down there," said Lana. "So, are we stuck?"

Amun smiled. "Opposite. I can tell it to go anyway, to..."

"You can override the safety measures in case of emergency," said Arjen in English. "Sorry. I get it." He turned to Warc. "If we clear the ones outside, can you make it to your friend?"

"Yes. How...?"

Arjen exchanged a look with Amun. "Just be ready to run."

Amun hit a few buttons on the screen, then entered an override command code. A rumbling sound could be heard. The ship tilted to one side, then the other. There was screaming and growling below but they couldn't hear it over the sounds of the engines. After each engine cleared the testing period, the screen prompted Amun for the next command. He raised his hand to the lever for the ramp.

"Okay," said Arjen. "Ready?"

They gathered by the ramp, Arjen, Lana, and Marlow while Warc waited for it to open.

"I am sorry for your friend," said Warc. "She saved me with her medicine."

"Thank you," said Arjen, "and for your father, the same."

Warc's face grew dim. He said no more. As soon as there was clearance, he ran down the ramp. Arjen and Marlow peeked out. Lana brandished the depleted Pelosin weapon and stepped down the ramp after him.

"Lana," said Arjen.

He grabbed the hammer and followed.

"Oh, come on." Marlow followed as well.

Lana was perched near a toasted corpse. There were no living Night Chasers in sight, only Warc, already some distance away. She reached back toward Arjen, holding out the gun and he took it from her. Lana wept for her exploration team who never made it back, then she took the hammer from Arjen and used it to lose the charred belt from Golen's body. She held the bones up, examining them for a minute, then tossed them away from him. They landed in the sand with a soft thump. Lana nodded at her work, then went back to the ship.

Chapter Ten

When the ship completed its systems check, there was another set of Night Chasers watching. They were further back, as the last group became a clear warning sign to keep your distance.

Williams sat at the controls with Amun at his side, translating the best he could.

"So, if I just push this," said Williams, "then enter where I want to go?"

"It will tell you if you're going the right way, but you have to land."

Williams moved the controls, then turned to Lana. "Seems straightforward enough. I won't know until we're in the air."

"Just a quick test run," she said. "Over the mountains, then land."

Williams saluted her and put his hand to the screen. "Initiating launch. Everyone, strap in."

There was a line of belts across the way made for Pelosin bodies, but good enough for the moment. Amun sat next to Williams, reading over a flight manual on screen as they felt the rumble of the engines. There was an immediate alert flashing on the screen.

"What's that?" asked Williams.

"The ramp, it is damaged," said Amun. "No problem. I can..."

"Override?"

"Yes." Amun clicked on the screen.

"We sure we *want* to override?"

Amun finished and leaned back. "For a short trip, yes. Not to leave Wyan, though."

Williams looked back at Lana and Arjen and shrugged. "Here we go." He increased the engine power and the ship lifted off the ground. The controls were touchy as he angled them toward the mountains.

"Shit, shit, shit," said Williams, feeling them lose altitude.

He manipulated the controls again, easing them up. The mountains were approaching too fast. He swerved to avoid an oncoming peak, then just missed the range underneath. The sunlight ripped through the windows, lighting up the cabin. "Slow, slow. Descend," Williams was yelling commands at the screen. Amun understood the tone of his voice, calling out instructions from the manual, while Williams executed them. The ship was coming in toward the wrecked village they'd parked the *Mack* at. He could see the grassy place they'd landed before, but was approaching too quickly. Amun reached over and hit a button. They felt the reverse thrusters kick in and Amun was thrown from his chair. Williams didn't have time to check on him. He was trying not to wrap them around one of the giant trees.

The Pelosin ship slowed and lowered to the grass at the tree line. They still had too much momentum when they touched down and the ship slid, tipping into the branches. There was a slam, a cracking of limbs outside and Amun was thrown again. He crashed into the back of the pilot's seat, as Williams tried to lean to the side and prevent the entire ship from tipping over. He cursed and begged aloud as branches scraped along the exterior, then there was a loud groan from the ship. Williams cut the engines and it fell into place, coming to a final stop. The other humans struggled with their buckles, then ran to check on Amun. He sat up with scratches and a dent on the top of his head.

"I'll be okay. Are we here?"

"We're back," said Lana.

The humans shared a group hug.

"Daylight." Julie looked out the viewing window. "I missed it so much. I never want to see nighttime again."

Marlow broke away. "Open the ramp. I have to find Avani."

"Just hold on," said Lana. "We all have people—"

Arjen pulled the gray lever.

"Thanks." Marlow ran down the ramp thinking of the quickest way back to the bunker. Then she had a second thought: would they be at the bunker still? Would Ice, Barchek, and Cannie just be waiting for her to return? Probably not at that point. It had been too many days. They had to have assumed she didn't make it. When Marlow looked around the wrecked village, she had so many memories of Barchek popping out from behind an old hut wanting to play. She wished more than anything that it would happen now, that she'd be holding Avani, that everything would be okay. There was nothing but the empty wind to greet her. After calling for Barchek, Ice, and Cannie a few times, Marlow stood, dizzy from turning circles, trying to catch a glimpse of any of them.

"The village," she said, under her breath, and took off running toward their former camp while the rest of the group looked on.

The path was familiar to her feet. The sun felt amazing on her skin. She shed the coat she'd been wearing, tying it around her waist. The dark rocks were beautiful with the light reflecting off their smooth surface, everything was, the green of the trees, the blue sky. Marlow was reminded why she understood Lana's desire to colonize. Shortly after they'd first arrived, when she'd had the chance to explore, she saw it.

The path began to open. Marlow saw grass ahead, giant trees and just the hints of their old huts. Some had been destroyed when the night came, but as she got closer, she saw some still stood. The bird pen was empty. Marlow couldn't remember what they'd done to hide them during the night. The lab was torn to pieces. The beasts had no clue what they were really looking for in there, only that there were things to destroy.

She slowed to a walk, resting a hand on a giant tree, taking in the place they'd called home for the last six months or so. The wind ruffled her hair. There was no sign of her friends, but again, why would they be hanging out in that old village? Why not go to the main one? If the Night Chasers killed most of the main village, why *wouldn't* Cannie go there? Maybe she was ready to reconcile with her tribe.

A sound cut through the air like a knife. Marlow's head snapped at her old hut. The door was slightly ajar and Avani's cries poured out. She ran, without thought, slipping in the grass with her overeager first steps. She reached the door and resisted the urge to slam it open, sliding in gently. Avani's cries filled the small hut, but she was nowhere in sight. Marlow caught a scream in her throat. There was someone sitting on her bed in the dark. She backed up and pulled the door fully open for more light. That was when she knew she was in a nightmare. It couldn't be reality because her dead ex-lover Rami sat on her bed. His head twitched as he stared at something in his lap. Marlow did a quick look to either side of the room. It was still empty, but Avani...

She approached Rami—if that were even possible—and looked at his hands. He was holding a small device. Avani's cries were louder than ever. Marlow wanted to scream.

"Rami? Rami!"

His head twitched up, one eye meeting her, the other stayed where it was, hanging in the socket. His face was crooked. It all felt out of place from how she remembered it from that different time, that different life. He didn't reply or even seem to recognize her. She snatched the device from his hands and clicked it off. The room was finally silent. Marlow turned as she heard footsteps behind her. There was a shadow in the doorway.

He spoke into a radio, "I've got target one," then looked up at Marlow and smiled.

A flood of terrible, repressed memories came into Marlow's mind. This was the man who'd stolen her from her house that day. The one who brought her in for the forced c-section. The one who'd killed Rami. At least, she'd thought that until now. Another thought hit her fast: they weren't much on last names in the Belt but the face, the resemblance was undeniable. He looked just like Lana.

Maynard Royal held up a taser and confirmed her suspicion. "I'll bring you to your daughter, if you bring me to mine."

Chapter Eleven

Lana led the group toward their village. Her legs ached, but were filled with a newfound energy. They'd survived the time of night. They'd wiped out most of the Night Chasers. There likely would not be another raid in four years. The Night Chasers couldn't have destroyed all the main village, nor all the people. Her spirits were high, though she didn't share it. Arjen walked beside her, but had a different look in his eyes, ever since she'd shared her full desires for the planet and the people.

Julie, Williams, and Amun strolled behind, happy to be out of the ship and in the light more than anything.

They spent minimal time in their village. Most found a change of clothes. Julie came out and flipped her Ray-Bans over her eyes. Williams gave a hearty laugh. Lana and Arjen were too focused on the next village and Amun just looked confused.

"They block the sun," Julie explained to Amun as they hit the next path.

Arjen looked down, remembering the Night Chaser that grabbed Marlow. He stopped on the spot. The blood-stained rock he'd used still lay in place, but the body was gone. Someone had cleaned up after them. *That was a good sign,* he thought.

The main village came into view. The log barricades had been taken down. The buildings stood in perfect condition. Only the forge was destroyed. At the well, Karath waited with her aides, just as she had when the time of night started.

Lana wanted to run to her, but her legs would not allow it.

"Karath," said Lana. "You are well."

"As are you," said Karath.

"The village...?" Lana looked around at its pristine condition. "What about your people?"

"They live."

"What?" asked Arjen.

"We have lost some," said Lana, "but we have fulfilled our promise. The Night Chasers have been taken care of."

"What about Ice, and the baby?" asked Arjen. One of the aides gasped at him talking out of turn. Karath ignored him, only addressing Lana.

"That promise is no longer. There is a new deal."

"What?" asked Lana. "But we—"

She stopped when she heard it: the hum of a Rock-Hopper. It descended from the sky like an artificial angel of death and landed near the well. The top opened as Lana and Arjen found themselves with the same word on their tongues. "Father?"

The group stood in shock as Robin Visser and Maynard Royal stepped out of the Rock-Hopper. They were accompanied by more of Maynard's security detail.

Maynard reached out his arms, but kept a distance between them. "Lana, look at all of this. This is incredible what you've done."

"What is happening?" asked Lana. "Why are you here? *How* are you here?"

"You weren't hard to track, though it was a long ride." Maynard straightened his belt loaded with his usual taser. "We're here for a couple reasons actually, but it's not what you're thinking. We don't plan to move in. First off, I want a grandchild." He held his hands up. "Now hold on, it doesn't have to be yours, but Belters are afraid that their babies won't turn out normal. We need *her*. I think you understand where I am going with that.

Number two, the Belt has split since your departure. You've struck up a civil war right when we were ready to unveil plans for a new expansion."

"What are you talking about?" asked Arjen.

Robin Visser took over, "We found a new body within the Belt that is just brimming with resources. We could consolidate many of our islands onto this one. There would be no more threat of 'Bubble failure as we'd have around the clock workers dedicated to only this one with more backups in place. With our population as it is, we must be forward-thinking. We expanded too fast before, not knowing the *situation* we'd run into with the children."

"Where is Marlow?" Arjen yelled.

"She's safely aboard the *Knox*," Robin said. "They're waiting. Now, decisions need to be made."

"What decisions? What about Avani and Ice? Are they with Marlow?"

"Just hold on," said Maynard.

"No, no," came a voice from around one of the nearby buildings. Bruuth came stumbling into the picture.

Maynard held up his taser. "Hold on, fella. You don't want this again, do you?"

Bruuth made a wide arc around Maynard to join Arjen and Lana. "They took Zane."

"What?" asked Arjen. "Zane's alive?"

Bruuth nodded. "I was taking care of him. He's hurt, but they stole him from me."

Arjen didn't have to ask what they wanted with Zane. If they had Marlow already, what else were they waiting for? Arjen couldn't help but stare down his father.

Robin frowned at him. "We need them both."

"Karath," said Lana. "Please, honor our agreement. We cannot let these men leave with our friends."

Karath didn't reply, she looked like she didn't want any part of their discussion and was ready for it all to be over.

"She broke your agreement before they even got here," said Bruuth. "She made a deal with the Night Chasers. She let them into our village to take your people and use them as they needed in an agreement to leave the rest of us alone. I'm sorry. I did not know."

"What?" Lana gave a death glare to Karath. "You let them take us? You—"

"I did what was right for my people," said Karath. "You don't belong here. It's clear you could not hold up to your promises. Now go. Leave us be."

"It's true, Lana." Maynard took a cautious step forward, his dark hair was combed forward and styled up at the front like a car crash. "You belong with us. If you agree to put this all aside, you can return as the Head Developer of the new land."

"Are you serious? You're offering me a job right now?"

"Not just a job. Power. The opportunity to do what you did here but with more support. You could help put an end to this civil war. We need you back in the Belt."

Lana looked behind her. The gears were already turning in her head. "What about my team? I didn't do this alone."

Maynard and Robin exchanged a look. Robin replied, "We only have room for one more, which will be Arjen."

"What?" asked Williams. "You're not serious. I've been a pilot for you for—"

Maynard held up a hand to silence him. "It is a long journey. We are not prepared to take on extras."

Williams took a step closer, stopping when he saw Maynard's hand go to his taser. "So, because my *dad* didn't come to pick me up, I'm being abandoned?"

"What about Marlow?" asked Arjen. "Will she be your lab rat again?"

"Marlow will be taken care of," said Robin. "We'll make sure she's comfortable, but you have to understand her importance."

"Jesus, Dad."

"We're talking about the future of the Belt. You used to understand this. You are blinded now."

"We were trying a different way, a better way."

"And see how that has turned out." Robin raised his hands. "You've failed here. It's okay to admit that. Now come home. There are good things for you to be a part of. You two together can help bridge the gaps between groups. Put an end to the uprising. There'll be a new land for you to help colonize."

Arjen crossed his arms, hoping to call his father's bluff. "Free Marlow to make her own choice or I'm not coming."

"Oh, don't play this game. You will be stranded here."

Arjen wondered who was bluffing whom. Surely, they saw the Pelosin ship...

"I'll go," said Williams.

"What?" asked Julie. "Thomas..."

"I'm sorry," said Robin. "The deal was not for you."

"Excuse me?" Williams pulled away from the group to confront Robin. He pointed a finger directly in his face. "You can't make this decision on your own. We need to talk to the judges first."

Robin shook his head. "You knowingly ignored communications from a government entity. Keeping them from your ship's leader." He motioned to Lana. "You came back within range and made no attempt to contact us. Your ship has been stolen. If you came back, the only place for you would be prison."

"I did no such thing. Lana knew about your communications. She ignored—" He couldn't finish his sentence as electricity jolted through his body and he fell to the ground in convulsions.

Maynard held up the taser. "Shall we? The *Knox* and crew are waiting. It's a long way back to the Belt."

Lana took a couple steps and turned. "Arjen?"

"You can't be serious," he said, reading Lana's eyes.

She'd said a lot more than his name, but he wasn't quite sure what.

Lana shrugged. "Then, goodbye." She leaned in and hugged him, whispering two words only he could hear, *"Long game,"* then stepped over to Maynard.

"What the hell, Lana?" Julie cried.

Maynard led Lana to her seat in the Rock-Hopper as Robin and Arjen shared a stare. Many of their unsaid words bounced around their heads like flies in a glass jar. It wasn't the time to spew family quarrels out for all to hear. After a few seconds, one of the guards grabbed Robin's elbow and led him to the small ship. Julie and Arjen helped up Williams as they stood together. The Rock-Hopper sealed as Robin and Maynard were already discussing their further plans. Lana stared at Arjen, straight faced. They watched the would-be Queen of Wyan fly away.

Before any of the humans could process the preceding events, Karath looked them over, then said, "You are not welcome in our village, *any* of you." Her pointed finger swept across them and included Bruuth.

Arjen turned to the group. "Let's head back to our village and regroup." Then to Bruuth, "I'm sorry about everything. If we'd never come..."

"The Night Chasers would have killed more of us," Bruuth said. "We don't know what is ahead. We can only learn from what is behind."

"It's true, my friend." Arjen watched Karath turn toward her house while her aides stayed to make sure the humans left. He put a hand on Bruuth's shoulder. "You stood up for us when no one else would. You are welcome with us for whatever is next."

Bruuth nodded, looking back toward the forge, likely realizing his normal way of life was over. "There are many stories to tell. I will bring food. You look hungry."

Chapter Twelve

They were back in the sunlight, but it still felt like evening when they gathered around the fire pit. Everyone took the time to bathe for the first time in almost a week. They found comfortable clothes and sat together with a strange air about them. Julie sat away from Williams; Arjen paced as Amun was tentative to do anything, reading their feelings with concern.

"It feels right, but it doesn't." Julie sported her Ray-Bans and a Nirvana shirt. "So many empty seats. Marlin, Walters, Admani..."

"I know." Arjen thought back to their first week on Wyan as they were settling into their new lives, the threat of the Night Chasers far enough away to still feel hopeful.

Even the last night on the beach felt like it was a year ago. So much had changed, and what was left was severed, as was displayed by the gap between Julie and Williams.

Arjen felt sick and alone. The pangs of his ruined relationship with Lana were still fresh. Everything would've been easier if he was sitting with Marlow as she held Avani in the air and she squealed the way only a baby could. If Ice would put him in his place with just a look that said she wasn't going to let him get away with shit, but that she also cared about him as much as anyone. Even Admani and Walters' weird relationship, it was something to talk about, a little entertainment for gossip when they weren't around. He was down to Julie and Williams who didn't want to talk to each other anymore and Amun and Bruuth who didn't speak English.

Still, he'd chosen to stay, to show some loyalty to those left behind. He had other plans, of course, but he'd have to work up the courage to initiate them.

They settled into their places as Bruuth parked a cart full of food in the circle.

"Eat, friends. I will put some grenners in the fire." Bruuth loaded up a wire rack they used for cooking as others dug in.

As their stomachs filled, they shared stories of their plight on the dark side of the planet while Bruuth continued to apologize for his people sabotaging their plans for the time of night.

Arjen took a big bite of a grenner, savoring the warmth and the spices the most. His meals over the past week had been less than flavorful, or nourishing for that matter. He wondered what his dad really thought seeing him with a big chunk of his hair burned off, emaciated and barely surviving on a different planet. It wasn't enough for Robin to make his only living son come back with him and it spoke to his cold heart. Part of Arjen wished they'd just tased him and tossed him on the ship. Made the decision for him, instead of leaving him to what remained.

He was licking his fingers when he caught movement out of the corner of his eye. He spotted Cannie first, then Barchek behind a tree. She was reluctant to follow her mother, but Cannie pulled her by the arm. Arjen stood and opened his arms.

"Friends. You're okay?"

They stood at a distance, shy and afraid.

"We couldn't stop them," said Cannie and Arjen noticed the unnatural bruising down her side. It wasn't unlike the normal coloring the females had. "They took Avani and Isolde."

Arjen felt his heart warm a bit. He hadn't heard anything about Ice's status. If they took her, it was probably to bring her back to her mother, Kaia. He hoped she was raising hell on the trip back.

"It's okay," said Arjen. "Thank you for all you did for us. If not for you, we would've lost more."

Barchek was looking around the group with hopeful eyes, as only a child can. "Marlow?"

Arjen shook his head. "She's okay but they took her too. She's with Avani."

"All good?" asked Barchek in English.

Arjen smiled. "Not *all*, but they're together...for now."

Cannie frowned. "What will they do with her?"

"It's a complicated story, something I've gotta deal with, not you."

"You will go? Won't you?" asked Cannie. "Marlow is our friend. You must help her."

"Yeah," said Barchek. "We belong together."

Arjen narrowed his eyes at her. "Seriously, Pat Benatar right now?"

Barchek looked confused. "No. I say she is my friend, too."

"Right." Arjen wasn't sure if he was being played by a seven-year-old alien. He ran a hand through his hair, wincing as he did. It was a habit he was going to have to stop until he healed all the way. "Will you join us to eat?"

Cannie and Barchek sat around the coals with the rest of the outcasts. Everyone's spirits were lifted with full bellies and a little companionship. Amun shared stories of Barchek's dad, Balowg, from the Pelosins' first few days on Wyan. Cannie chimed in. Arjen retrieved Percy's telescope to watch the sky. As the cart of food emptied down, Barchek pulled out one of the last husks and squealed.

"Look."

Arjen turned to see her holding Honey. He smiled at the memory of the real duck and how much Ice and Marlow loved her.

"Avani's gonna be pissed," said Arjen.

"Shit-bitch," said Barchek. "We have to bring it back to her."

Cannie patted her daughter's shoulder. "They are past the stars, Barchek."

Barchek looked to Arjen who was examining the sky again.

"Two days," he said.

"Huh?" asked Julie. "Then what?"

"In two days, Melinger will be as close as it gets. We'll take Amun to search for his people. We'll look for ours and the *Mack*, as well. Then...well, then, we'll return the duck to Avani."

Acknowledgments

Once again, I have to start with my wife, Erin. She's read and given thoughts to a lot of my stories, including this one. Next would be Jennifer (Barchek) for being the first reader of Interstellar Islands, and the first reader of The Night Chasers. It's proof that with loyalty, dedication, and unwavering friendship, you can get an odd-looking, potty-mouthed, alien child named after you. Please start your training regimen to play this role in the movie someday. I owe you that at least. To the awesome, Stefanie with an F for the artwork. Is www.designsonthecobb.com taken yet? Thanks to Aunt Sharon as well for reading early drafts, and other things yet to find a publishing home. Thanks to Arlo and Christine at Rogue Phoenix Press for letting me continue down this wormhole. Big thanks to everyone who purchased, reviewed, and promoted the first book. This not only made the second a possibility, but warmed the heart of a strange, bald author, who spends too much time in his office coming up with alien species. Thanks to those that made me sign copies and deliver them around the country. I hope to raise the value of those at least back up to the cover price. Thanks to Hannah for taking the book across the pond, and others for contributing to the collages. Anders...it's too late to check your messages now. Maybe on the next one.

About the Author

Scott lives in western North Carolina with his family of redheads and hopes the county laws will allow him to one day raise ducks on his property. He loves his pizza stone, watching white squirrels try to figure out his bird feeders, and heavy music.

Also by the Author
at
Rogue Phoenix Press

Interstellar Islands

The world finally had its third and then final war. Two remaining teenagers, Marlow and Zane are left surviving in a church bunker with nothing but a couple ducks. They've watched everyone they love, pass on from the toxic conditions and know they aren't far behind them. When they are found by a team scavenging for supplies, the teenagers don't believe the claims that they are from the asteroid belt, the last settlement of humans that made it off Earth just before it all went to hell. They don't believe they live out there on Interstellar Islands with artificial atmospheres. They don't believe but they don't have much choice but to board their ship and see where it takes them. Whatever the people from the belt have in store for them can't be worse than what's left on Earth. Can it?

Part I
Prelude

A cold, gray breeze dragged across the barren land once known as Inland Florida. Metal fencing surrounded the backlot of Bride of Christ Pentecostal Church, though no one knew the name, as the sign had been repurposed many years ago. Two ducks were inside the fencing. One, Marvin, lay on its side taking its last breaths and the other, Honey, was dipping its bill into a bowl of water.

Zane watched them from the roof of the church, shaking his head, causing his dark hair to swing in front of his small brown eyes, shielding his view for a few seconds. He was perched like a bird, looking out as far as he could through the unnatural fog. The wind cut through him and he wrapped his coat tighter, letting out a long crackling sigh as desolate tears welled up in his eyes.

Honey looked up when the back door to the church opened with a creak.

"Zane? Will you come down from there?" Marlow called up. She had a blanket over her shoulders, trailing in the dirt as Honey approached, looking for food.

"What's the point?" he called back, not looking away from the ominous gray. "What's the point of any of this? Look at Marvin."

Marlow whipped her head, a long braid of hair swinging with her, and hurried over to the dying duck.

"Why didn't you tell me?" she asked through intermittent coughs. "I coulda..." She trailed off, holding the fragile duck head in her palm. "Oh, Marvin."

Zane laughed a bitter laugh. "What? You gonna resuscitate him, again?"

She looked up towards him. "It's a she. Marvin is a she."

He laughed again, more lighthearted this time. "True." His reply was lost in the wind.

"Would you come down here?" Marlow called.

He sighed again, wiped the tears from his eyes and climbed down.

The chapel was filled with plants, mother-in-law tongue, ferns and dwarf pines, among others. Most of the leaves were browning up and falling off. Marlow stood near the back, holding a steel trapdoor open with one arm and Marvin tucked under the other.

"Come on," she said. "You really shoulda been wearing your mask."

Zane grunted, shrugged and followed, catching the door from her as they descended into the underground bunker.

The bunker had been built by a preacher with a zeal for Armageddon, Pastor Jerry Hill, who warned his congregation time after time that the end was near. Though it hadn't been exactly as described in the Bible, he wasn't far off. It had started with the threat of a nuke by Pakistan, then an actual one launched by the US. Soon, North Korea, Russia and other countries joined in and World War III was well under way. This was forty-five years ago, in 2045. Three quarters of the population was lost during the war and the aftermath, but humans are remarkably resilient. The Earth had a resurgence about twenty years back. People went back to smaller communities, farming and taking care of each other. Power grids were restored for some areas. Nations were re-established, but many years of lawlessness couldn't just be undone. Countries once strong. were now weak and recovering. Others took advantage of that.

The Final War had happened two years ago. Zane, Marlow and their families took shelter at the church bunker during it. "Built for times such as these," Pastor Hill said, but the air was saturated with death. He, and most people with more than a few decades of using their lungs, passed on first, along with children.

It was five degrees the day Marvin the duck died, and it started a string of events Zane and Marlow couldn't have dreamed of.

Chapter One

Marlow set Marvin on a card table, sliding a couple plants with her elbow to make room. Marvin had stopped breathing, and Marlow was bending down to perform duck CPR when Zane grabbed her shoulder.

"Just...don't," he said. "She's dead."

"But maybe I can..."

Zane shook his head.

She sighed and took a step back, still focused on the duck in the dark room. "Then we butcher her and eat her tonight."

Zane threw his hands up. "What's the point? We're down to one fucking duck." His slight Indian accent normally made her laugh when he cursed, but not now.

"We'll go out. We'll—" She tried to continue, but a coughing fit overtook her.

Zane put an arm around her shoulders when she stopped. He wanted to tell her that her cough was getting worse, that it was probably lung cancer or whatever it was that took their families but what good would it do? He was afraid he wasn't far behind, as his own chest felt tight most nights. They hugged for what could've been five solid minutes, both parties recalling memories of their families finding each other as they sought shelter. Finally, they broke away and Marlow looked up at him, wiping tears as she did.

"Let's eat this fucking duck."

Zane wanted to protest but couldn't. *Let her have a last meal,* he figured.

Marlow butchered Marvin, apologizing to her that things had turned out the way they had. They built up their fire pit within the fence and Honey watched as they turned Marvin on a spit. Thankfully, she didn't seem to recognize her and quickly lost interest, scratching in the dirt for long-gone bugs or other edibles.

They sat down inside the church sanctuary, sharing a pew with a plate of duck meat between them. Honey had finally cornered a cockroach and was stomping it into submission as she pecked at it. It was the most entertainment they'd gotten lately.

"Do you think we're the last two people?" asked Zane, staring forward at the window frames taped over with plastic sheeting.

Marlow loosened a chunk of meat from the bone and chewed greedily. "Probably not."

"What if we are?"

"I'm sure there are others. Just not in this wasteland that used to be Florida."

"Do you think they'll ever make Earth *right* again?"

"Maybe, if there's anyone left to do that."

"You just said—"

"I know, Zane. I'm just saying, I'm sure there are people, I just don't know if they *can* make Earth right again."

Zane set a half-finished piece of duck on the plate. "So, why are we even bothering then?"

She looked at him, grease staining her lips and chin. "Because, we have to try, we promised our parents we would."

Zane slapped the pew in front of them. "That was all fine and good when they were alive, but now? No one's here to hold us to that. No one's here at all."

"Then do it for me, Zane. Survive a little longer for me."

He huffed. "Fine." And picked the duck back up.

~ * ~

After Marlow settled in the bunker for the night, Zane took one more trip to the roof of the church. It was his place to think. Eighteen months ago, his dad would do it, looking for a rescue helicopter or some sign of peace. His hope was always in vain. No one ever came for them and eventually, his father didn't have the strength to climb the ladder anymore. He'd died just over a year ago, followed a month later by Marlow's mom, then finally, their last companion, Jason. He was closer to their age, eighteen and vibrant, as much as he could be, given the conditions. Zane could still remember the choking wheeze of his last few breaths. The sound scraped up and down the walls of the bunker, as he lay clutching Marlow's hand while Zane paced behind them. In some ways, he blamed himself for Jason's death, deferring to him to take scouting duty more often and Jason had never complained. He'd just go out, looking for anything useful to keep them alive a little longer and his reward was death. Zane's reward for hiding in the bunker was to watch all his friends and family die out before him. He had half a mind to throw himself from the freezing shingles of the church roof, but he'd promised Marlow he'd stick around. Once she went—and it wouldn't be long—all bets were off.

Zane hugged his coat tighter. The temperature had dropped to the negatives, just a normal July night in Florida. The cold air kept his mind awake. He could almost hear his dad saying, "Once the politicians come out of hiding, they are going to need us to help rebuild. You are young and strong, you can help, have a normal life and maybe a family one day." Zane shook his head at the thought and how wrong it had been. He couldn't blame the guy for having hope but he knew better now.

His teeth were chattering when he headed for the ladder. He caught the first rung and almost slipped when he heard a whooshing sound in the distance. What used to be a norm during the Final War was now odd, to hear sounds of any kind in the distance. Zane craned his neck, trying to catch a glimpse of something, anything else, but the sound was gone. He finished the climb and went back into the bunker, locking the door as he did.

Made in United States
Orlando, FL
18 November 2022

24694777R00147